SHADOWS OF THE SKY

THE SEVENTH WHISPER, BOOK II

DYLAN HAGUE

Hydra Publications

ISBN: 978-1-948374-32-3

Hydra Publications

Goshen, Kentucky

www.hydrapublications.com

To B. and Cam, who listened to me yammer on about my ideas. I owe you each a cider.

For Aslan, who is three years old at the time of this dedication. Sorry, Peanut, but you'll have to read this one on your own.

Once more, to all readers and lovers of fantasy. We are the wizards now.

GLOSSARY

GLOSSARY OF WORDS AND PHRASES

Here you'll find translations for most of the phrases in this book that are written in the languages of this world. If you find anything not recorded here, it's probably an expletive. Don't worry too much about it.

CIDARI (ELVISH)

Kapsüsen nu - "I missed you."

Reilan ko - "fair skies."

Amon Äti, t'visti da hävi! - "Mother of Mercy, heal this wound!"

Silvia, mina Vaeli di mina Lieli... palëa si páka! - "Silvia, my Light and my Song... show me the way!"

Pïli a raki, Paiasidé... Addane mina në ká'su? - "Clouds have broken, Sunshine... Will you let me see your eyes?" an excerpt from an ancient ballad written from an elven soldier to his wife after he returned from war. Very romantic, a favorite among Cidari natives.

Kase mina, Kutamé. - "Look at me, Moonlight."

Viltar - "mage-knight."

MAREHO (MERFOLK)

hemkest - lit. "Home city." usually refers to Twipari itself, but can also refer to Tamia as a whole if speaking to one not native to Tamia

Ha maene - "Well met."

Aha ki koi? - "What say you?"

Ai - "Yea."

Ka - "Nay."

Pare ana - "Very good."

K-kanu - "My Queen."

Kaniha i Makala! - "Eighty on Makala!"

fidas - "cousin."

OLD ERIDIAN

Íloi - "We drink." Usually used as a toast, similar to, "Skol," or "Salud,"... or just "Cheers."

ÚDAN (DRACONIC)

Kur bit'düg - expletive, lit. "f--k my life." Don't say it in front of your parents.

fu thrák kuri - "you f--king freak."

skrí - "s--t."

kur - "f--k."

veno - "friend."

Böth napen fe - "Give me your name."

Zir-ik Kéldi, Udári, on Zin fïlg mefï. - "I am not Kéldi, Dragoon, but I will fly with you."

JHUBAN (GHARPASAN)
Acha dan - "Good day."

LUSHVAYTT (DWARVEN)
dref - "s--t."

VUMSAKK (ORCISH)
Nasa-Taed, oshtell hur kriip. - "Tree-Father, heal this wound."
Bel mis! - "Be mouse!"

VOLOKI
pizuri-ditke - lit. "wraith-baby."
Ushvizna min Vilshe! Ushvizna yi! - "Release my Wizard! Release her!"
Mi trushku - "I'm fine."

"*O*i, Gloomy! Get up, we got a problem!"

Denin frowned as the rough voice of the Danesmen came through his tent flap. It had been a long night, and an even longer month, since he arrived in the Township of Dane. He was unaccustomed to the cold of the Ías Fuil, but that's not to say he was any stranger to the cold, itself. He just didn't like it. Denin heaved himself up and shrouded himself in his cloak and hood, already clothed and armed. The cloak was vital, a gift from his father before he left. He never left the tent without his hood up. *That's why most of the Danesmen came up with their nicknames*, he thought... Well, that, or the bags under his eyes.

When Denin emerged from his tent, he found the six hunters he was traveling with shaking in their boots, trembling before some faint glow. Denin looked up to see the image of a thin man, young in face, wreathed in wispy wrappings about his body. Around him in the air hung a chilling haze and, in the creature's sunken eyes, there was only death. Some sort of restless ghost, likely the spirit of a Dane boy who wandered too far from home and froze to death.

"Lovely," Denin groaned again as he gripped his weapons. "Just what I like to wake up to. Everyone, get back!"

In one hand, Denin held a long rapier, and from his other hand hung a long black whip. With two commanding steps forward, Denin cracked the whip out wide, the sound hanging in the air as it echoed across the mountainside. The ghost drifted back for a moment as it locked eyes on Denin. As its lips curled back with a hiss, the Danesmen gasped in fright as rows on rows of sharp, jagged teeth revealed themselves.

Denin gritted his teeth and took another step forward, flourishing his blade out wide. The ghastly thing lowered itself to the ground, its feet hanging in the air as it clawed at the dirt. Under its ethereal fingers, the land seemed to rot and die.

"Back to Volok with you," Denin barked. With a blink of motion, Denin cracked the whip once more, this time striking the thing in its face. Ectoplasm burst out from its face, and a notable gash appeared over the creature's eye. It hissed again and lunged forward, its hands outstretched like claws. Before it could sink its fingers into Denin's body, Denin thrust his sword into its belly. The blade sunk into the phantom's semi-tangible form, and ethereal fluid spurted across Denin's arm. Its snarl twisted into a wince, then flattened out as the thing wailed, its body dissipating into nothing.

Denin cracked his neck as he tucked his weapons away once more beneath his cloak. "Now then, if you boys are done soiling yourselves, we can get a move on."

"How did you do that...?" The leader of the Danesmen stared in confusion at the stranger.

"The weapons are consecrated, blessed by a Cardinal of Xanith," Denin explained. "There's a Temple back home to the lady." This was a lie, of course, but they didn't need to know that.

They'd been hiking for the past five days. Apparently at the top of this Gods-forsaken icicle of a mountain was some kind of guardian spirit that the Danesmen needed to beseech. The attacks on the village were growing more and more frequent. While nothing had yet breached the walls of the settlement, it still frightened the townsfolk to hear the ruckus outside each night.

Denin had only been in town for a short while, but he proved to be stronger than most of the guardsmen in the village.

Because of course he was.

After hiking a bit longer, Denin came up alongside the leader of the Dane hunters. "Tell me, again, why we're going up here," he said, his voice low and airy.

"Curse on it, boy, I've told you a hundred times now," the hunter growled. "We need to speak to the Watcher."

"I get that," Denin replied, "but what *is* the Watcher? A lesser god?"

The older man chuckled. "No, he's no god. He was once one of ours, a Danesman. His father was a Monk who lived in the Temple of Kh'anora, back at the bottom of the mountain. They were chosen by the Udásíaki to be the Watchers—Guardians of the Ías."

"Udásíaki?"

"Ice dragon. Big thing, huuuge..." the old hunter stretched his arms out to emphasize his point. "Lives under the mountain. Keeps things running. They say his kin were buried here in the Burned Ages, and that's where the mountains come from."

"That sounds ridiculous."

"Don't let the Udásíaki hear you say that," the hunter said with a grin. "Anyway, the Watcher is ageless, and he has powers. He can travel from peak to peak in a breath, he can sleep in the snow for days and not freeze. He needs no food or water."

Denin frowned. That sounded all too familiar.

"But," the hunter continued, "he can't live in the Township. If he did, it would freeze over."

"I imagine he must be lonely," Denin mused.

"He says it's all right," the old man replied. "That little one from the Shores, the Princess, she used to come visit him sometimes. But she hasn't been around in a while. Guess being Queen of the Mermaids keeps you away, eh?"

Denin shrugged. He'd heard about the Battle for Fartide, but that was months before his arrival. Had he been around when it happened, he might have gone to help fight. But there was nothing to do about it now.

In a few hours, the lot of them arrived at a cavern near the mountaintop. The leader of their pack stepped forward.

"Watcher!" he called into the inky shade. "Kaada! We need your help!"

Denin stared into the cavern, chewing at his lip. He was unsure of what to expect from this Watcher character, but he had some ideas, and he wasn't particularly excited about them.

A faint breeze sounded behind them. When the seven men turned, there before them stood a young man with olive skin and eyes of dark grey. His black hair was cut short, and his white clothes were lined with frost, the snow mingled into his fur collar. On his hips were two curved daggers, and a small bow poked out over his shoulder.

"Gentlemen," the new fellow said, his voice warmer than Denin expected, "is there something wrong?"

"Monsters, boy," the elder hunter whispered as he stepped forward. "Creatures in the night. They come more and more each day, and we don't know why."

"Steady, old man." Kaada took the man by the shoulder. "What of the Mayor? Has Lord Edwin said anything about it?"

"That's why we're here," Denin spoke up. "He sent us to find you. Said to tell you we need your protection."

Kaada paused for a moment, then stepped toward the cloaked figure. "I don't recognize you," he said. "... What's your name?"

Denin furrowed his brow. "Alec," he replied. "Alec Ducard. I'm a mercenary in from Davenstead."

Kaada inched closer to Denin, narrowing his eyes. As he drew nearer, Denin lifted his head enough that his pale blue eyes locked with the white-garbed warrior.

Trust me.

The Watcher blinked for a moment. "We don't get many folk from Davenstead," he smiled, extending a hand. "I'm glad you've come. I'm sure Lord Edwin is paying you well for your services."

"It's enough to keep me around, yeah," Denin answered with a faint half-smile, taking the hand in his and giving it a solid shake. The Watcher's hand was cold, almost as cold as his own.

Well done, boy.

Denin winced a bit at the intrusive voice in his head.

"I suppose we ought to go have a look." Kaada smiled as he looked about at the Danesmen. "I'll go on ahead. See you all there!" With a wink, the Watcher's form dissipated into a frosty haze and whirled off into the air.

"All right, boys," the leader called. "Let's head home!"

The men all cheered as they turned to make their way back down the mountain.

Break from the hunters. Follow the Watcher.

That'd be too obvious, one of them would notice.

Take the leader first. He'll cover your trail for the others.

... Huh. Good thinking.

It ought to be. I've been doing this much longer than you.

Denin rolled his eyes as he sidled up once more to the leader, placing a hand on his back and weaving his will into the man's mind.

Cover for me, Denin's voice sounded in the eldest hunter's mind.

The old Danesman nodded as Denin slipped off from the group and into the trees.

"Hey, where's he going?" one of the younger hunters asked.

"Don't worry about him," the leader replied. "He'll meet us back at home. Just come on."

Denin smirked as he drifted away from the eyes of the Danesmen. He had to admit, the old man knew his tricks. As soon as the group was out of earshot, Denin closed his eyes and slipped into the shadow of a nearby pine. As his fists clenched, he felt his being shift as he transformed.

The oldest hunter led his men on back down toward the Township, and he looked up to the sky with squinted eyes. A wisp of dark mist disappeared into the distance.

It struck almost as soon as he made it to the foot of the mountain. The hunger took hold, and Denin dropped to the snow, whole and trembling. It was a detestable sensation, the crippling enervation and boundless might at the same time. He could not bite back the animal growl in his throat as he crept across the ground, the snow hardening under his icy fingers.

His eyes darted back and forth all around him, until he spotted a lone figure wandering up through the trees. She wasn't a Danesman, as a Danesman would have been smart enough to dress warmer. Probably some brigand up from the mainland, separated from the rest of their group.

Denin focused for a moment. No one else around but

the group of hunters on their way down the mountain to the village. They were days out. Denin dug his fingers down into the frozen earth as he stared at the woman.

She would do, for now.

* * *

DENIN WAS BACK IN THE VILLAGE THAT NIGHT. He approached on foot from a distance, his strength renewed as he threw his hood back. His crimson hair cascaded over his ears, concealing their pointed tips from the guards who opened the gate. Sticking to the shadows even in the moonlight, Denin made his way west through the hamlet toward the mansion at the edge of town.

At the bottom of the stair leading inside, Denin could see the frost-covered spirit from the mountaintop. Speaking to the Watcher was the township's Mayor, Lord Edwin. Edwin wore a long blue robe trimmed with white, his silver hair pulled back into a tail. He looked at Kaada through gold-rimmed spectacles as he spoke, and he took Kaada's hand in a familial manner. Concentrating, Kaada listened as best he could to their conversation.

"... sort of creatures are we talking about?" Kaada asked.

"Omens, I should think," Edwin replied with a grim tone. "Wolves of raven fur, large birds, even some serpents of unusual size. None have yet entered the gates, but they feel... I don't know. It's as if they're heralding something. I fear we may be on the verge of attack."

"An attack by what, though? I can't be of much help if I don't know what I'm to be hunting."

"I wish I could give you a clearer answer..." Edwin frowned as he looked down at his feet for a moment. "Have you any blessed weapons?"

"No," Kaada answered. "I had a holy dagger once, but I lost it in the Shadowlands. You remember, when the Giantlings came out to try to take Frostdrake."

Edwin nodded. "Well, next best thing, then. We've some silver arrows readied for you, and some raw silver left over for you to gild your blades."

"Silver?" Kaada asked. "This... Ed, this sounds more serious than I expected. What do you think might be out there?"

"Son, I don't know what to think. But I can't take any chances."

Kaada frowned for a moment, then nodded. "I'll take whatever you can spare. Thank you."

As the Watcher turned to walk away, Edwin placed a hand on his shoulder. "Kaada... It's good to have you back." the Mayor smiled. "You know I loved your father, and you know I love you."

Kaada smiled back. "It's good to be home, Ed. At least, for a while."

Denin slunk back into the shadows as Kaada walked by on his way out to the nearby inn. It seemed preparations for war were underway.

They are unprepared.

Denin frowned. *I don't know. This Watcher fellow carries himself like a seasoned huntsman. He might be the force Dane needs.*

The Watcher cannot stop the coming tide. Only the Boltwalker could hope to weather the storm now, and he remains in the Plains to the East. He grows complacent in Laithe Kingdom.

But what if he makes his way here? What will you do then?

Why do you think I sent you, boy?

Denin furrowed his brow as his fingers traced the intricate pommel of the longsword on his back. Even sheathed and untouched in days, Denin felt its power. Felt it and hated it, much as he felt and hated his own.

This is what you were born to do, Denin. Monitor the Boltwalker, just in case. If he comes, then bring me his blade. But let him live with his shame.

And if I can't? If he makes me kill him?

There was a breath of silence in Denin's head. He didn't need to ask again; he groaned, as he knew exactly what the old man would say.

You know what you are. You have them for a reason.

Denin shook his head. Gods, please, let the Bolt-walker stay in Laithe.

While you're here... take the Watcher.

... You think I'm powerful enough?

I do. I know what you're capable of.

Denin grimaced. Of course he did.

He stepped into one shadow, and out another. Behind the inn. He had his eye on the Watcher. The ghost wandered around the building for a moment, looking out at the town. Denin could see him sigh. He must have so much going through his mind, being home again.

Denin winced as he reached out with his mind. His

own consciousness crept up to the phantom. From inches away, he could feel all the emotions swirling inside the Watcher. Melancholy and mirth in a swirl of...warmth. This town was his home.

Denin gritted his teeth. Then, he struck.

1

*C*aeleen wrinkled his nose at the mingling stench of wet dog and old blood. His knees ached from staying low in the tall grass of the plains outside the newly erected settlement of Alryne, following the trail of viscera and fur. He rubbed at his eyes, trying to combat the weariness as he considered his situation; Alryne was a part of Haven Kingdom... or Q'let Kingdom, as they had called it before Cestus renamed it. So in a sense, these attacks shouldn't have been any of his business. But all evidence pointed to the attacks coming out of Nighthand Keep, a small fortress just at the edge of Laithe, which made it Mull's responsibility to see justice done.

At first, Cestus seemed intent on solving the problem himself. He sent a company of guardsmen out from the Capitol to find the murderer, likely to claim any reward offered. But, when they found the claw marks and shed fur mixed in with all the blood in the alleyways where the attack took place, the guards made it clear that they had no intention of dealing with wild things for so little pay.

By then, word had reached Viraati Lien, and Mull had sent his own force to investigate. Naturally, Caeleen was chosen to lead the party, being the best active hunter in Laithe Kingdom... perhaps in all of Eridan, but that was neither here nor there. The young Ranger requested that his old companion, Baron, join the hunt, but the Beastslayer, now Spymaster of Greyfort, seemed to have retired from active duty, now serving as chief instructor for the Grey Claw, Greyfort's corps of soon-to-be monster hunters. So instead, Caeleen brought along the twins Thraun and Marish Glenn, two of the scouts he had been helping train for the past five months, and Raimi, one of Viraati Lien's spies.

And of course, Caeleen went nowhere without Leon Farrough, his squire. Not for lack of trying; Cae wasn't comfortable being served or waited on. Leon was sixteen, older than Cae had been when he started training. But the boy could keep up and keep quiet and, indeed, seemed like he'd make a fine Ranger someday, so the Whisper agreed to teach the boy his trade. Of the five of them, Leon seemed the most disheartened when Cae decided they would stable their horses in Alryne and follow the trail to Nighthand on foot, but the boy held his tongue.

Caeleen's fingers dug into the dirt as he pinched a bit of flesh from the ground. The bloodied meat was still moist, which meant they were close. The Ranger frowned. This should never have happened; Baron had wanted to bring in a group of Slayers to clear out Night-hand and reclaim it for Mull some time ago, but the Grey King pleaded patience. He wanted Nighthand to be a final test for the Claw. But circumstances forced the King's hand, it would seem.

"Something I don't understand," Leon started as he crept up from behind. "If we already know the attacks are coming from Nighthand, why don't we just go in and take them? Why track them all the way from Alryne?"

Caeleen sighed. "A good question, Leon," he replied. "That was Mull's first instinct, too. But our King decided we needed to see the site of the attack for ourselves, to be certain we knew what we were getting into. And, aside from that..." Cae rolled back on his heels and sat down as the other three of his crew caught up to them. "I thought it would be good for you. You don't get many opportunities to practice your tracking, do you?"

"Not so much lately, I guess," Leon sighed. "I admit, I've gotten rusty."

"I think you're doing all right," Cae replied. "Suppose it's kind of my fault, too, I should give you the chance to lead the hunt more often."

"I'd like that, m'lord," Leon said with a smile. "It'd do me good."

Caeleen arched his brow. "Come on, kid. We've been over this. I'm no lord. Look at me." He gestured at his coat, covered in dirt and full of holes. "You really think Mull's court would let someone like me sit at their table?"

Thraun chuckled. "I should think not. Not like that at least, Sir! When's the last time you washed your hair?"

Caeleen eyed the young scout-in-training with a smirk. "My point is, I'm not a lord. Don't think I'd really want to be, either; my talent has always been for hunting and fighting, I'm a dreadful politician."

"But you've had your hand in politics before, haven't you?" Raimi added. "Some two years back, was it not you there with Baron and Queen Siahra when she petitioned the Emperor for his aid?"

Caeleen's smile faltered, and he cast his eyes to the ground. "It was, yeah... that was a rough year for everyone, I think. But we got through all right. Besides, I don't exactly think I helped. Just kinda... showed up and waved my sword around."

A silence hung over the party for a time until Leon finally spoke. "I've been giving it some thought," he started. "Marish, you said you thought it might be Q'leti held up in Nighthand, right?"

"Yeah, maybe," the scout replied. "I mean, it makes sense. They need to feed their wolves, and Alryne is the closest settlement to Nighthand. Those claw marks have to come from somewhere..."

"But why were there no boot prints?" Leon mused. "There were plenty of paw prints all over the place, but no footprints. And the paw prints we saw were all pretty big..."

Caeleen furrowed his brow. "Leon, what are you thinking?"

Leon shrugged. "Well... what if it's not wolves, per se?" The squire looked up at his Knight. "What if it's werewolves?"

Marish went pale. "Oh, Gods..."

Caeleen cleared his throat and got back to his feet. "If it is, then we'll deal with it. Kid, you have my axe?"

Leon nodded, reaching over his shoulder and pulling out a worn single-bladed axe, just the right length to wield with one or both hands. On its wooden shaft, in Old Eridian script, was carved the Laithe Knights' Creed: *Lem-ho ar Raich, cred-ho ar duaine-e.* "*My hands for the King, my heart for his People.*" Caeleen had the same words inscribed on the blade of his sword, Gem'shil.

Cae nodded. "Anyone remember why we bring an axe on a hunt?" The Ranger looked to each of his three students. "Come on, I know at least one of you remembers."

Marish scratched her head, her black hair rustling about. "Because...because swords were designed for fighting noble races, not animals. You can kill an animal with a sword just fine, but an axe is more effective."

"Very good, Marish!" Caeleen smiled. "Leon, hold onto that thing. You'll probably need it more than me, and you know the axe better than I do."

Leon tilted his head as he returned the axe to his back. "What about you? What are you gonna fight with?"

Caeleen smiled and tapped Gem'shil's hilt with his fingertips. "Just because it's not ideal doesn't mean it doesn't work."

The five of them continued on, with Leon leading the way. The squire did his best to follow the trail, and Caeleen monitored the path as they ran along. Every now and again he would call out tidbits of advice and occasional corrections to the Knight-to-be, and young Leon acted on them accordingly. Faithful and obedient, the boy was, and confident enough to lead the way. Cae was quite proud of him.

It took them another three days to reach Nighthand on foot. Along the way, Caeleen sent a message to Viraati

Lien by sparrow, requesting reinforcements. If were-wolves had taken hold of Nighthand Keep, they would need more than just five hunters to take it back.

The party stopped short at the edge of the tall grass just outside the entrance on the afternoon of the third day. The trail of blood was fresher and bolder red on the ground leading up to the stone archway. Raimi had gone ahead to look for the folk taken from Alryne or, at least, what was left of them.

And, there while they waited, Caeleen turned to his students. "I need you three to listen very closely right now," he said. "These aren't just some game we're about to fight. And it's not just thugs. Whether it's Q'leti or werewolves or whatever in there, Nighthand has a repu-tation. Whoever is holding this place, they're dangerous. *Very* dangerous. So, remember: don't split up, don't start a fight you don't have to, and do *not* be a hero." Cae looked to the twins. "You two have everything you need?"

Thraun nodded as he and Marish gripped their weapons, Thraun with his shortswords, and Marish with her shortbow. "Wish we'd had time to pack that salve we had at the house," Thraun mused. "What was it, fairybloom?"

"Fairybloom salve would have dried out by now," Marish said. "We don't need it, anyway, just... y'know. Don't get hurt."

Cae smiled and shook his head before turning to Leon. "You ready, kid?"

"Ready as I'll ever be, I guess!" the squire answered with a shrug as his hands gripped the axe. "Shouldn't we wait for Raimi to get back?"

"Raimi is already back." Three four turned all at once to see the spy crouching amongst them once again, her twin daggers already drawn. "I've looked around, and things are... a little more complicated than we expected."

"What's the matter?" Caeleen whispered.

"It seems Marish and Leon were both right. There were Q'leti here, but they've all been captured. The Keep is under the control of a pack of werebeasts. Two were-bears guard the entrance, mostly werewolves patrolling the halls. At least eight, or nine. A third werebear guards the dungeon where the Q'leti and their wolves are being held..." Raimi turned grim eyes toward the Ranger-Knight. "There weren't any survivors left from Alryne. I'm sorry."

Caeleen cursed under his breath as the twins looked with stern eyes to one another. Leon cast his eyes to the ground.

Raimi gave the four a moment before she continued. "I didn't see him, but I heard some of the Q'leti mention their leader. It sounds like this pack is led by a werewarg."

"Oh, Gods," Cae groaned, "not a werewarg."

"A werewhat?" asked Thraun.

"A werewarg," replied Cae. "You know what a warg is, yeah? A really big wolf with a short snout? Well, a werewarg is like a really big werewolf with a short snout. I've only ever seen their kind once before, when I was a kid living in the Dokk. Thing was ten feet tall, at least. Dreadful, nasty things. Hard to kill." Caeleen frowned and drew his sword, pulling his hood on over his head. "Thraun, Marish, leave the leader to me and Leon when we find him. He's prepared for this, and I don't want you two getting hurt. All of you hang back while I take the guards, don't move until I signal."

The Ranger emerged from the grass and strode with confidence toward the front gate, pulling a silvered dagger out of his belt. As he drew near, out of the darkness within the entrance lumbered two great beasts, the werebears Raimi had mentioned, walking on two legs with their arms hanging close to the ground. Their bodies were large, and their yellow teeth showed beneath their snarling lips, saliva dribbling down their chins as they growled at the hooded figure.

"In the name of Lancelot Tyran Mull, King of the Grey Plains of Laithe, I hereby place you, and your ilk, under arrest." Caeleen held his head high as he spoke, his eyes just reflecting a glint of light under the shadow of his hood. "Come quietly or face the King's justice."

The beast on the right tilted its head. "*No King. Only Fad-Ficali,*" it growled and huffed in the Bear-Tongue. "*He will... want your pelt.*"

Caeleen smirked. "*Come, take it,*" he growled back.

The second werebear lurched forward and drew in a deep breath. It meant to roar, to let out a great rumbling thunder.

Cae drove the breath out of it with a length of mithril plunged into its belly. He pulled the blade out and slashed across the ursine creature's throat with his dagger, the wound hissing and sizzling at the touch of silver.

The first werebear's beady eyes widened as its partner dropped twitching to the dirt, and it swiped broad at the Ranger. Caeleen ducked under the claw and plunged the silver into the monster's breast. Smoke poured from the hole in the beast's heart, and the were-bear fell to the ground.

After a moment, the beasts' corpses began to shrivel and shrink, their fur receding, until all that remained were the bodies of two half-orc men. Caeleen turned back and raised his sword toward his party, and the four ran out from the grass to join him.

"I didn't know you were a Creature Tongue..." Raimi whispered, her brow furrowed. "Some think it unnatural, Sir. Mind who you do that around."

Caeleen shrugged. "Nature-magic is in my blood. Just a gift from Kh'anora, the way I see it."

Raimi nodded. "Suppose so. Still, best be cautious about it when we get back home. C'mon, let's get this done."

Nighthand was a sizable castle. Not as big as Viraati Lien, or Castle Cestus, but big enough to get lost in. Moonlight poured in through the windows, bathing its rooms and halls in a faint blue light. It wasn't much to go on, but Cae's eyes were keen enough to guide their way.

Caeleen crinkled his nose as they entered the Great Hall; the musk of animal was pungent. How long had this pack been here? Putting the stench out of his mind as best he could, Caeleen led his team through the Hall, and into a smaller corridor off to the side.

In this corridor was a patrolling werewolf, black-furred, and about seven feet tall, its back turned to the hunting party. Caeleen knew it had heard them the moment they stepped into the hall, as he just saw its ears prick as they entered. It made no movements toward

21

them, but it knew they were there. It was smart, it wanted them to sneak up on him. Marish wouldn't have it. A shot from her bow, and a gurgle from the wolf's punctured throat, put an end to that.

Once Marish had retrieved her arrow from the human woman's remains, the five of them advanced up the stairs. On the stairs, however, was a second werewolf which spotted them just before the first landing. It growled and leapt upon them before they had a chance to strike. Its claws tore through Caeleen's jerkin, but could not penetrate the silent chain shirt he wore underneath. Still, the blow was enough to toss him into the wall.

As the beast turned to advance on the Ranger, Raimi darted forward, her daggers punching hole after hole into the werewolf's ribs until another half-orc man dropped, motionless, to the stone stairs. Leon helped Caeleen back to his feet, and they continued on.

Just off the first landing, and through an old trophy room full of rusted and worn-out arms and armor, the five found themselves in another large chamber, the throne room. Sitting upon the stone throne at the end of the room was the largest werebeast Caeleen had ever seen. Leon nearly let out a gasp, but Marish clasped her hand over his mouth just before he could give away their position. Caeleen led his companions through the deepest shadows to stay out of the beast's sight. Silent as a mouse, the Ranger pulled out his dagger.

"For the King!"

Caeleen's neck cracked as he turned to watch Thraun throw himself at the werewarg. Before he could leap forward and stop the trainee, a blur of dirty white fur descended on him from behind the throne. The sound of ripping leather echoed in the chamber as Thraun skidded across the floor.

The werewarg let out a roar and rose from his throne, standing at least ten feet tall. Thraun wobbled to his feet, blood dripping from his right breast as he stared down the white-haired werewolf advancing on him.

"*Hold!*" Caeleen barked in the Wolf Tongue as he stepped out of the shadows, holding his weapons out wide. "*If you strike this boy down, I'll have all your pelts hanging in my cabin!*"

The white werewolf tilted its head. "No. You invaders," it growled in stilted Eridian. "You attack us in our home. Why?"

"This is not your home, creature," Thraun hissed, still clutching at his wound. "You took this place from the ones who held it before. The Q'leti."

"I have no time for this." The werewarg glared at the Ranger as he spoke, his speech clearer than that of his minion. "You've killed some of my children, I know. For this, I should take your head. But I give you one chance: leave now, or die."

Caeleen returned the werewarg's glare with a fiery stare of his own. "Afraid I can't do that, friend," he started. "I assume you're this 'Fad-Ficali', yes?"

"I am," the beast replied.

"Good!" Caeleen pointed his blade at the creature. "In the name of Lancelot Tyran Mull, King of the Grey Plains of Laithe, I hereby place you under arrest. Come quietly, or..."

"Or we'll carve you up and turn you into a nice lining for our boots," Thraun cut in with a grin.

Caeleen frowned. "... More or less, yeah."

Fad-Ficali glowered at Thraun for a moment. "...Dron." He growled at the white wolf. "Kill the boy, but leave the green one to me."

Dron's lipped curled back to reveal vile yellow teeth as he flung himself at Thraun. The Scout-in-training lifted his arms to shield himself...

Shk-shk-shk! Three daggers sunk themselves into the white wolf's thigh! The werewolf collapsed and retched with pain as Raimi and Marish leapt out of the shadows to attack.

"Treachery!" Fad-Ficali bellowed. "I'll have you *all* in my teeth!"

Caeleen grinned as Leon appeared at his side, the squire's hands wrapped tightly around the Knight's axe. "You'll die trying," he replied. "For the King!"

In a blur of motion, Caeleen had his foot planted on the werewarg's chest. Pushing off with all his might, the Ranger landed a kick square to Fad-Ficali's jaw as he flipped back to the ground before him. Fad-Ficali snarled and swiped wide in the Ranger's direction, but his claw met the back of the squire's axe.

"Please, just surrender!" Leon pleaded. "We don't want this to end in bloodshed!"

"I kind of do, honestly," Raimi called over her shoulder as she danced around the swings of Dron.

"So do I," Marish growled as she bandaged her brother's wound.

"Agreed," Thraun hissed.

"Sorry, Leon," Caeleen said as he dipped back into range of Fad-Ficali's claws and parried a punch with his pommel. "It's four against one. This only ends one way."

Leon ducked beneath the clamping jaws of the werewarg and looked wide-eyed to his teacher. "W...so are we really doing this?"

"Get your head in the game, kid!" Caeleen shouted over the beast's guttural sounds. "This is part of the job! You wanna be a Ranger, you have to *fight*!"

Raimi passed between Dron and Marish again, leaving a smattering of red marks on his white snout as she twirled. Catching his left claw by running it through with her dagger, the spy leaned in close and bared her teeth in the werewolf's face. The rancid vapor of his breath made her dizzy for a beat, just long enough for Dron to sink his teeth into her shoulder. With a vicious shriek, Raimi bit down inside her cheek and spit in the white wolf's eye.

The creature reeled back, yelping, his eye sizzling—a pellet of liquid silver. A dangerous trick taught to her by Baron, but it proved effective. Dron threw a wide swipe back in Raimi's face, leaving four deep gashes along her jawline. The spy hit the floor hard, and Dron dribbled saliva onto the cold stone as he advanced.

Fad-Ficali growled and sneered as he swung again and again, each stroke of his claws missing the green-garbed Ranger by a hair. Caeleen leapt back as the werewarg pressed forward, and cursed under his breath as a leap from the beast closed the distance between them in a heartbeat. Making broad swipes with his dagger, Caeleen held Fad-Ficali back with its silvered blade for but a moment before the creature swatted the dagger out of his hand. Before Caeleen could dive away, the world shuddered around him as Fad-Ficali boxed his ears. All fell silent, but for the ringing, and the werewarg loomed over the Ranger, now wobbling on one knee.

A dash of red splattered across Caeleen's face as the head of his axe buried itself into Fad-Ficali's side.

The warg-creature tumbled to the side. Leon kicked it away, jerking the weapon out and twirling it about in his hands.

"For the King!" The Squire's voice cracked as he took up the battle cry, throwing himself at the beast with the axe whirling all about him in a blur.

Even with blood seeping from his side, Fad-Ficali fought viciously, batting away several swings of Leon's axe. But the Ranger-in-training would not yield the offensive, spinning about like a top and striking fast and hard, leaving wounds all along the werewarg's arms.

Caeleen shook the daze from himself and scrambled to his feet, clutching his sword in his left hand. Sparks danced along the blade as Caeleen darted low to the ground, scooping up his dagger as he rushed back into the fight. Carving a long streak of red into Fad-Ficali's back, the Whisper leapt onto the beast's shoulders and jammed his silver into its neck. The sizzling flesh under the dagger brought Fad-Ficali to his knees, and Leon brought the axe down into the werewarg's skull, putting an end to it.

Caeleen flipped forward off the dead beast's shoulders as it transformed, and flung his dagger at Dron, who now held Raimi's head in his jaws. The silvered weapon buried itself up to its hilt in Dron's exposed throat. With a short gurgle, the white wolf fell dead. What remained of Dron dropped to the floor, and Raimi fell with him, cradling her face as red dribbled from her open wounds. Dron's body receded to reveal a stunted, tusked form with green-tinted brown skin and a thick grey beard—a dworc, half-dwarf and half-orc.

Caeleen turned back to Fad-Ficali out of curiosity, and threw his brows up in surprise to see a wrinkled old gnome, his thick, white mustache touching his chin and covering his mouth. Caeleen couldn't help but wonder how long it had been since the werewarg had assumed its true form, if he had been living off the undying strength of his beast-shape for years, maybe even decades, trying to stave off the effects of age. He knew some were-creatures used their animal forms' longevity as a sort of false immortality, but... well, their stories usually ended the way Fad-Ficali's had.

Caeleen sighed, looking around the room at his students. "That, uhh... that could have gone better."

Marish looked back in a panic. "Sir! Over here!"

Caeleen rushed forward, skidding on his knees to reach Thraun's side. "How bad is it? Is it deep?"

Thraun grunted as he pulled his hand away from the bandage, blood already seeping through and running down his torn leather vest. "Not too deep," he grunted, "But it bleeds. Stings like Volok, too."

Caeleen cut the bandage away with his dagger. Marish was about to protest until she saw the Ranger's fingers come to the opening in her brother's flesh. Caeleen closed his eyes, and his fingertips emitted a faint golden glow. "*Amon Äti, t'visti da hävi,*" he muttered, reciting the short prayer he'd learned so long ago. As the Elvish words left his lips, the torn flesh in the scout-in-training's side closed, leaving only a pale scar underneath the blood.

"Thank you, Sir," Thraun managed through a sigh as the pain dissipated. It was then that the sound of heavy footfalls came from behind the main door at the other end of the chamber.

"Raimi," Caeleen called, "how many werewolves did you say there were patrolling?"

"Eight, or nine," the spy replied, putting pressure on her own wounds. "But there are likely more about the grounds. They couldn't have taken this place from the Q'leti with so few numbers."

Coming to his feet, the Ranger approached her and repeated his spell, closing the gashes in her face and leaving only faint scars in their place. She'd need to see a priest about those bites later, but she would be able to carry on for now. "And we killed two patrolling... so that leaves six, or seven. At least." His eyes darted to Leon, wiping the blood away from the head of the Knight's axe. "So, squire... think we could take seven werewolves?"

"With all due respect, Sir," Leon stammered, "Not a chance. Not without Sal'tera."

Caeleen shrugged and brandished Gem'shil once more. The boy was right; he really should have brought the holy blade. "Well, I don't suppose we have a choice. Eyes up, everyone!"

The hunting party gathered together, facing the large doors at the end of the room, weapons drawn.

The doors burst open, and in marched a sizable force of soldiers, each in gleaming steel armor, and grey tabards, bearing the gold lion of Laithe Kingdom on their chest. In their hands were bloodied axes and polearms, and scattered amongst them were a number of older scouts, their short grey coats covered in blood, with arrows already nocked in their shortbows.

Amidst the soldiers strode a man arrayed in sturdier armor fashioned in the likeness of a lion, with an axe in each hand and a sword the length of Leon across his back. His helmet was plated with gold that ran back to imitate a long mane, and he pulled the visor up to reveal the man's grizzled face, scars cutting across his nose, and through his thick mustache.

"Sir Edmund!" Caeleen cried out as a grin spread across his face. "Gods bless you, you made it! The King got my sparrow, then?"

"Aye, he did!" Sir Edmund nodded, smirking under his scars. "Sorry we took so long to get here, lad. Got a bit sidetracked by a pack of wolves on the way down here, I'm afraid."

"Oh, *viik*," Caeleen started, "was anyone hurt?"

"Ha! I ought to be askin' you that, boy!" Sir Edmund shook his head. "Five hunters taking a castle full of were-beasts on their lonesome! What were you thinking?"

"I was thinkin' it'd make a good test, honestly," the Ranger replied with a shrug. "It got a little rough, and we all made some mistakes, but I'd say it went rather well." Cae spun back on his heel, his hair swinging about as he did so. "On that note! We better get on our way back to Alryne to get our horses! On our way home, I'd like a word with each of you in private so we can talk about what we all did wrong." He started to turn away, but stopped short and pointed to the spy. "Ah, that is... except for you, Raimi. Y'know. Not my student and all."

"Of course," Raimi replied with a smirk.

"Before that," Sir Edmund cut in, "we ought to get down to the dungeon and take a look at the captives."

Edmund led the march down into the depths of the Keep, his axes gripped in hand. As they walked into the dungeon, another werebear rose from the floor in front of a small cooking fire.

"Never seen an animal with a penchant for cooking before," Edmund remarked with a wry smile.

This creature was larger than the werecreatures the hunting party encountered on their way in, but still not as large as Fad-Ficali had been. Edmund grinned underneath his mustache and slid his visor down before charging the beast.

Leon moved to aid the older Knight, but Caeleen held out a hand to stop him. "Let him have his fun; he came a long way."

Edmund and the werebear both reached the center of the room in three great strides, and Edmund got the first strike. Before the creature could even raise a claw, the axe in Edmund's left hand sunk into its face, taking several teeth on its way out. With a quick, twirl, Edmund struck with the same axe, knocking the werebear in the temple with the back of the axe head. The beast staggered for a moment as Edmund swung both axes about him and laughed, circling his opponent.

The werebear roared as best it could through broken

and missing teeth, and threw itself onto Edmund. It threw several swipes at the Knight, most of them bouncing off of the steel plate of Edmund's forearms, until one stroke slipped through and sunk into the helmet, knocking it away. The Knight grimaced, the scars on his shaved scalp now bare for everyone to see.

Edmund grunted as he broke from his guard long enough to strike the incoming claws of the werebear with an axe from the right, splitting the werebear's hand right down the middle and holding it in place. Bringing the other axe down on an overhead arc, he severed the arm just below the elbow.

The bear shrieked and batted the axe out of Edmund's left hand with its remaining claws. Fire dancing in his eyes, the Knight clenched his fist and caught the werebear's jaw with a wide hook that sent it sprawling to the floor. Tossing the other axe aside, Edmund drew his sword, whirled it over his head once, and brought it down. With a resounding *clang!* ringing out over the sound of torn flesh and splintered bone, the sword's tip sunk into the stone floor as the werebear's head rolled away.

"And stay down," Edmund growled.

The werebear's fur receded and transformed into that of a dirt-covered woman with grey skin, her severed head bearing two curled horns.

Not many ghari in Eridan, Caeleen thought, *and even less ghari were-creatures.* Perhaps the pressure of being that outlandish drove her away, brought her to a pack who didn't mind her claws. If it was enough to drive humans to leave civilization, how much easier would it be to afflict one so different. It shamed the Ranger, but there was little he could do.

As the older Knight slung his sword back over his shoulder, his scouts came pouring into the room with bows drawn, peeking into the cells lining the walls. They packed each cell full with dwarves, the Q'leti, with matted hair and crusty beards, covered in filth and tattered leather and cloth scraps hanging from their bodies. In the cells at the end were their wolves, their fur filthy and matted together with blood, many of them little more than skin and bone.

Caeleen stood beside Sir Edmund as the cells opened and the dwarves shuffled out, his brow furrowed.

"I know we can't let them keep Nighthand, Sir," the Ranger said, "but we can't just leave them to die in the wilderness. It's not right."

"They made their decision, lad," Edmund replied. "There's nothing more we can do for them, unless they surrender and face judgment for their crimes."

"Don't you think they've been punished enough, though? Q'let was their home, and the Foundsmen drove them from it without much choice."

"The Foundsmen drove their ancestors out, not them. It was their choice to pillage and kill; no one forced them to."

"We don't know that, Edmund."

"Longwatch, you've too much a heart, and too big a mouth for your own good, sometimes. I hope you know that."

"Would it kill you to show some empathy, Sir?" The

Ranger gestured toward the tattered clothes of the Q'leti, many of them children. "Gods above, they're suffering."

"Empathy is a luxury we cannot afford in our line of work, lad. You need to learn that now, before it gets you into trouble." Without another word, Edmund started away to inspect the prisoners.

Caeleen grimaced and skulked back out to join his party.

"Sir?" Leon asked, placing a hand on Caeleen's back.

Cae pinched his eyes and blew a puff of air roughly from his nose. "Let's just get back to Alryne," he hissed.

THE HIKE BACK TO ALRYNE WENT SLOWER THAN THE chase from it. With nothing pressing them, the company were free to take their time, and were on the way back for five days, cutting across the long grass the way they had come. It was fortunate that Cae and Raimi both carried bottomless bags with them, symbols of their station as field agents for the Lion's Throne, in which they could carry firewood and food to keep them warm and fed without burdening them.

Eventually they returned to Alryne and, after a day in town to rest, Cae came to the stables where they had left their horses. The Ranger grinned as he came upon his beloved steed, Tüli. The young horse was ashen in coat, with a dark grey mane and amber eyes. He had been a gift from Mull when Caeleen had returned to Greyfort after the Battle for Fartide. And, Gods, was he fast; with a little effort, the two of them could make the trip from Greyfort to Brookridge in under two days.

"*Kapsüsen nu, Tüli,*" the Ranger whispered into the horse's ear while feeding him an apple from his bag. "Ready to ride on home, boy?"

Tuuli snorted in response, nuzzling into Caeleen's shoulder. Cae laughed and reached for his saddle.

"Sir?"

Cae spun around to see Marish standing in the doorway. "You said you wanted to talk to each of us about what happened."

"Yes, I did!" Cae nodded as he left the saddle for a moment. He stepped forward and put a hand on Marish's shoulder. "First and foremost, let me say this: that was a great shot you took when we got in there. It's hard to hit a target in the throat, and even harder to do it from behind."

"Thank you, Sir."

Cae smiled. "But," he continued, "when we got to the throne room, that was where you slipped up. Can you tell me what you did wrong?"

Marish frowned with thought. "...It...it wasn't helping Thraun, was it?"

"Not in itself, no," the Ranger replied. "But, when you went to help him, you left yourself exposed. You turned your back to a werewolf."

Marish shrugged. "I figured Raimi could hold him off. She's a trained spy."

"I see your reasoning, but that doesn't change the fact. She needed your help, but you were still bandaging

Thraun. If you're going to do field medicine, you have to able to do it quick. We'll work on that, okay?"

"Yes, Sir." Marish bowed her head. "I'll do better."

"I know you will." Cae smiled and clapped the girl on the shoulder. "Now, go on, pack your things. And send your brother out here, would you?"

Marish nodded and hurried off. As soon as she was out of the way, Caeleen slipped behind the door to the stable and waited.

A bit later, Thraun shuffled through the door, looking around when he saw only the horses. Before he could turn back around, Caeleen slipped forward and smacked him on the back of his head.

"You rushed a werewarg," the Ranger said.

Thraun rubbed his head where he'd been struck. "I thought I could handle it!" he protested.

"It was a *werewarg*, Thraun. What were you gonna do, let it cut you open and then strangle it with your entrails?"

"I've killed wargs before!"

"Wargs aren't the same as werewargs. Thraun, we've talked about this. You can't just rush headlong into a fight like that. You're not a soldier, you're a scout."

"Well, maybe I should be a soldier!" Thraun threw his hands up. "I'm terrible at sneaking around, and I hate using that bow!"

"Thraun, you're one of the best sneaks in your class. You're a great tracker. And not every scout has to use a shortbow; we could get you an arbalest if you need something else."

"I don't want to shoot things, Sir!" Thraun clenched his fists. "I'm a fighter, I'm not an archer!"

Caeleen paused and put a hand on Thraun's shoulder. "Try to calm down. I can't help you if you're not going to listen."

Thraun glared at his teacher for a moment before sucking in a deep breath and letting his hands dangle. "I'm sorry, Sir. I just..."

"I know," Cae smiled. "It's okay. Not every scout does it the same. If you like, we can shift your focus, start training you as a skirmisher. You're a great swordsman, almost as good as I am. But you've already come so far in your scout training. Don't throw that away so quickly, all right?"

Thraun cast his eyes to the ground and nodded. "I won't, Sir."

Cae clapped the boy on the back. "all right. Go get your stuff. We're setting out today."

The ride back to Greyfort took about three weeks, since the hunting party joined with the soldiers and scouts Edmund hadn't left at Nighthand. Cae did his best to keep his annoyance to himself, knowing he and his party could travel quicker by themselves, but Leon and Raimi could see his irritation in the set of his jaw and the way he gripped his reins. They laughed to themselves and kept on riding.

When they arrived at the gates to the City of Walls, the sound of trumpets rang out loud and clear to herald their return. The Whisper winced as the brass rang in his ears; two years of being a Knight, and Caeleen was still unaccustomed to being heralded.

The train of warriors snaked through the city right up to Viraati Lien. There, a group of servants waited and took Tüli's reins and led him and the other horses away to be fed and brushed.

The soldiers departed with the servants, and Caeleen and his party followed Sir Edmund into the throne room. There sat King Mull, as broad and strong as ever, but with a streak of white hair running through the brown locks under his crown. The white was right where his scalp had been broken in a hunt about a year back, when a wild roc had struck him right off his horse. Mull had gotten his payback, and the roc's beak was fashioned by the castle's Magesmiths into a lovely set of armor, but the mark had been made.

"Welcome home, Sir Edmund!" Mull called out as he rose from his throne, his arms out wide. "And to you, good Ranger! I take it your work is done, then?"

"Indeed, Sire!" Edmund bellowed with a grin. "Nighthand is yours once more! The beasts are vanquished, and the Q'leti have been driven back into the wild! I've left a garrison at the Keep, and they await your orders!"

"Excellent!" The King replied. "You're to be commended for your efforts. Perhaps we'll hold a feast in, let's say... three days, eh?"

"That sounds lovely, Sire!" Edmund bowed low before his King. "If it's all the same to you, I believe I'll retire. I heard on the ride here that the Lady Andelyn is playing tonight at the Fixin's, and I don't want to miss that!"

"You're dismissed, Sir Edmund," Mull laughed. "Go, enjoy your evening."

Edmund bowed once more and strode out of the throne room. Mull came down the stairs then and put his hands on Caeleen's shoulders. "Are you all right, Ranger?"

"We're fine, Sire," Cae replied with a sigh. "I wish I could say the same for the victims from Alryne."

"I heard," Mull said. "I'm sorry, lad. We can't save everyone, I'm afraid."

"I know... I'll admit, we probably would never have made it home, if not for Edmund and his company. But these four fought hard, and I'm proud of them." The young Knight gestured to his hunting party.

Mull nodded. "You certainly know how to pick 'em, don't ya?" The King grinned, and Caeleen chuckled.

Mull stepped back and looked at the hunting party. "So! I hope you'll all be at this feast, then. Come in your uniforms, we want you all presentable. That includes you, Whisper. Scrape that stubble off your face. And do something with your hair, won't you?"

"As you wish, Sire," he sighed. "But, if I may, I'd like a word with you about our treatment of the Q'leti."

Mull nodded his head. "Come to me tomorrow, lad. We'll talk in the morning; I'll meet you at the city gate." Mull smiled at the party once more. "The lot of you are to be commended for your bravery. I'll see you all at the feast. You're dismissed!"

The party all bowed low and departed, going their separate ways. Thraun and Marish headed off to their family's farm just outside the city, Raimi went to report to

Baron on their mission, and Cae and Leon rode back to the Grey Wood.

There, in the wooded hills, not too far from the nest of the griffin Kaon, was Caeleen's little cabin. It wasn't much, but it had all the essentials; stables for Tüli and Buck (Leon's horse), a few targets in the back, a kitchen, a pair of bedrooms, a washroom, and even their own globe and caster. They'd cost Cae nearly three months' wages, but he was glad he'd picked it up; every so often he'd use them to speak with his sister Venya in Evenwood, or check in on his friend Nightsister Iómi in Highhaven, or receive orders from Mull regarding threats reported by his scouts, or... well, a good many things, now that he thought about it. The washroom didn't see too much use; Cae and Leon had taken to washing down by the river to save themselves the trips up and down from the cabin to the riverside with their buckets. Still, it was nice to have.

Once Tüli and Buck were stabled, groomed and fed, Cae and Leon got to work on a simple dinner of rabbit stew. Cae had an arrangement with Glenn Farm which supplied him with fresh vegetables. He was learned enough in cooking that he could tend to himself, but they found that Leon was better at the cutting and trimming of meat. Preparing their evening meals had become something of a ritual for them, a means of easing the tension out of them after a rough hunt.

As they sat waiting for the stew to finish heating, Leon looked across the table at his teacher. "So... you wanted to talk to each of us about something?"

Caeleen nodded. "Care to take a guess at what I needed to talk to you about?"

A silence hung over the pair for a moment. Leon hung his head and broke it with a sigh. "I hesitated."

"You hesitated."

Leon shrugged. "I'm sorry, Sir. I know we've talked about this, and I really am trying to work on it..."

"I know you are." The Ranger nodded. "I guess I should have drilled you harder about it the past few months to get it out of your system before we headed for Alryne. I know you don't much like fighting."

"It's not that I don't like fighting," Leon stammered. "It's just, I... y'know."

"You're still having the nightmares, aren't you?"

Leon nodded, his eyes on his hands folded on the table. "It... I can still smell it some nights."

Cae nodded. Leon had been a farm boy, one with dreams of becoming a dancer, before he was taken in by Mull to be a squire. His family, the Farroughs, had lived on their farm close to the edge of the Grey Wood. Two years ago, a wolfbear that had come from the Widewood had slaughtered his parents and brother right in front of him. Cae remembered that hunt with sharp clarity; it had been in the wretched beast's cave that he found Sal'tera, the lightning-throwing Blade of the Covenant. That hunt had earned him a Knighthood, and led to Leon being entrusted to Caeleen's keeping and tutelage. But Gods above, the Ranger would give anything to undo the damage done to that boy.

"I know what you're going through, believe me. It happened to me, too..." Caeleen reached across the table and took the boy's hand, trying to ignore the chill as he remembered the sight of his father's blood, and the stench of dragonfire stinging his nostrils. "... I still have nightmares, too."

Leon frowned. "What...what do you do? How do you fight the fear?"

Cae sighed and pulled his hand back as he turned away. "It... it isn't easy. But, in time, you'll learn to turn that fear into drive. If you don't fight, it could happen to someone else."

Leon ran a hand through his short blonde hair. "I know, Sir. I just wish it would turn a little faster."

"Well," Cae replied with a smile, "you turned it fast enough this time, I guess. You saved my life, Leon."

Leon paused for a moment, then nodded. "I guess so, yeah."

"Kid, let me tell you. People will always agree that fighting with an axe is easier than fighting with a sword. But make no mistake, using the axe the way you do is an art. I've known dervishes from the deserts of Cidarian, and not even they can do what you do."

Leon smiled at his teacher's praise. "Thank you, Sir."

Cae smiled. "You'll gain confidence with time, I'm sure. You just need practice."

About that time, the stew began steaming and filling the cabin with the smell of good meat. "C'mon, let's eat."

---

2

*T*he next morning, Caeleen waited at the city gates with his hood drawn as Mull came riding up. The Ranger raised his brows when he saw the King rode alone, no guards or anything.

"Morning, Griffin!" Mull called with a tired smile. "Come, ride with me down to the coast."

Cae grimaced, not yet accustomed to the callsign Mull had given him. "As you wish, Sire," he replied, his head bowed low.

Mull shook his head and chuckled. "That's Lion to you, lad. Speak to me as a hunter, not a servant."

Caeleen smirked under his hood. "Fair enough."

It was about a half-hour ride to the coast. Caeleen did his best to conceal his amusement at having to rein Tüli in; Mull's black warhorse was large and strong, but couldn't hope to keep up with Tüli's speed. They rode in relative quiet to the beach just outside the city and slowed as they rode south along the waters of the Silver Ocean so they could speak.

"So," Mull said at last, "you wanted to speak to me about the Q'leti."

"I did," Cae replied, pulling his hood back. "I... Look, I know what all the other Knights say about me."

Mull cocked a brow. "Which things? That you're too soft, or that you need to wash your hair more often?"

Cae allowed himself a quick laugh before his grimace set in. "They don't exactly hide their contempt, that much I'm sure you know already."

"Aye, they can be harsh. I've heard some of their... whisperings about my policies. It seems some of them would prefer if I made more like our Emperor."

Caeleen hadn't quite intended to do it, but he turned and spit on the sand as they rode by. His face flushed, but relief washed over him as he heard a hearty laugh boom out of his King's chest. "I know, I know, he'd probably call it treason, but... Gods, I just can't stand him."

"Neither can I, lad," the old Lion grinned. "But I suppose he's a necessary evil. What's the alternative, hmm?"

"You could challenge his rule," Cae suggested. "Throw down your sword before the Gilded Throne. You're a fantastic warrior, Sire. Whoever he picks as his champion, you could take them." Caeleen figured it a fair assumption that the Rite Electorate would concede to Mull's challenge, considering his service as leader of the Royal Hunt. It was also a fair assumption that Cestus would choose a champion to fight for him, because... honestly, what was he going to do? The Emperor was a twig of a man, past his prime.

Mull shook his head. "I'm not an Emperor, lad. I'll

not sit on a chair while my fellow men do all the dirty work."

Cae frowned. "Well...back to the Q'leti."

"Yes..." Mull let out a ragged sigh. "I'm not fond of the way they're treated myself, to tell the truth. Haven Kingdom should be theirs, there's no denying that. But it's beyond my power to do anything for them there."

"But it's not beyond you to change how they're treated here in Laithe, Lion," Cae insisted. "This is your Kingdom, no matter what anyone says. We could help them, we don't have to shove them around and drive them from their beds."

Mull nodded in agreement. "What did you have in mind?"

Caeleen pointed farther south, back inland. In the distance, Nighthand Keep was just barely visible at the edge of Krem Zhul-Mkat. "See all that open space there? There's plenty of room for a new settlement. It isn't a permanent solution, but it would be a good start. Give the Q'leti a place to call home until they can go back to their *real* home." The Bowmaster shrugged. "I mean, what are *we* doing with it?"

Mull gazed out at the grasslands in the distance, the crinkles at the corners of his eyes deepening with his pondering. "Perhaps... Ranger, how potent is your sister's magic?"

"Venya?" Cae asked, his head tilted. "She's... well, she's only been a proper Druid for two years, but she's pretty powerful. She can work the building trees now, she told me before we left for Alryne."

"Could she build a shelter for the Q'leti?"

"Probably. She used to work on a farm, too, so she could probably help them get their own crops started."

Mull smiled. "How would she like to visit the mainland?"

Cae grinned. "I think I like where your head's at, Lion. I'll see if she's up for it."

Mull grinned. "Hold on, hold on. I'll have to run it by my advisors first. I think they'll agree though, thank Xanith."

Caeleen nodded. As the two of them turned back to return to the city, Caeleen let a smile play at the corners of his mouth. "Now about this feast..."

"Uniform, boy. The one with the stripes and the puffy shoulders, the Bowmaster's coat. You'd best be in it." Mull grinned. "And pull your hair back."

"What? Sire, come on!" Caeleen laughed.

The two of them stabled their horses outside the Fort's Fixin's when they returned. Here and there about the dimly lit tavern were a handful of folk still in waking up or nursing their heads... Sir Edmund among them, having had too much the night before by the look of him.

Leon was already at the bar waiting for them when they went inside, making idle conversation with Cici the barkeep. Caeleen smiled as he dropped onto the stool beside his squire, and the older woman set a pint of Redgrove Cider in front of him. Behind the bar, Caeleen could see the little form of Wini Amilë, Cici's granddaughter, rinsing out glasses in a bucket of hot water.

"How goes it, Ranger?" Cici asked.

Cae took a draft of the cider and nodded. "Goes all right, ma'am," he replied. "Just biding our time until the feast."

Cici turned to Mull, who sat on Caeleen's other side. "And, good morning to you, Sire! What brings ya to the Fixin's today, hmm?"

"Just getting out for a bit, Miss Amilë," the old monarch replied. "How fares your daughter? Any word from her in the globe?"

"Not so much the last few days... but, last time she called, she said she's doing well." Cici cocked her head toward Caeleen. "I suspect he's heard from her more recently than I have."

Cae shrugged. "Haven't heard from her in a while, but I think Isi probably has."

"And how is Lady Rumoré?" Mull asked.

"She's doing well!" Leon piped up from the other side of Caeleen. "We saw her the other day by the riverside, cleaning some of her old robes. I heard there was a big fight in the tavern over there about a week back."

"Oh, Gods," Cici moaned. "If I had a copper for every fight that broke out in here, I could probably afford a bigger building!"

Cae turned to his squire with a look of amusement on his face. "Leon, that was almost four months ago."

Leon's eyes widened. "It *was?*"

Mull chuckled. "Well, is she all right?" he asked.

Leon nodded. "She said it wasn't a big deal. Couple of guys with a couple of knives, nothing that serious."

"That sounds serious to me." The King's face was suddenly grim.

Caeleen cocked an eyebrow. "Sire, please. This is Isi we're talking about. A few knives are nothing to her. Trust me, I've seen her in action." The Ranger traced a finger along the long scar on his cheek.

"Hmm..." Mull eyed the scar for a moment, then nodded. "I suppose you're right."

Cae smiled, then drained the last of his cider and wiped his mouth. "Well, we'd best head out on patrol. Suppose we'll see you all at the feast. Leon, let's get to it!" With a swish of his cloak, Caeleen and Leon headed toward the exit.

"In uniform, boy!" Mull called after him.

Cae tossed a lazy salute over his shoulder as he and his squire walked out the door.

THE AUTUMN AIR IN THE GREY WOOD CHILLED Ranger and squire through their coats as they skulked their way through their rounds in the Grey Wood. There were a handful of parties that aroused concern from the young hunters as of late, although nothing too out of the ordinary for the region.

At the moment, the two sat high in the trees and watched as a small pack of goblins gathered in a small clearing. The pack had been on the move in from Haven Kingdom for the past day or so, but had yet to show signs of hostility. Cae decided it would be wise to monitor them, just in case.

Just as the two began to tire of their observation, a distant *thoom-thoom-thoom* reached their ears.

Exchanging a quick glance, they each nocked an arrow and turned their eyes in the sound's direction. It didn't take long for them to find the source of the sound; from the trees several yards out emerged a lumbering figure, thick in limb, but still comparatively lanky for his height. He stood at least thirty feet tall, and each stride brought him forward almost the length of Caeleen's whole body.

Caeleen recognized him right away and stood up to his full height in his tree.

"Adma!" the Ranger called out, loud and clear. The goblins in the clearing all craned their necks to see the source of the sound.

The giant smiled as he spotted Caeleen and Leon in their trees. "Oh! Good day to you, little masters!" He bellowed, his words coming out a bit slow. "How fare you on this day, hmm?"

"All is well on our front, friend!" Cae replied. "Mind your step, though, we have some guests down here, and it'd be a shame if you were to squish any of them!"

"Hmm?" Adma looked down to see the critters, chattering among themselves in the clearing. "Ah, yes! I've been waiting for these little ones!"

"Have you, now?" This time, it was Leon who spoke up, his voice shaky. "Might we ask why?"

The giant chuckled. "Afraid I'm up to no good, are you? Worry not, my friend, I only need their help with some building. I'm building a boat, you see!"

"A boat!" Caeleen exclaimed. "Whatever could you need a boat for, Adma?"

"I hear the fishing out in the Silver Ocean is wonderful this time of year," Adma replied. "I haven't had fish since that lad Acandis was last in Laithe. Oh, I wonder what happened to that boy?"

"Acandis?" Leon frowned. "I'm sorry, friend. I'm afraid Acandis passed away many years ago."

"Did he?" Adma frowned under his moss-laden beard. "That's a shame. He seemed a good lad."

"I hear he was a wonderful ruler," Cae agreed. "But you have me curious. How are you going to find all the wood for your boat, Adma? You know we have an agreement about the trees here in the Grey Wood."

Adma nodded. "I asked in the city. That nice lad, Mully, agreed to give me some of his wood for my boat, if I brought some fish back for the people. A very polite lad, that Mully!"

Cae laughed. "Polite wouldn't be the word I'd use for him, but maybe he just acts different around me!"

Adma chuckled once more. "Well, we'd best be going. Good day to you, little friends!" The giant lowered a hand to the goblins at his feet, and they clambered up his arm and clung to his back and shoulders as he lumbered away.

Leon let out an audible breath.

Cae turned to his squire and smirked. "Never met a giant before, eh?"

"No, Sir!" The Ranger-in-training replied, a nervous laugh bubbling up under his words.

Cae laughed and returned his arrow to its quiver. "Come on, we've got more to do today."

"How big do you think his fishing nets will be?" Leon asked.

Cae laughed as they two hopped down from their perch in the trees.

Sometime just after noon, the pair made their way to the banks of the Grey River. They often came here toward the end of the day to bathe and launder, since the river was a bit too far from the cabin to move water into their bathroom.

But today was different; the two had caught word that a message would come that Caeleen had been waiting some time for. Not enough word came to him about the goings-on in Tamia, but every now and again a hupawi, a river siren, would make her way downstream with word from the land of the merfolk. Caeleen leaned against the bridge with his arms crossed, absent-mindedly tapping his foot on the damp ground.

Leon watched the river quietly for a time, then finally turned to his teacher. "Sir, would you mind not tapping so loud?"

Caeleen jumped subtly, his foot stopping as he returned his attention to the present. "Hm? Oh. Sorry, pal. Just a little antsy is all."

"Why?" Leon asked. "What's got you so worked up?"

Cae shook his head. "I dunno, I just... I haven't heard much about how things are going over in Fartide in a few months. I like to keep up with how rebuilding is progress-ing, how the people are getting along, that sort of thing."

"And how the Queen is doing, I bet," Leon added. The comment wasn't sly, as most people were about that particular topic. So many people loved to tease Cae for his concern over Queen Siahra, always joking that he *had* to fancy her. But Leon was always genuine. The boy understood.

Cae nodded. "I worry, y'know? It can't be easy, what she's trying to build."

Leon nodded, leaving the thought to linger there. Cae was right. King Arian had left mighty big shoes to fill when he passed, and Siahra had her hands full enough with repairing the damages to her capitol city. Cae would have been happy to stay and lend a hand after the Battle for Fartide, were he not so busy on his grand quest to save his mother and all that.

Before either of them could make any further comment, they pricked their ears to the sound of a distant singing. The melody seemed lazy, and filled with a quiet mirth as it drifted in the air, though its source could be found nowhere.

Cae popped up from his place against the bridge, and pulled back his hood, smiling as he spotted the shape in the water approaching. Its trail danced playfully about in the river for a moment before a more distinctly human shape emerged from the surface.

The woman bore a slightly darker shade of the beige skin Caeleen remembered Siahra having, and her scales were a pale violet that shimmered as her tail shifted into the shape of two dainty legs beneath a long purple skirt which seemed to dry quickly as she walked ashore. Cae noted, with a vague curiosity, that the slender fins gracing the woman's arms did not disappear as she came upon land. Perhaps this was one of many differences between the maotu and the hupawi.

Caeleen and Leon both bowed instinctively. The woman smiled and offered a small curtsy. "I suppose you are the Ranger I have heard so much about?"

"Might be so," Cae replied. "Caeleen Longwatch, Bowmaster of Greyfort. This here is Leon Farrough, my squire. And you?"

The siren tossed her black hair over her shoulder, letting it land on her back in a wet mass. "My name is Sivi."

"Sivi," Cae echoed. He wondered what it meant in the siren-tongue. He wondered if the sirens even had a language apart from that of the mermaids.

"I heard you might like to hear about the things happening in the *hemkest* lately."

"We'd like that, yes," Leon added. "Poor Cae's been losing sleep over it."

Sivi laughed, a little musical giggle. "Well, I'm glad I could help."

Cae shot Leon a quick look before turning back to the siren. "So how is Tamia? How is the Queen?"

Sivi frowned for just a moment. "I will be honest, woodsman... things have been strange in the Sea as of late. A cold wind blows in from the west, and it brings strange tidings."

"Strange? How?" Cae asked.

"It... something is making the people cold. Not in their flesh, but in their hearts. They grow distant, quiet. After a while, they become angry. We do not know why.

And in the depths, things are stirring. Ugly things, like the dragon brought with him."

Cae grimaced, remembering Sturamtönn and his horde of sahuagins. He was unsure if anyone had killed that kraken the wyrm brought with him, but he knew they had done well in clearing out the remnants of the horde's ground forces.

"And yet, Siahra stands strong." Sivi smiled. "Her teachers have made her a great rider, and she leads the Mo-Lamai without fear."

"That's wonderful!" Cae thought aloud. "I remember she told me she always wanted to be an Oceanguard!"

Sivi nodded. "Her wisdom grows beyond her years. Even now, she sends for counsel from many great minds throughout the Sea. Among them, in fact, is Grand Mistress Suressa."

"Hmm? Grand who?"

"Suressa is the leader of my people," Sivi explained. "The rivers of the Three Kingdoms are her realm."

"How come we've never heard of her?" asked Leon.

Sivi shrugged. "Perhaps you do not pay enough attention." She winked at the boy, and he cast his eyes to the ground timidly.

Cae shook his head. "Well, I'm glad to hear how well she fares, despite the circumstances. Maybe if things ease up here, I might could pay her a visit sometime."

"Perhaps, yes!" Sivi replied. She scratched at her arm for a moment. "Oh...forgive me, woodsman, but I must be on my way. Hupawi do not fare so well away from our waters."

Cae gave another little bow. "Thank you so much for your words, Sivi. Blessed tides."

"And to you." Sivi inclined her head with one last smile before turning back and sliding gracefully into the river. Leon and Cae could hear her siren song drift off downstream for a moment before it dwindled and faded from earshot.

Leon smiled. "What a lovely voice."

Cae smirked. "And they say I'm the smitten one."

"Hey, what's that supposed to mean?"

Cae laughed aloud as he led the way back into the Grey Wood.

As the sun began to dip toward the west, the pair made their way uphill from their cabin toward a large nest. They visited this nest often, as it was home to a very special family of griffins. As they vaulted over the lip of brush and twig, Cae smiled wide as three griffin cubs scampered forth to greet them.

Two pounced on him and knocked him to the floor, while the third and smallest leapt into Leon's arms. As the pair laughed and scratched at the cub's ears, their parents strode forward. Cae grinned up at his old friend.

"*Afternoon, Kaon!*" the Ranger growled and purred in the Griffin-Tongue. "*How've you been lately?*"

"*Good afternoon, Ranger!*" Kaon replied. "*We've been well. The children are just about ready to go on their first hunt!*"

"*That's wonderful!*" The Ranger grinned as he turned back to Leon. "Hear that, Leon? Isn't that great?"

Leon frowned at his teacher. "... Sir, you know I don't speak Griffin."

Cae paused for a moment, then let out a bark of laughter. "Sorry, pal. I always forget!"

"You always do this same bit, too," the squire replied. "And it's still not funny."

Cae shrugged as a cub nipped at his ear. "The cubs are almost ready for their first hunt!"

"Oh!" Leon grinned. "That's really cool!"

Cae nodded and turned back to Kaon. The two exchanged a glance. They shared a strong trust after what they had been through together; it had been Kaon who bore Caeleen on his back during the Battle for Fartide, where the sea-dragon Sturamtönn was slain. Since then, Caeleen and Kaon had fought together a handful of times since he returned to Greyfort. Caeleen's Eagle companion, Alahir, remained in the Dokk to aid his sister in her watch over the mountains in Caeleen's place, so having Kaon around made things a little more familiar for Cae. It had helped him adjust to his new life.

"When will you be taking them?" he asked.

"In the coming weeks, I should think," the griffin replied. *"Zhira believes we ought to do it early this season."*

Zhira, Kaon's mate, nodded. *"If we wait too long, it may become too cold. Winter came early last year, we don't want to miss our chance."*

"I agree," the Ranger replied. *"If you two need any help getting them ready, let me know. Leon and I would be glad to help."*

"We can't ask that of you, Ranger," said Zhira. "You've been very good to our family since you arrived *here, and I thank you for that. But a griffin's first hunt is a family matter."*

Cae nodded with a smile, turning and showing an open palm to his old friend. Kaon nodded, looking to Leon. The squire stared back, and slowly lowered the cub he was holding to the ground. Kaon squawked and shook his head in amusement.

"Let's get going, we should get back home before dark." Cae grinned as he shrugged off the two cubs still pawing at him and leapt off down the hill, Leon tailing after him.

The sun was just dipping down past the horizon when Cae and Leon returned to their cabin. They were tired, of course, but there was still one last thing for the pair to do. Behind their cabin was a sizable pen. The two of them leapt over the small wooden fence and sat down in the flattened down dirt for a moment to breathe.

"You did well today, Leon," Cae said.

"Thank you, Sir," Leon replied between drafts from his water flask.

Cae smiled as he pulled out a flask of his own. "You're getting faster, you know. You're almost fast enough to keep up with me now."

Leon furrowed his brow. "Almost? Really? Come on, I've totally got you by now."

Cae laughed. "Kid, you're good. But you're not that good. Not yet." The Ranger stood, brushing the dirt from his coat and grinning. "But we'll get you there."

Leon stood up as well, brushing himself off. They stood facing each other for a moment, then drew their training weapons. Leon gripped an axe similar to the one Cae lent him, and Cae flourished his dagger and sword.

Caeleen made the first move. Darting to the left as he charged, he planted with his foot and launched himself toward Leon's flank as he swung with his shorter blade. Leon deflected the dagger with the handle of the axe as it began to spin in his hands, and with a quick pirouette the squire threw a powerful stroke horizontally, intending to force his teacher back. Cae instead ducked beneath the swipe and swept the boy's legs out from under him.

Leon just barely caught himself on the way down, swirling on his arms for a moment as he launched himself back to put distance between the two of them. Cae smirked; Leon worked his dancing skills into the way he fought.

Leon spun his axe over his head before vaulting off the fence toward his teacher. The axe head bounced off of the mithril blade, and the recoil left a small opening in Leon's front. Cae took the shot, throwing an elbow into the squire's jaw, just hard enough to knock the boy back. He didn't want to hurt the lad, just teach him.

"Don't let a parry throw you off like that!" Cae quipped as he brandished his mithril blade. "C'mon, you weren't this clumsy with that werewarg!"

Leon grinned and shook his head. With a skip that brought him high into the air, Leon tossed a kick toward his teacher's head. Cae moved out of the way easily, spinning around as his squire landed behind him. When the boy's next swing came faster than the Ranger had expected, he almost tripped over himself. Cae was impressed; Leon had used the momentum of his kick to spin himself the right way in the air before landing!

Leon's strokes began to come faster, the head of the axe bouncing off of Caeleen's weapons, quicker and quicker as the squire spun and danced around his tutor. Cae's grin was wide; the boy was doing far better than he'd expected. Suddenly, Leon planted his foot and, turning the axe backward in his axe, swung the blunt end of the weapon into Caeleen's side.

The Ranger dropped to a knee and coughed out a single "ha!" as he rolled over his shoulder. Getting his feet back under him, Cae brought his blades together, one beneath the other over his head, to block the axe coming down over him.

Klinnng!

The two froze as the steel blade of Caeleen's dagger snapped, half of it dropping to the dirt.

"Oh!" Leon stammered. "Oh, Gods! Sorry, Sir! I didn't mean..."

"Nah, nah. I guess..." Cae twisted his face in bewilderment as he looked down at the broken weapon. "Wow. I guess I messed up the block. Did...did I put the sword in front? I meant to."

"I don't think you did," Leon replied. "Wow... didn't think I'd swung that hard."

Cae frowned. That had been his father's dagger. "Ah, well," the Ranger sighed. "I've been meaning to get the old thing replaced, anyway."

Leon shrugged. "Think that's enough for today?"

Cae laughed. "Probably." The two looked out westward. The trees were too thick now to see the horizon, but they could both tell that the sun was already gone, and the sky had already grown dark. "Let's grab a bite, then hit the hay."

* * *

THE NEXT TWO DAYS WENT BY RATHER QUICKLY, AND soon came the day of the feast. As he scraped at his wet face with a small hunting knife to clear away the bits of beard that were sprouting again, Caeleen was still a little hazy on the details of the event. Was it to honor his students? Sir Edmund and his soldiers? It certainly wouldn't be to honor Caeleen. Mull knew how particular the Ranger was about excessive praise. Better to go unnoticed than put on a pedestal; working in the background made his job much easier. Everyone knew there was a Ranger in the Grey Wood, but no one ever asked about him. Caeleen liked it that way.

Leon was already dressed in his squire's uniform, the grey lion cub emblazoned on the right breast of his red tunic.

Caeleen frowned as he pulled his Bowmaster's uniform out of his closet. It was a darker green than his regular coat, and the heavy leather made it harder to move his arms, despite the puffed-out shoulders being made of a looser fabric. White stripes ran down the arms all the way to the cuffs, and the right breast was adorned with the stylized symbol of a griffin in white. The hood sewn into the coat was smaller than the hood of his cloak and came in too close around his head when drawn. It, too, was trimmed in white. The tail of the coat came down just below his hips, and they hugged his legs a little too tight for his liking. The uniform constricted Caeleen's movement, made him dangerously slow. He only ever wore it to formal events such as this one, or... well, whenever else Mull told him to wear it.

It took him a few minutes to pull the whole ensemble together, pushing his lion-head pauldron on over the top of the left shoulder and crushing the puffy shoulder of the coat down as he did so, but eventually he got the thing on and presented himself to Leon.

The squire grinned. "You look miserable."

"I *feel* miserable." Cae tightened the strap of his bow and quiver, and he groaned when he couldn't get them into a comfortable position. "This sucks."

"It's a nice outfit, though," Leon mused. "Isn't that the point?"

"I'd much rather wear what you've got on." Cae gestured to his squire's tunic. "At least, you can lift your arms all the way up, and you still look nice."

Leon grinned, waltzing up to his Knight and throwing an arm around his shoulder. "Come on, let's just go. The sooner we make our appearance, the sooner we can get you out of this thing."

"Right," said Cae. "And, before everything gets started, we need to go see Baron. He had something he wanted to talk to me about, I think."

The ride to Greyfort was quick, just shy of half an hour once the two got going. The ride slowed a bit once the pair entered the city but, soon enough, the horses were back in the royal stables, and Cae and Leon crept along Viraati Líen's back passages and secret stairs, until they came upon the Spymaster's Quarters.

There, bent over a map of the Empire with that long, thin blade in place of his left forearm, was Spymaster Baron, still a mountain of muscle despite his cushy new station. Cae smiled at his old companion; they hadn't been given much chance to speak since the Battle for Fartide where that arm had been lost. But Cae knew Baron had been keeping an eye on him as often as he could.

"Been a while, old man," Caeleen said as he approached the table. "How's the whole intelligence thing going?"

"Intelligence is good, you should try it sometime." Baron offered a wry smile as he looked up at the Ranger. "... You should do something with your hair before the feast."

"*Skri!* I completely forgot!" Hurriedly, Cae gathered up his hair and pulled it back into a bun. A sloppy bun, yes, but it looked better than it had before.

"Language, boy," Baron growled. "You're a Knight of Laithe, you can't just fire off vulgarities whenever you like."

"What did he say?" asked Leon, shuffling forward into the dimly lit room.

"I'm not going to answer that," Baron laughed.

"Ask me later," Cae said with a wink. "So what's up? What did you need to see me for?"

Baron frowned. "Well," he began, "it may be nothing. Or it may be... well, it may be something serious. You know I have spies throughout the Empire."

"Naturally," Cae replied.

"Well, some of my eyes in Tamia have reported some... odd goings-on throughout the Diamond Shores. Fauna not native to the region, wargs and bats and ravens prowling along the roads and in the wilds. Wandering groups of vagrants attacking travelers for food, and some just sort of... there, mulling about and not doing much at all. Isolated pockets of winter weather."

"Winter weather? Like snow?" Caeleen furrowed his brow. Sivi had told him things were strange out west lately, but... "*Snow* in Tamia? In *October*?"

"That was my reaction, too," the old Beastslayer replied. "It may just be changes in climate causing odd weather patterns and migration of these creatures. The homeless folk I can't explain, but... I might have suspicions."

Cae grimaced. He knew exactly what Baron was implying. It bordered on treason, suspecting the Emperor of targeting the merfolk, but... well, he'd already gone after the elves. Was it truly that big a leap?

"Either way," Baron continued, "they might all be unrelated. But they might not. Some new records salvaged from the Burned Ages have given more light to phenomena we'd once thought only myth. These records suggest that these occurrences may be evidence of malevolent Voloki magic."

"Voloki? Gods be good..." the Whisper shuddered. The thought of demons roaming the Three Kingdoms chilled the Ranger's blood. Beasts and dragons he could handle, but demons and devils...

"Again, I might be way off the mark," Baron assured

the boy. "But, if I'm not... Caeleen, you're the best hunter in Laithe. Maybe the best in all the Empire. You'll be needed on the front lines."

"We can't go to war with Volok, are you crazy?" Cae threw his hands up. "What are we going to do, storm the Four Hells?"

"Calm yourself, Ranger," Baron hissed. "I'm not asking you to lead an army. But I might ask you to leave Laithe for a time."

"Leave Laithe?" Leon stammered. "Caeleen is a Knight of Laithe, he's *the* Bowmaster. Who'll watch over the Grey Wood?"

Baron stared at Leon for a moment. "Why do you think we brought you here today, boy?"

A thick silence hung in the air. Leon's eyes widened. "... I... Sir, I'm just a squire."

Cae turned to look at his student. "That may be true... but you're almost ready."

Leon threw his eyebrows up. "What?? No! I can't, I'm not a..."

Cae frowned. "Leon, I get it. You're still just a kid, I know. But you've been doing better than I let on. I wasn't much better a hunter than you when they named me Whisper of the Dokk."

Leon stared at his teacher for a moment, unable to speak. "Sir... I don't know what to say."

"Don't say anything for now," Cae replied. "Just know that things will get tougher for a while. I'll be asking a lot more of you to get you ready for your Trial."

"What *is* my Trial, anyway?"

Cae frowned. "It'll be a lot like the scouts' final test,"

he replied. "But it's gonna be harder. That's all I can say." The Ranger turned to Baron again. "So what does this mean for me, then? Will I be heading to Tamia?"

"You might be," Baron replied. "If reports like this continue to come in, and I decide it's worth investigating, then I'll talk to Mull and we'll probably have you deployed to Fartide. You'll serve Queen Siahra as a Knight of the Shores for a time and, if you come across anything that might be causing these events, you'll put a stop to it. If the creatures attack anyone, you'll put them down. If it snows in any of the townships, you'll be there with cloaks and blankets. If you come across the wanderers, you'll find them shelter. And whatever else the Queen demands of you..."

"I think I get it." Despite the grim implications, Cae couldn't help but smile. He and Siahra had worked closely with one another when he had joined her to liberate Fartide from Sturamtönn. Omani had named him Siahra's Companion and, while he still was unsure what that meant, he was honored to fight at her side. It would be good to see the Diamond Queen again.

"Wipe that grin off your face," Baron chided, jokingly. "You'll be there to hunt demons, not swoon over the Queen."

Caeleen's face reddened. "Swoon? Swoon?? Excuse you! I do n—I, nuh-uh, no! I do *not* swoon!"

Baron chuckled. "all right, I've kept you long enough. Get going, you don't wanna miss the feast."

Cae's cheeks were still burning when he and Leon hurried out of the room. Swoon? *Swoon?*

* * *

"You look terrible, Sir," Thraun joked as Caeleen sat down beside him at the long table in Viraati Lien's audience chamber, now filled with Greyfort's nobility.

"Shut up," Cae grinned as he gingerly punched the scout-in-training in the shoulder. "Still look better than you, kid."

Marish leaned over the table to see past her brother. "Ignore him," she said with a laugh. "You look very nice, Sir. That uniform suits you."

"Well, aren't *you* a dirty little liar?" Cae replied with a grin. "How are you two? Your training going okay?"

"Better now, yeah," Thraun replied as Leon sat down on Caeleen's other side. "Seems skirmishing is a good fit for me. Thanks for that."

"I'm glad you're taking to it," Cae said with a smile as he reached for a cut of turkey on the table. "You'll be a great scout someday, Thraun."

"Does that mean I'll be famous?" the boy joked.

"Not by a long shot," the Whisper replied. "But you'll keep your people safe."

Marish patted her brother on the back. "Fame would just make our jobs harder, anyway. This is enough."

"Agreed," Leon replied over Caeleen's shoulder.

Cae smiled. "So," he started, "Trials are coming up soon. You two ready?"

"Maybe," Marish answered. "Just depends on what we'll be doing."

"It won't be that bad, I promise." Cae bit into his slice

of turkey to hide his grin. He knew exactly what they'd be doing, but he wasn't about to tell them.

The four dug into their food, piling their plates high with meat, potatoes, bread, and all the best vegetables from the harvest this season. Cae had just sunk his teeth into a beautifully plump tomato when Mull stood up from his seat to look out over his people.

"Friends," the old king began, "lords and ladies and hands of Greyfort. Thank you for coming this evening, to honor the souls who fight for our safety and peace." This remark was met with polite, yet vigorous, applause. "Now, I know we all have a lot of eating, and plenty of drinking to do, so I won't talk too long." Many folk laughed, and Mull grinned.

"Firstly!" Mull swept wide with his right hand. Cae noted he was wearing one of his roc-beak bracers and gestured near the head of the table on his right. "Sir Edmund! Our fierce defender, who led our forces to seize that long-lost stronghold, Nighthand Keep! *Íloi!*"

Sir Edmund stood up, wearing his brown surcoat proudly as he waved to the nobles, now raising their voices in excitement. Edmund was popular among Greyfort's people, Cae had noted.

"Thank you, Sire!" Edmund bellowed. "My life for the Walls!" With a flourish of his hands, the broad-shouldered Knight bowed deeply before his King before turning and raising his fists high, roaring triumphantly to the people. They roared in response. After a moment of laughing, Edmund took his seat, still grinning wide under his mustache.

"Now," Mull called over the dying-down voices of his

people, "Edmund and his men were not without aid. Before their blades even reached the wolves of Night-hand, we had forces in the Keep at work to take the castle. Indeed, the leader of the beasts ruling over the Keep was felled not by a soldier, but by a squire!"

A sudden ripple of murmurs came from the gathered people, and Leon blushed.

"Yes, and these few, these fine hunters, were led by none other than the Griffin of Líen, himself!" The King's hand swooped down and indicated the four sitting at the table on the King's left. "Sir Caeleen, of House Long-watch! Bowmaster of Greyfort, Whisper of the Grey Wood! Íloi!"

Caeleen let out a quiet sigh as he and his three students stood up from their seats to the sound of much tamer, perhaps even timid, applause. His jade eyes locked onto Mull's as he pulled out his dagger in his off-hand.

"My hands for the King, and my heart for his People." Caeleen's voice was even, but projected, as he and his party stood erect and performed the Ranger's Salute—the dagger, gripped tightly in the right hand, held over the heart. A few voices whooped as the applause raised, before they sat back...

"Creature-Tongue! *Monster-man!!*"

Everyone fell silent and turned to see an older man, his red hair intermittently greyed, point a shaky finger at the Ranger as he shouted his slurred accusations. "This man! He speaks to the beasts! He's a beast, himself, he is! He's an animal!"

Mull's eyes burned as he glared at the heckler. He was about to let out a terrible shout, to have the man dragged away, but Caeleen held up a hand, subtly nodding to Leon. Mull held his tongue as the Ranger vaulted over the table and strode up to the man. Even without his acute sense of smell, he could almost taste the stink of booze radiating from the man.

"An animal, am I?" Again, Caeleen spoke loud enough to be heard throughout the room, but he did not shout.

"One of them!" the man spat. "One of them terrible beasts, like the one that killed them Farroughs! A monster! What, you plan to bring your animal friends here, kill us all? Are ya?"

Caeleen put a finger to his lips, his eyes cold. The heckler paused for a moment. "Do you hear that?"

The man sneered and shook his head.

"That's the sound of a hundred-thousand terrible beasts out there, prowling about, skulking after their prey, and *not* coming here for you and your family." The Ranger took a step closer. "And do you know why they don't come here?"

The heckler blinked a few times. "N... no..."

Caeleen narrowed his eyes. "They don't come here because I do my job."

In a flurry of motion, Caeleen drew his bow, nocked and drew an arrow, and fired.

An instant later, the crowd let out a collective gasp as Leon gripped the same arrow tightly in his right hand. Not missing a beat, the squire nocked it into his own bow, drew, and fired. Another gasp, and several shrieks, sounded as Caeleen caught the arrow. The Ranger turned back to the heckler, whose own face had gone stark-white. The young hunter cocked a brow and smirked.

"You're welcome."

Caeleen tossed the arrow into one of the large fire pits and strode out of the chamber, Leon following close behind.

"Hail to the Rangers!"

Caeleen stopped and turned back. He smiled at Sir Edmund, who roared his praise.

The timid applause of the rest of the room followed shortly after as Knight and Squire walked out of the chamber.

* * *

"DID YOU THINK THAT WAS FUNNY, LONGWATCH?" Baron glowered at the Ranger, still hovering over the same table he'd been at since before the feast.

Caeleen shrugged as he propped his feet up on the table across from the Spymaster. "I mean, kind of."

Mull shook his head from the other end of the small table. "Caeleen, we've talked about this. You've heard what people say about you, the rumors."

"Well, we certainly heard them tonight," Leon said with a frown. He crossed his arms over his knees, which were tucked into his chest as he scrunched up in his seat at Caeleen's side.

"You're not helping, squire," Baron growled.

"Neither are you two." Cae crossed his arms. "Honestly, what's the big deal? Let them think I'm crazy, let them think I'm a monster. If it keeps them out of my woods, that just makes my job easier."

"You still don't understand, Caeleen!" Mull barked. "You are a public figure! Whether you like it or not, people know you. You're not just the guardian of the woods anymore, boy. You're a Knight. You're *my* Knight! Everything you do reflects on me. If people think you're out of line, they will lose confidence in me."

"Cestus has been waiting for a chance to take Laithe," Baron continued. "He can't very well just march the Imperial Legion in here and take Greyfort, not without starting a war."

"Cestus won't go to war with us." Cae shook his head. "Everyone knows he's got his eyes on the mines under Krem Zhul-Mkat. Next time the Legion goes to war, it'll be against the dwarves."

Mull grimaced. "All the more reason for him to want Laithe in his pocket. He wants our soldiers. Cestus has got eyes everywhere, his own spy corps far more wide-spread than our own. He's waiting for a chance to discredit me, put a new King on my throne. One loyal to him."

"He can't just kick you out!" Leon cried. "You're a King!"

"But he's our Emperor," Cae said, with a sigh. "It's well within his power. That's why we've been laying low for so long, we don't want things to get any worse."

"But they will," Baron hissed, "if you two show out like that again."

Leon leapt up from his seat. "Your Highness!"

"Sit down, Leon." Cae's voice was soft, but stern.

Leon furrowed his brow, but he took his seat.

Cae rubbed his eyes, wearily. "Look, I'm sorry for the outburst at the feast. I should have let you handle it, I know. We'll do better."

Mull crossed his arms. "But...?"

Cae locked eyes with his King and held his gaze for a moment. "The people can say what they want about me. But they will *not* speak ill of my squire when he takes my place."

Mull waved the thought aside. "I'd never let that happen, you know that. Leon is a wonderful lad."

Leon turned just a hint of red. "Thank you, Sire."

"You two should get going," Baron said. "Trials are coming up, and you both need to be ready."

"Agreed," Cae said as he stood up. "And I'll cast to Ven tonight about what we discussed earlier, Sire."

Mull nodded, and Knight and Squire left the room.

The ride home was grim. Leon had suggested they stay at the Fixin's for the night and leave early to return to the Wood, but Caeleen shook his head. They needed to be in the Wood at dawn, and not tired from the ride when they got to work in the morning. He hated pushing the boy so hard, but he needed to be ready when he...

Cae shot up straight in his saddle as the two disappeared into the Wood. Something was wrong. His eyes darted about in the darkened forest, his vision slowly adjusting. What in the Hells was this chill? He knew it was getting colder this time of year, but...

There. In the shadow of a pine on his left. Out of the inky black crept a single wolf.

Cae dismounted, Leon following suit, as Tüli and

Buck circled back around to wait just outside the edge of the forest.

Slowly and silently, the Rangers drew their weapons.

The black-furred beast slunk closer, sniffing at the ground as it approached. Its eyes glowed with a pale orange hue. A low growl tumbled out of its form as it inched ever closer to the pair.

Cae carefully dropped to a knee and aimed with his bow, an arrow nocked and another two arrows in his draw hand, holding his breath as he focused on the animal.

"Sir, wait." Leon pointed with his free hand.

Out of the woods crept three more wolves, each of the same ebon fur with that eerie glow in their eyes. As they raised their eyes, they found themselves encircled by the pack.

Cae gritted his teeth. "*Come on, then,*" he demanded in the Wolf Tongue. "*Let the boy alone, I'll take the lot of you, myself.*"

"Be at peace, Rangers."

Caeleen's eyes widened as he recognized the voice of the Old Man. Shooting back up to his full height, he whipped around to see the green-garbed Hunter with the massive greatbow on His back. Kh'anora, God of the Forest and Nature.

"My Lord," Cae stammered. "I... forgive my aggression. Things have been difficult as of late."

"It's quite all right, Mister Longwatch." The old Wood God smiled. "I ought to have been in closer contact these past months. You've done well for yourself, lad."

"Thank you, my Lord," Cae replied. Dropping to a knee, he beckoned for Leon to do the same.

The squire came forward and knelt beside his teacher.

"And you must be young Mister Farrough!" Kh'anora smiled. "It's a pleasure to meet you. Mister Longwatch speaks often, and fondly, of you."

Leon's expression spoke of bewilderment more than anything. "I... forgive me, I'm not entirely sure who... I, umm... Sir, who—"

"This is Kh'anora," Cae replied. "Our Patron."

Leon's face flushed, and he brought himself low to the ground before Kh'anora's boots. "Woodfather!" he whispered. "Forgive my disrespect! I didn't know!"

Kh'anora laughed. "It's quite all right, lad. Up, up! Let Me have a look at you!"

Leon and Caeleen got to their feet, and the old God clapped His hands to Leon's shoulders, nodding as He looked over the squire. "Yes, yes. You're a strong lad, I can see it. You'll be a wonderful Ranger in your own right soon enough."

"Th-thank You! I, I don't know what to say!" Leon stammered.

Kh'anora smiled and shook His head. "You're alright, lad. But I must warn you, things will be difficult from here on out. You need to be ready for more pressing training. Starting tomorrow, I should think!"

"Oh, yeah." Cae nodded.

Leon let a nervous laugh escape his lips before straightening back up. "I'll be ready."

"I know you will," Kh'anora replied. He smiled, then turned to Caeleen. "I need a word with you, lad."

"What's the matter?" Cae asked. He glanced around

at the wolves still circling them. "And... no offense, but this doesn't really seem like Your style. Maybe Volok's, but not You."

"You catch on quick."

Cae jumped as he noticed the veiled and hooded figure behind the Wood Lord.

"*Kur!* I—sorry!" The Ranger stammered as the figure stepped forward. They were shorter than either Cae or Kh'anora, just shy of Leon's height. Crimson hair poked out beneath the veil which hung low beneath the wide hood of a black cloak. Thin hands reached up and pulled both back to reveal a young face, light-brown skin, with eyes of the deepest black framed in locks of blood-red. Beneath the cloak, Cae could see black robes lined with the same silver as that of Kh'anora's coat. The Knight's blood chilled as it dawned on him.

"Volok?" His voice was shaky. He'd heard whispers of the visage of Volok, Goddess of Death and Judgment. Admittedly, he expected Her to be more... frightening.

The Woman nodded. "I am," She replied. "Kh'anora has told Me much about you. I thank you for your service, Longwatch."

Cae nodded, still wary. "I... Fates alive, I wish I could sneak up on people like that."

Volok smiled, and a quiet laugh came from Her chest. "Perhaps, one day," She replied before Her visage grew stern. "I assume you've heard about what has been happening in Tamia?"

"Yes, my Lady," Cae answered with a nod. "Mull and Baron believe it to be a sign of... well..."

"Death magic." Volok rolled Her eyes. "I swear, that woman will be the death of Me..."

Kh'anora chuckled. "The death of the Goddess of Death? Isn't that a little amusing?"

Volok eyed the other Ethereal with a smirk. "Yes, Brother, the humor isn't lost on Me."

"What woman?" Leon asked curiously. "Y-You mean Your other half?"

Volok tilted Her head curiously for a moment. "My other... oh! That's right! A common misconception, dear, but yes."

Caeleen's brow furrowed. "Misconception? What do you mean?"

"Don't worry about it," Volok replied. "Here, I have something for you." Cae couldn't tell from where She had pulled it from, but in the Ethereal's hand was a small charm. It appeared to be made from some kind of smooth black stone, in the shape of a feather.

Cae took the charm in his hand. "Thank you, my Lady," he said as he fastened it around his neck.

"It won't tell you exactly what, or where, the things are that are causing all this mess," The Goddess explained, "But it will give you an awareness when they're near."

"I suspect you won't need to be told *exactly* where they are," Kh'anora added smugly. "Mister *Finest Hunter in the Empire*."

"You stop that," Caeleen chided with the faintest hint of a smile on his lips. "I'll do my best for both of You. And I'm certain..." he turned then to his squire "... that you'll be fine on your own here until I return."

Leon's eyes were still wide and his hands trembled as he balled them into fists, but he nodded.

Cae smiled. He turned back to the Ethereals, but They were both gone. Neither Them, nor the wolves, were anywhere to be found, and not a trace of Their presence remained, save for the charm around Caeleen's neck.

3

*T*he next three weeks were some of the most difficult since Leon had begun his squireship. His archery drills were faster, he ran his tracking exercises with no aid, and sparring each evening had become significantly more intense. It made Caeleen proud to see the boy push through. At the same time, a sort of guilt ate at him that, perhaps, he was pushing the lad too hard. He was good, there would be no denying that, but he was only sixteen... well, seventeen, now. Poor boy had a birthday come and go during this dreadful crunch.

The orange and red and brown of autumn had finally showed in earnest, which made Caeleen smile. Autumn had always been his favorite season. He even had another coat and cloak made just for the season, the coat a deep earthy brown and the cloak a rich crimson, rather than the greens he wore during the spring and summer. It helped him to better blend in with the trees during their marvelous transition.

On the first morning of the fourth week, the day of

the Trials, Leon had been outside tending to their training weapons when Caeleen shuffled out, holding their pink caster crystal aloft.

"Sir?" the squire cocked a brow. "What are you doing?"

Caeleen glanced over and smiled at the boy. "Inviting someone over," he replied. "Someone special."

Before Leon could ask any more questions, Cae pointed the crystal at a large oak not far outside the training pen.

A moment went by. Then all at once, the tree shuddered, its leaves rattling in their branches as some drifted to the ground before slowly swirling about the trunk.

Cae and Leon watched in awe as a shimmering light emerged from the old oak. Out of the light stepped a figure and, suddenly, the light vanished. The figure was a girl who looked to be about Leon's age. Her long golden hair ran in waves down to the center of her back, and in it was woven blooms of red and gold flowers, and thin vines of green that seemed defiant of the chilly autumn air. Her skin was pale and her eyes were an icy blue, and the dress she wore was a pale red, layered with shades of brown and gold. On her back she wore a cloak of red much like the Ranger's, and in her hand she held a tall staff of old wood that pulsed with green and gold light coming from deep within. Leon noted that the ground seemed not to give beneath her bare feet, that even the fallen leaves she stood on did not crackle or bend, as if she were entirely weightless.

As soon as the figure appeared, Caeleen grinned and

ran forward, vaulting over the wooden fence of the pen. "Ven!" he called, throwing his arms around the girl.

She let go of her staff, which stood on its own, and flung her arms around his neck. "Cae!" The girl's voice was soft, but clear. "Fates alive, it's so good to see you!"

Cae pulled away and looked the girl in the eyes. "How have you been? How's Ma?"

"She's doing great," Ven assured him. "She sent something for you!" Out from under her cloak, the girl produced what appeared to be a fingerless leather gauntlet of sorts, one made for the left hand.

"A new armguard!" Cae exclaimed. "Gods, I've been needing one of these, my old one is practically threads by now."

"That why you never wear it anymore?" Leon grinned as he came forward.

Cae smirked and pointed at his squire. "Now don't you start, too!"

Ven laughed. "Oh, and Alahir wanted me to say, 'Hello' for him! He says the hatchlings are flying well now."

"Oh, great! I should call down there sometime, check in on them."

"Well, yeah... but call Mom sometime, too, okay?"

"I...yeah."

Ven nodded with a smile before reaching a hand out toward Leon, her staff drifting out of the way as she did so. "It's wonderful to finally meet you, Leon!"

"You honor me, Lady Earthspeaker!" Leon replied, taking her hand and bowing low for a quick moment.

Cae cocked a brow as Ven laughed. The Druid

turned back to Cae as her staff returned to her hand. "I don't suppose we have time to waste, do we?" she asked. "We'd all best head for the capitol."

"Agreed," the Ranger replied. "Leon. You ready?"

Leon stood straight and nodded, a fire suddenly sparking in his eyes. "I am."

"Good." Cae smiled as he clapped the boy on his shoulder. "Bring the horses around."

* * *

"Good people of Greyfort! My friends! It is time for the Festival of Trials!"

The crowd thundered with applause as King Mull bellowed from his dais in the small stadium just outside the walls of Greyfort. Nearly the entire city had turned out for the Festival, and the stadium was completely packed, with throngs more people standing outside hoping to see the action in the large illusory globes set up outside. The Trials were, more often than not, the most excitement that Greyfort's people would see in their days. Cae thought that fortunate, and he thanked Kh'anora that this would likely be the only bloodshed the children of the city would ever see.

First came the Trial of the Claw. Cae was admittedly surprised to find that the city guard had managed to capture the beast they brought into the arena as a final test for the crown's official Beastslayers. The creature was draconic in nature, though it had no wings, walking instead on four powerful legs. Dazzling blue scales covered the beast's form, and it wielded four angry heads that thrashed about as it roared.

Caeleen had done research on these beasts. Dracohydra, they were called. But, until now, he had been at least in some part unsure of its existence. But not only was this beast real, it was also very, *very* angry. The Claw were the only ones to perform their Trial as a group, aside from the Trial of the Squires. And it was obvious that they needed to, as the dracohydra came close to turning several of the six trainees into bloody ribbons. But, after a fine display of tact and teamwork, (and plenty of preparation, Cae was certain) the beast went down, and the crowd cheered as the Claw stood proud before their King and saluted him. Cae looked to the old hunter beside him to see him practically beaming. Baron had poured his whole heart into training the Claw, and they had proven themselves more than ready to serve.

Afterwards came the Trial of the Soldiers. Their tests were simple: each faced a beast, mostly bears or wargs, and were given only a spear and a shortsword to kill it with. Three of the thirty-four trainees failed the Trial, having to be saved by the guards from a grizzly end at the hands of their beast. Cae couldn't help but sigh; it wasn't their fault, but it was still disappointing to watch.

And then came the Trial of the Scouts. There would only be Trials for the twins today, as the remaining trainees would not be ready until next spring. First was Thraun; the boy practically skipped out of his tunnel, his swords drawn as he cried out to the people for their applause. After a moment of playing the crowd, Thraun turned and bowed before Mull.

"A wonderful day for a Trial, Sire!" The scout-to-be called. "I hope my performance today is to your liking!"

"I'm sure it will be, lad," Mull replied with a hearty chuckle. "Good luck to you!"

"Very good!" Turning on his toes to gesture broadly to the crowd once more, Thraun's grin widened as he spun around to face the tunnel opposite his own. "So then! How shall I prove my mettle, eh? What is my Trial?"

The answer came in the form of an arrow that whistled over Thraun's boulder, sinking into the wall behind him. The crowd suddenly gasped. Thraun's smiled dropped as Caeleen emerged from the shadows.

"I am." The Ranger smiled coldly, his jade eyes locked on his student.

Thraun blinked several times before brandishing both his blades, his smile returning. "Fair enough! What do I have to do?"

Caeleen allowed himself a grin as he pointed to a large hourglass in the box where Mull's dais sat. "Fifteen seconds. If you can last a quarter-minute against me, then you pass. Are you ready?"

Thraun's jaw clenched as he bent his knees and prepared to move. "I'm ready."

The arena was silent as the whole city waited. An official held the hourglass in both hands and looked closely to ensure both combatants were ready before he brought the glass down onto the ledge of the box.

Thud.

Just as the time started, Caeleen nocked another arrow and fired. Thraun was already out of the arrow's way, darting his way across the dirt floor of the stadium. Caeleen dashed in a circle along the rim of the arena as he fired again and again, each shot barely missing its mark. His fourth shot grazed across the leather pauldron on Thraun's left shoulder just as the boy lunged forward, thrusting his right sword at the Ranger.

Caeleen lurched just barely out of the way, making a swipe with the arrow he had drawn to push Thraun back. The arrowhead cut through a single belt across Thraun's chest, and the pauldron he'd grazed slipped right off. Thraun didn't seem to notice as he quickly twirled, swiping again with his right hand.

Cae bent back as he let his bow drop to the ground, and his dagger, a brand-new mithril piece, was already drawn. It glanced off the steel in Thraun's grip, deflecting it just enough. Caeleen flipped back, a blur of brown and red as he wheeled through the air. Sal'tera was out by the time his feet touched the ground, and Thraun was already upon him.

Blades clashed against one another again and again; white sparks dancing off of the holy blade and across the dirt as they fought but, in direct confrontation, it was clear that the Ranger had the mastery.

Thraun faltered for a heartbeat as he realized he had clashed blades against the Blade of the Covenant, but he hid his surprise beneath a crooked grin.

Suddenly, Thraun dropped to the ground and made to sweep his teacher's legs. Caeleen hopped over the attack, landed a solid kick to Thraun's jaw before the boy could stand back up. It looked bad, but Thraun rolled back over his shoulder and was on his feet again, spitting out a bit of blood as he prepared to charge again.

"Time!"

Thraun froze as the crowd exploded with cheers. A smiled cracked his stern face, and the boy crumpled in the dirt, laughing aloud with relief. Caeleen sheathed his weapons and ran forward, dragging the boy to his feet and clapping him on the shoulder.

"Congratulations, Scout Thraun!" Caeleen said, clasping his hand around Thraun's forearm in a warrior's shake. The new scout returned the gesture proudly.

"Thank you, Sir!" Thraun replied, grinning ear-to-ear.

"Wonderful work, lad!" Mull bellowed from his seat. "Welcome to the Grey Scouts!"

Thraun and Caeleen turned together and saluted their King as shouts of "*Íloi! Íloi!*" rained down upon them. As the excitement died down, Thraun trotted off back through his tunnel as Caeleen took water. A few moments went by, and then out of the tunnel emerged Marish.

"A lovely day for a show, isn't it?" Marish called out to her teacher.

The crowd were quick to erupt into applause, and Marish smiled up at them.

Cae let the corner of his mouth twitch upward; the slightest arch of her brow gave away her reluctance.

"Don't worry," Cae called to her. "They're just excited to see another fight. Give it a week, they'll move on."

"Good to know." Marish grinned as he drew her own

bow. She preferred a shortbow to the bigger recurve Caeleen wielded. Though it had less impact than the bigger bow, Marish could fire off arrows faster with the smaller weapon. Caeleen knew this well, and he had worked her to the bone on her accuracy. No good loosing a hundred arrows if they all miss their mark.

"Less important for a scout than a spy, but I see your reasoning," Cae replied as he drew his blades and pointed to the hourglass. "Fifteen seconds. Are you ready?"

Marish narrowed her eyes, and her jaw clenched just like her brother's. She nodded.

The arena went quiet. The air went still, save for the gentle breeze blowing overhead.

Thud.

In a flash, Marish loosed an arrow. Caeleen ducked aside as it sailed by and began charging.

Marish began strafing around, the way Cae had before, but she fired six arrows in the time it took Cae to loose four. Most of the shots just missed their mark, but the fifth arrow managed to just nick the clasp on Caeleen's cloak, and it fell from his shoulders. Caeleen felt the weight lift off of him, and he grinned as he cut the sixth shot out of the air with Sal'tera, a crack of electricity bursting from the blade as he did.

Gently tossing her bow away, Marish drew her own longsword and closed the distance.

Caeleen prided himself on his speed in combat, but he readily admitted that Marish was naturally faster. Because of her steel being heavier than his mithril, however, the two were on relatively even ground in swordplay. Her polished blade danced between her hands and clashed repeatedly against the Ranger's weapons.

Here and there, Cae could simply duck out of the way of her strikes, but neither fast, nor far, enough to counter. She had him matched with the sword, and he knew it.

Unfortunately for Marish, Cae had yet to teach her sword-and-dagger and, in a blur, he locked his blades around hers and flung her sword aside.

With a quick pirouette, the Ranger through a broad swing toward the girl's head with the flat of his sword. Marish bent back out of the way and seemed to spin for a moment on her hands before throwing a kick back in Cae's face. The Ranger grinned as he jumped out of the way, knowing it had been his own squire who taught her that move. When she got to her feet, the scout had two daggers at the ready, and was about to lunge.

"Time!"

Again, the crowd howled with excitement as they applauded the new scout. Marish let out a hefty sigh as he daggers dropped from her hands. Cae put his own blades away and took her arm in the same warrior's shake he had given her brother.

"Almost got me, not gonna lie!" Cae whispered, with a wink. "Congratulations, Scout Marish!"

"Thank you, Sir!" Marish replied, clapping her opposite hand onto the Ranger's shoulder.

"Spectacular!" Mull cried. "Welcome, Miss Glenn, to the Grey Scouts!"

Again, the cries of "*Íloi! Íloi!*" boomed all around them as the pair saluted their King.

"Alright, good folks! What say we take a bit for food, eh?" Mull announced. "In an hour, we'll have one last Trial. Go, eat and drink!"

Caeleen collected his cloak and clasp and shuffled back through the tunnel he came from. Walking past the Claw, it surprised him to see them still carving up the dracohydra.

"Hey, good work out there!" Cae called. "Don't know if I could have done it better myself!"

One Slayer, a young-looking elven man with deep crimson locks, looked over his shoulder, and smiled. "Not by yourself, anyway."

Cae chuckled. "Ain't that the way?"

The elf nodded and went back to his work. Baron stood there with the Claw and, when Cae approached, he nodded to them and joined the Ranger on his way out.

"So, I never actually asked..." Cae started as he looked over at his friend. "Can...can you still feel it?"

Baron cocked a brow as he looked down at the stump where the rest of his arm used to be. "You know..." he mumbled. "Sometimes, yes. It itches, or it'll turn numb. But it isn't too much of a bother these days. Not near as much as it used to be, anyhow."

Caeleen nodded. "So I know you had some trainees in the Spy Corps this year. What do you have in mind for their trials?"

Baron grinned. "I have some of them following a few of the more prominent folk of our fair city. Raimi is helping me keep track of them, and provide some challenges."

"Sounds fun," Cae replied. "Anyone on me?"

"Come, now, Griffin," Baron answered with a grin. "Where would the fun be in just telling you outright, hmm?"

Caeleen laughed, and the two of them eventually found their way to the King's company. There they sat and ate, Caeleen at his sister's side.

"Lady Earthspeaker," Mull started between bites of goat, "I hope we aren't pulling you away from your duties in the Dokk at a bad time."

"Oh, not at all!" Venya replied. "Things have been calm in the Mountains as of late. And, even then, our village Overseer has things mostly in hand either way. He certainly has a talent for keeping things under control."

"Oh? Might I have heard of him?" the King asked.

Venya shrugged. "Perhaps. He was a Dragoon in the Cidari Army two centuries back. Koromaer Liuk'tär... well, Koromaer Dragonstain, as we call him."

"Liuk'tär... the name does sound familiar," Mull mused. "I'm not sure I can place it, though."

"Actually, I've done a bit of research," Cae chimed in. "When he led his forces on Ruin's Peak, two of the travelers among them were from here. Richter and Ophelia Longwatch, our ancestors, were a Ranger and Druid of Greyfort, and probably patrolled the Grey Wood."

"How about that!" Mull chuckled. "Seems the apples found their way back to the tree!"

"Perhaps there are graves to these two in your village?" the old Chancellor asked. "It might be appropriate to travel to Evenwood, and honor them for their service to Laithe."

"I would advise against it," Ven replied. "While the Dokk is calmer lately than it has been in some time, there are still wild beasts about. Besides, between the two of them, only Richter has a proper grave. When Ophelia passed, she grew a large sycamore around herself on the edge of a fairy sanctuary a day's hike from the village. Under this tree is where we bury all the Whispers. Only members of House Longwatch are permitted to visit the graves... unless we're burying a Whisper, that is."

"Seems fair enough to me," said the King. "Back to the matter at hand, though. I suppose Sir Caeleen has filled you in on what we have planned?"

Ven nearly spat out her drink. "Ah! I'm so sorry, I just... I'm still not used to this 'Sir' business."

"Real nice, Thrushy," Cae said as he elbowed his sister.

"That's *Lady* Thrushy to you, *Sir*," the Druid chided, elbowing the Ranger back. "But yes, Sire, Cae told me what you had in mind. I'm more than happy to help, but exactly how large of a settlement will I be growing?"

"Pretty big, I should think," Cae answered. "There are a lot of Q'leti out there who need a place to call home."

"Have you discussed it with them yet?" Ven asked. "Maybe they don't want our help."

"Would that excuse us from doing what we can for them?" Mull asked in response. "We have to do something, I should think. The Q'leti are starving, and we have the power to help them look after their own."

"The Q'leti are a proud people," Baron added. "Lady Venya may have a point. Our intentions may be benevolent, but we need to be careful about how we approach them. We don't want to offend them."

"We still have to try," Cae answered. "After seeing the state they were in at Nighthand... it just wouldn't be right not to do anything."

"I agree," Mull said. "Either way, let us establish the settlement. If The Q'leti don't want it, we'll find some use for it. Perhaps as an embassy for the Gharpasans, or for the folk of Honey Island."

"A wise decision, Sire!" said The Chancellor.

"Sounds good," Cae added.

"That settles it," Mull said. "We'll begin construction on this settlement in two days."

After their quick recess for luncheon, at long last came the Trial of the Squires. This was the event everyone had come to see, the birth of this year's Knights. Members of Mull's own Pride, as he called them. Not every Knight was given a squire, but those who did oft dreaded this day. Cae seemed not to worry, though. He knew Leon would be ready... probably.

Leon stood with his chest puffed out before the roaring crowd as Mull returned to his seat at the dais. To his left was Duncan, Sir Edmund's squire, a large boy of eighteen years in a metal breastplate and greaves over a leather surcoat and trousers, with a pair of iron mallets at his sides, and a large sword strapped to his back. To Leon's right was Eda, squire to Sir Bellam, a Battlemage. She wore a short robe, wraps around her arms bearing many glowing inscriptions, and leggings of worn leather, and she carried only one weapon: a thick wand hewn from building-tree wood with a sharp tip forged of runic iron.

Comparatively, Leon couldn't help but feel excessively armed. On his back was a recurve bow, shorter than Caeleen's but larger than Marish's, and an axe similar to the one he borrowed from Cae. At his waist were two daggers. He carried more weapons with him than even Caeleen did. He was only able to, he knew, because his back was stronger than his teacher's... likely from carrying Caeleen's things for so long. He once would curse under his breath about the burden, but the squire was thankful for it now; Caeleen was good at disarming, so he would need all the help he could get.

"Good folk of Laithe," Mull called out, "it is now time for the Trial of the Squires." The King's voice was sterner now than it had been before. "The three brave souls you see before you have trained hard, and now they seek to join my Pride. Should these Squires Three succeed in their Trials this day, we shall name them among the Knights of the Grey Plains. Your chief defenders! May their strength never falter, and may their hearts burn bright!"

Leon planted a fist firmly over his heart. "For the King!" he cried. Duncan and Eda did the same.

Mull smiled down, grim but proud. "Good luck, you three!"

The King lifted a hand and out stepped the three Knights in line with one another. Edmund, Caeleen, and Bellam, each arrayed in their own gear and adorned with the lion-head pauldron of their station, faced down their respective squires. Each offered a salute according to their occupation. Caeleen gave the Ranger's salute, Edmund brought his fists together over his chest, and Bellam held out an open palm. The squires mirrored their instructor's salutes. Then, all six drew their weapons.

"Fifteen seconds, then?" Duncan called. "Think I got this one."

Edmund shook his head as he lowered his visor. "Sorry, lad. Not goin' to be that easy."

Eda frowned, brandishing her wand. "If it isn't a test of endurance, then what are we doing?"

Bellam grimaced as a blue light gathered around the large sapphire at the head of his staff. "It's a test of everything we've taught you. You have to show that you can surpass us, so that one day, if the need arises, you'll be able to supplant us."

Leon let out a gulp as he nocked an arrow. "So that means that, if we want to be Knights..."

Cae nodded, training an arrow of his own on the boy. "You have to beat us."

Mull grinned. "Let the Trial begin!"

As soon as the words left the King's lips, the whistle of two shafts of wood filled the arena, followed by the sound of bursting splinters as the Rangers' first arrows crashed into each other. The air cracked as Eda and Bellam loosed their spells, fire and ice tearing across the dirt. A handaxe tore through the air, only to be batted away by a mallet. War cries tore loose from their wielders' throats, and the crowds roared. The Trial was on.

Leon rolled out of the way of two arrows shot

together and loosed another arrow at his teacher. Caeleen was well out of the way by the time the shot whizzed by, three more arrows in his draw hand, and he fired again. Leon whirled to the side before dashing behind the roaring form of Duncan, now locked in a tight grapple with Sir Edmund.

Caeleen strafed, ducking under a stray bolt of arcane light Bellam had deflected from Eda's wand. When he reached Duncan's back, Leon was gone.

The Ranger just barely heard shifting dirt behind him. He turned and tried to parry, but Leon's fist cracked across his jaw before he could. Caeleen staggered and dropped his bow, and Leon drew his axe. The weapon swirled in his hands like a twister, and Cae gritted his teeth as he drew blades of his own.

Duncan came soaring past them as they clashed.

"Dunc!" Leon called as he twirled around his teacher. "Do you need any help?"

"I'm good, little man!" Duncan grunted as he picked himself up, drawing his sword. "I'll yell if I need ya!"

"Aye!" Leon replied, just before the pommel of Cae's new dagger dashed across his chin. The squire allowed himself to spin with the momentum of Cae's strike, putting that force into his axe as he swung with the axe's back forward. The blunt of the axe knocked the dagger clean from Caeleen's hand. Caeleen leapt back, dipping and diving out of the axe now tearing madly through the air at him.

The Rangers tumbled across the ground as a small explosion rocked the stadium, and Bellam crashed through the wall. Dame Eda had won her Knighthood, as expected. Duncan bellowed out a triumphant cry and took the offensive as Sir Edmund craned his neck to see where Bellam had gone.

Leon spun back to his feet, and Caeleen hopped back into stance. Leon grimaced; his axe had flown all the way across the arena. In a flash, the boy had his daggers out and brandished them as he circled his teacher.

Cae smiled, now having his own dagger back and still gripping his holy blade. White sparks danced off the sword as Cae brought the tip around and pointed at his squire, holding the blade steady with the dagger beneath.

"Are you going to shoot me, Sir?" Leon asked with a shaky smile.

"Depends on what ya try next," Cae replied with a wink.

A solid *krak!* sounded behind them. "Agh, *dref!*" Sir Edmund hissed as he crumpled to the dirt clutching his broken nose, his helmet several feet away. Sir Duncan held his blade to the back of his teacher's neck and grinned proudly.

That left only Leon.

"Looks like it's down to us, kid," Cae said.

Leon snarled and bent his knees.

Cae's eyes bore into him, and Sal'tera began to glow, the hum of hallowed magic hanging in the air.

Leon spun to the left.

"*Uro!*"

The air exploded. The bolt flew past, blasting a hole into the arena. Leon flung a dagger and darted forward. The short blade sliced into Cae's hand, and the sword fell to the dirt.

Before the Ranger could react, Leon drove a knee into his stomach. Spittle flew everywhere, and Cae dropped. Leon pressed his dagger to the Ranger's throat.

"Yield."

The crowd was silent. Cae coughed, gasped for air, and smiled.

"I yield."

The air was electric as the people of Laithe screamed with excitement. Letting out a hefty sigh, Sir Leon dropped his dagger and threw his arms around Caeleen's neck.

"You did it, kid," Caeleen said breathlessly as he grabbed Leon's arm with a grin. "You're a Ranger now."

"Thank you, Sir," Leon whispered, his voice shaky and his eyes wet.

The three squires gathered once more and knelt in the center of the arena. Mull stood and looked over them at the edge of his dais, his smile wide and his cheeks rosy.

"Squires Three," The Lion of Lien began, "long and hard have you studied and trained under your teachers, and this day you have earned your place in my Pride. I name you now Dame Eda Cedrin, Sir Duncan Morley, and Sir Leon Farrough, Knights of the Grey Plains of Laithe." Mull's smile spread into a grin as his hands rose. "Rise now, *Knights* Three, and meet my eyes!"

The three young Knights stood proud as they lifted their eyes to their King. Each gave the salute of their occupation, and together they bellowed out the Knight's Creed.

"My hands for the King, and my heart for his People!"

* * *

"A round for the Knights Three, Miss Cici!" Sir Edmund called as he led the small gathering into the Fort's Fixin's. "And one for their teachers as well while you're at it!"

"Volok's backside, Ed, ain't there another tavern in this blasted city?" Cici joked as eight officers and a Druid walked into the already crowded tavern. Quickly, the other barkeeps set about preparing ales for the King's men and maidens.

"None as lively and lovely as the Fixin's, Miss Cici!" Caeleen added with a chuckle. As they walked in, the older Ranger turned and smiled at the Lady Andelyn, the famed Songstress of the Redgrove, who had just finished a song with her troupe. The crowd bellowed their cheers and tossed their coins into the boxes at the edge of the stage.

"Thank you all, thank you so much!" Andelyn called. "And welcome to the conquering young heroes in our midst! A round of applause for the new Scouts and Knights, eh?"

Thraun and Marish blushed as drunken cheers filled their ears. Leon and Cae grinned at their friends.

"Lady Andelyn!" Dame Eda called. "It is an honor for mine eyes to behold you, sweet maiden of the lute! Never have I laid sight on countenance fairer than yours!"

"Thank you, Dame!" Andelyn replied, her cheeks turning red.

"Eda?" Bellam asked quietly, "Are you already drunk?"

"So what?" Eda grinned, her face now a burning vermillion. "I'll celebrate my way, you celebrate your way."

Folk wandered in and out of the tavern the length of the day. Eventually, Lady Andelyn and her troupe came down and joined the gathering from the Trials. The lot of them talked and ate and drank for some time and, eventually, Cae took a room in the inn for the night and allowed Leon the chance to settle into the cabin by himself, to get started adjusting to life alone. Folk began to depart then, and Cae dropped into his bed and passed quickly into sleep.

It was just after midnight when the knocking came upon his door. Caeleen jolted back awake and leapt from his bed. It surprised him when he opened his door to see the Lady Andelyn standing before him.

"Oh! Hey, uh, Lady Andelyn," Cae stammered, still half-asleep. "How can I... how can I help you?"

"Is anyone else in here?" the Bard whispered.

"Not at the moment," the Ranger yawned. "Why?"

Andelyn pushed her way into the room and shut the door. Her eyes were cold, a drastic change from her demeanor onstage. "I have a message for you from Davenstead."

"Davenstead?" Cae tilted his head. "I don't know anybody in Davenstead."

"No, you don't. But I know you're on your way into Tamia."

Cae jolted awake. "How do you know that?"

"That's not important now," Andelyn replied. "What *is* important is my message. I've been in contact with Kànen No'vistus, the Bard of the Wild Butterfly."

"Kànen the Dragonslayer?" Cae raised his brow. "That's pretty big. What does he want with me?"

Lady Andelyn grimaced. "I'm sure you've heard rumors coming out of Haven Kingdom about the Wild Rose."

"No, I haven't heard anything... wait, Wild Rose? The serial killer? Thought he died a decade ago!"

"Not dead. We captured him. Interred him in Under-lake, a prison underneath the... you get it." Andelyn frowned. "Until recently... Wild Rose escaped last year. We've been trying to hunt him down, but he's a skilled sneak. We haven't caught him. We've had reports of killings across Haven, and our spies reported sightings of him for a whole year, but..."

"Couldn't keep up with him," Cae sighed. "Believe me, I get it. I dealt with similar *skrí* back when I ranged in the Dokk."

"I'm sure," Andelyn replied. "Well, we've recently received word. They have spotted the Wild Rose in multiple places across Tamia. People are disappearing more often there anyway, so we believe he's using the events going on there to cover his tracks."

Caeleen's blood went cold. "What about the capitol? Have they seen him near Fartide?"

"Not yet, but it would be no surprise." Andelyn replied grimly. "We need you to bring the Wild Rose to Siahra's attention."

"I'll do my best," Cae assured the Bard. "But I'll

likely have my hands full with the weird happenings in Fartide already."

"Caeleen, please. Rose is immeasurably dangerous. Davenstead has shut its gates, no one in or out until he's found."

"Davenstead is on lockdown? Gods..." Cae crosses his arms. "Look, I'll do what I can. In all likelihood, we'll happen upon him anyway."

"That's all I can ask of you, then." Andelyn turned and went back to the door. "Thank you, Ranger. On behalf of all Eridan, thank you." Without another word, Andelyn slipped back out of the room, leaving Caeleen alone with his thoughts.

---

4

*T*he grasslands between Greyfort and Nighthand were about a half a day's ride out for the small group. Cae suggested he could have brought Ven himself on Tüli, and even have the both of them back before dinner, but Mull insisted on being there himself. Leon wanted to tag along, but he knew he had his duties now in the Grey Wood.

So three rode on, Lion and Whisper and Earthspeaker, into the grass-covered plains. The sun was already beginning to set behind the clouds, leaving the world around them in washed-out blues and greys under orange-gold beams. The grass was well into its turn from green to gold, but patches of green still stood out here and there.

Mull was the first to dismount when the three of them came to a stop. The old King looked out over the way, noting Nighthand Keep in the distance. It was prominent on the horizon, perhaps close enough to reach before nightfall were it still summer. He smiled; this new settlement would be an excellent waypoint between the Keep and his own city. Out of his own saddlebag, he produced a sizable bag of soft velvet, about the size of a one-year-old, which he handed to Venya.

"*Curapo tagora*," Venya whispered as she peered into the bag. "I've always wanted to try my hand with such a large sample of seeds."

Mull cocked a brow. "You do know how to do this, yes?"

"Of course," Ven replied. "The wall around Even-wood is nearly covered in building-tree now."

Cae frowned. "What was wrong with the wall before?"

"Nothing really," the Druid said. "But the timber was old and starting to give a little here and there. The Over-seer and I thought it would be smart to fortify it with something... Kind of makes me wonder why he didn't have Earthspeaker Ophelia use the building-tree to make the wall to begin with."

"Perhaps we could discuss it later?" Mull suggested with a smirk. "I do hope to get back to my Palace sooner rather than later."

Venya rolled her eyes and emptied the bag onto the ground. "Both of you please step back," she ordered. "I don't want anyone getting swept away."

Cae and Mull backed away, and Venya slowly raised her hands to the sky. A subtle green glow began to shimmer at her fingertips, spreading down her hands all the way to her elbows. The Druid flicked her wrists, and almost at once, a gust of wind rushed past the three from behind and took the seeds swirling up into the air.

Cae and Mull nearly fell on their faces, but Venya stood firm, her green glow erupting into a brilliant emerald light as she brought her hands around in a circle and down toward the ground. The sudden gale pushed down into the earth, burying the seeds all about.

Venya clenched her hands into fists and, at once all around, there burst forth clusters and trunks of dull-brown wood. Venya stretched out her fingers again and raised her arms, her hands trembling and a wind whipping all about her. The wood began to spread and weave together, forming walls and structures, some stretching high into the sky, and some snaking along the ground. In the center of it all formed a sort of longhouse, similar to the one Cae had visited in the Widewood belonging to Khat'ran the Spider-King. The building-trees continued to weave together and stretch all around, forming many buildings and towers and walls, as Venya's hands continued to whip all about.

Finally, the Druid let out a grunt as she threw her hands out wide, and the wind about her seemed to burst. Cae and Mull fell flat on their backs, and their horses jumped and whinnied in surprise. The green light dissipated, and the air grew still. There, in the dying light of day, stood a wide, waiting town, formed entirely of beautiful wood. Shades of green began to settle into the wood, and small blooms of autumn flowers poked out at the base of the trees. All around Venya, the grass had returned to a rich green. Cae sat, his mouth agape.

"Gods above," he stammered. "Ven, that was incredible."

Venya turned and smiled. She stumbled for a

moment, her staff whipping forward into her hands so she could lean against it.

"Lady Earthspeaker?" Mull jumped to his feet. "Are you alright?"

"I'm good, I'm good..." Ven replied with a sigh. "Most Druids don't make structures so wide so quickly, since it takes a lot out of them."

"We could have done this over a few days, that would have been no trouble," Cae said as he helped his sister stand up straight. "You in that big a hurry to get outta here?"

"Someone has to keep an eye on things in the Dokk," Ven replied. "Koromaer can't handle everything himself."

"That's fair." Cae shrugged. "Still, you could hang around for a few more days, at least 'til I head out for Tamia."

"I suppose I could..." Ven turned to the King. "If Your Majesty permits it."

"Lady Venya," Mull answered with a smile, "you are welcome in my city anytime."

Ven smiled and dipped low into a curtsy. "Since it's getting dark," she said, "we might as well stay here for the night."

Cae nodded. "That's good thinking, don't wanna get caught on the road at night."

Mull frowned for a moment, but he nodded, and the two of them helped Venya onto her horse. Together, the three rode into the empty settlement.

"What should we call it?" Cae asked. "Maybe New Q'let, in honor of the Q'leti homeland."

"I don't know," Ven mused. "We're not trying to replace Q'let. We don't want to be hurtful."

"We'll give it a name in Old Eridian," Mull said. "Something fitting, but strong... how about *Duin Durach?*"

"What does that mean?" Ven asked.

"'Oak Fort,'" Mull replied. "I thought it made sense. The walls look solid, and they're... oak-ish enough."

Cae cracked a grin. "Oak-ish?"

"Y'know what, boy?" Mull chided with a grin of his own.

"Here," Ven interrupted. "We'll stay in the longhouse tonight."

Cae helped Venya into the structure as Mull led their horses not far behind, bringing them to the stables just outside the longhouse. The King brought with him two bedrolls, one of his own and one for the Ranger, made of thick brown bear pelts that Caeleen had taken himself. By the time he had the horses settled down and he entered the empty longhouse, Venya had already crafted a hammock of rich green vines for herself, and the two from the Dokk were settling down. Cae was the first to find sleep, followed soon after by his sister.

Mull lay awake a while longer with his thoughts, but found rest eventually.

* * *

THE NEXT DAY WENT ALMOST WITHOUT INCIDENT. The three didn't depart for home until shortly after midday; Ven had assured Mull that everything was in order, but the King insisted on going over everything himself. Ven led him through the settlement and went over everything she had crafted at length, while Cae stayed behind and saw to the horses. Tüli snorted as the Ranger strapped the thick sleeping pelt to his saddle.

"Been a long few weeks, eh?" Cae asked as he stroked Tüli's grey mane. The horse nestled his head into the crook of Cae's neck. The Whisper smiled and gently pushed his horse back, then strapped the King's pelt to his mighty warhorse.

A chill darted up Caeleen's spine. His hand clutched the feather charm around his neck before he realized he'd reached for it. Something was nearby, something... *wrong.*

Tüli whined and reared up on his hind legs as Caeleen turned all round. Nothing looked out of the ordinary, but the Ranger could feel eyes on him. He was being watched.

Securing the horses to a post in the stables, Caeleen slunk into the slowly growing shadow of the longhouse and nocked an arrow in his bow. Peering out from around the side, he cursed under his breath when he saw nothing. Whatever was spying on him was either exceptionally good at hiding, or was capable of invisibility. It wouldn't be impossible to find, but...

There. A small hut a few yards southeast. Caeleen furrowed his brow. There was a faint shadow cast atop the intricately woven structure, a shadow of something that did not appear to be there. The shadow appeared in the shape of some large winged creature, something similar to an altóg, a large batlike creature the size of a full-grown bear. Bigger, in fact. Cae could tell that the shadow, itself, was large; there *was* something there, something hidden by magic.

In as swift a motion as he could muster, Cae leapt out of the shade and fired an arrow at the roof of the hut. The arrow whistled in the air for less than a second before sinking into the invisible thing, accompanied by a spurt of black liquid. A shriek pierced the Ranger's ears, and a crack of thunder rocked the area, a wave of force blowing the Ranger off his feet. The hut seemed to crumble to ashes without flame, and the chill in the back of Cae's mind was gone.

"Ranger!"

Cae whipped around to see Mull and Venya rushing toward him. The archer held up a hand.

"I'm alright!" he called. "I'm fine, I just..." a frown set in on the Ranger's face as he looked back at what remained of the hut. "There was something here. Something was watching me."

"A spy?" Mull asked. "Was it one of Cestus's?"

"I doubt it, Sire," Cae replied. "Whatever it was, it wasn't natural. Some sort of black magic kept it out of sight. It might have something to do with the events going on in Tamia."

"What exactly is going on in Tamia?" Venya asked.

"We aren't entirely sure," Cae said, "but I've spoken to Kh'anora and Volok about it. The Ethereals believe the incidents in Tamia are the result of some kind of Voloki death-magic, or at least its presence."

"Voloki?" Ven whispered. "Fates preserve... Cae, I don't like this."

"Neither do I, Thrushy," Cae replied. "But something is gonna have to be done. If we don't get out there and figure out what's happening, and how to fix it, more people will get hurt."

"Death-magic has a tendency to spread," Mull added. "If we don't find the root of these occurrences, they may soon come to Laithe. I don't want that in my Kingdom."

"Hold on, hold on!" Ven held up a hand. "Voloki death-magi? I...Cae, listen. When we heard about the dragon, I thought Overseer would die of fright. This is... this is too much. Tell me you're not actually doing this!"

"I am," Cae said. "Ven, this needs to be done. I won't let this spread to Evenwood. I need you in the Dokk to keep things in order, in case it doesn't work out."

"He'll be fine, Lady Earthspeaker," Mull insisted. "Your brother is a fine huntsman, and one of the fiercest warriors I've ever known. He'll return home once all is well, I promise you."

Ven frowned at the Grey King for a long moment before giving a somewhat curt nod, her eye cast down. "We should be getting back to the capitol," she said.

"Actually," said Cae, "I'm gonna ride through the night into Brookridge, probably stay there for a couple days. You're welcome to come along if you feel like it, Ven."

"Fine," the Druid replied. "What's in Brookridge, though?"

"Need to visit a friend of mine, see what she knows about the Voloki." Cae let a little smile turn the corners of his mouth. "Plus, it'll just be nice to see her again."

* * *

THE TOWN OF BROOKRIDGE WAS LARGELY THE SAME as it had been the last time Caeleen was there. Under the star-laden sky, Cae and Venya rode into a hamlet already settled down into sleep. A few lights were still burning in the town, but only one structure was fully lit: the Temple of Silvia, the most recent addition to Brookridge, and home to many of Haven's finest healers. Cae admitted to himself that it had been sometime since he came to visit, and he felt a bit of heat rush to his tired face as he stabled Tüli.

Ven drew her staff and let down her dress, her trousers and boots seeming to disappear in a shower of green sparks as the long flowing garment fell over her legs, and Cae pulled his red cloak around him a little tighter as the two walked to the Temple.

The Temple itself was a fair bit smaller than the one in Greyfort, and the interior was drastically different; there was no chapel section to the building, but the whole temple was a large infirmary. Beds and slabs of stone sat in circles around a large bowl of water in the center of the chamber, over which floated a brilliant golden flame. Several white-garbed Clerics, most of which Cae assumed were just beginning their studies, seemed to drift about amongst the few citizens in the beds here and there, occasionally coming to the bowl to gather water in their pitchers.

At the back of the Temple chamber was a mural depicting the likeness of Silvia, this one a painting rather than a stone carving like the one in Greyfort's Cradle

District. At the foot of the painting was a small shrine, just a few candles and a collection plate. Cae made his way to the altar, followed by Ven, and dropped a few silvers into the plate.

"Mother of Mercy bless you, Ranger."

Cae turned with a smile as he recognized the voice. There stood Cleric Adept Isiliel Rumoré, beaming back at him. Her long raven hair was pulled into a long tail that fell down over her shoulder, and her silver eyes seemed to shimmer a bit with contentment. She wore what appeared to be a traveler's robe, a battered white coat with red trim over the vest and trousers of a hiker. The long coat looked to have had sleeves once, but they had been removed, leaving the elven maiden's arms exposed, and leading Caeleen to notice how much... well, *bigger* Isi had become. She was Caeleen's height now, and her arms were thick with muscle, toned and strong, and covered in the faded marks of many wounds. Across the White Mage's nose were three long jagged scars that cut straight through her freckles.

"*Usah viik!*" Cae exclaimed at the sight of his friend.

"Sir Longwatch, please," the Priestess said with a laugh. "You're in a church, mind your language."

"Sorry! I just... wow!" Cae shook his head and smiled. "You look great! Have you been working out?"

Isi looked at her old companion with a cocked brow. "Perhaps," she joked. "It helps ward off bandits and monsters if you look more imposing. Oskar has been a great help in my training since he joined the Clergy."

"Oskar? The blacksmith? Ha! Good on him getting into the good fight." Cae laughed and threw his arms around the Cleric. He meant to speak more, but coughed suddenly as she lifted him up off the ground.

"It's wonderful to see you, Caeleen," Isi said.

"You, too!" the Ranger croaked as his friend put him back down.

Venya couldn't help laughing. "Honestly? I needed to see that. I really did."

Isi turned to the Druid and lowered her head. "*Reilan ko*, Lady Earthspeaker."

"*Reilan ko*, Priestess." Ven bowed in like manner. "Thank you, again, for what you did for my mother."

"Think nothing of it," Isi replied. "I'm sure the two of you would have done the same for me."

"If we knew how!" Cae added with a laugh.

Isi shook her head and smiled. "Siahra was right, you *are* an idiot."

"I do my best," the Ranger said with a shrug. "C'mon, let's go to the Oxen. Gotta ask you about some stuff."

The three of them walked out into the cold of the autumn night and headed for the Oaf and Oxen. Cae let out a hefty sigh as he walked into the tavern. It had been some time since he was last here and, even in the dead of night, he felt comfortable in the small inn. Only two others were present in the tavern area, and one of them had fallen asleep at his table.

"So," Isi started as the three of them sat down at the bar, "how have you been, Caeleen? How are things in Laithe?"

"They're alright," Cae said. "Leon passed his Trial, finished his training. He's gonna be taking my post in the Wood for a while."

"What? That's wonderful!" Isi replied. "You must be so proud!"

"I am!" Cae continued. "He's worked so hard, and he's earned it. He's a fine Ranger, and he'll be a fine Knight. I just... I'm worried."

"I understand that," Isi said. "Anytime I have to send one of mine out to Ecrin or Alryne or, Gods forbid, to Davenstead..."

"What's wrong with Davenstead?" Ven asked.

Isi grimaced. "Wild Rose," she replied. "He's back."

Ven's eyes widened. "You're lying."

"I'm not," Isi replied. "He escaped some time ago. We're not sure if he's staying in Davenstead or not, but..."

Cae held his tongue. The Voloki worried Ven enough, he thought to himself. She didn't need to know he was hunting a madman.

"But enough about that," Isi said finally. "How are Cici and Wini?"

"They're good!" Cae answered with a grin. "Wini's getting so big now! She's started helping out around the Fixin's during the day. Cici's doing good, too; we've been talking to some folks from Honey Island about stocking more of their whiskey. Seems to be a favorite, so that'll be really good for business."

"Honey Island? Biggs says they have pretty great wines," Ven added. "What do you suppose their secret is?"

"Years of experience, I guess," Cae mused. "But, whatever! Cici wanted me to ask you about Iómi. How are you two doing?"

Isi's eyes widened, and a bit of blush came to her face.

"She... I, umm..." The corners of the elven maiden's mouth twitched upward just enough for the Ranger to notice. "We... She's good. We're good."

Cae smiled. "Good to hear... Honestly, I wish I could bring my questions to her, but I don't want to get in the way of her studies."

"I could pass some along, if it helps," Isi suggested.

Cae nodded. "Maybe, but I might just swing by there on my way into Tamia... if I have time."

"Why are you going to Tamia?" Isi asked, a smile now playing on her face. "What, did you just miss the Queen that much?"

"I'm not doing this with you, too," Cae said with a wry smile. "There are a lot of weird things going on over there right now. Mull wants me to take care of it, since I'm good for that sorta thing. But I need information about what I'm gonna be hunting, which is why I'm here."

Isi cocked an eyebrow. "I'm afraid I don't follow..."

Cae let out a sigh as he ran a hand roughly through his hair. "Some of the things happening out there line up with some more recent findings from the Burned Ages. We think there might be a Voloki death-mage of some sort out there, or..."

"Or devils," the Cleric whispered, her brow now furrowed. "Caeleen, are you... tell me this is a joke."

Cae shook his head. "I really wish it was, but, no. I've already spoken with Kh'anora and Volok about it, but I figured it would be wise to consult you before I go. The Clergy keeps up with demonology and techniques for combating the Voloki, right?"

"We do," Isi answered, "but we don't have much in our records here. The Brookridge Temple is still relatively young, we haven't had the time to build up a library like the one in the Institute, or even the one in Greyfort."

"I've already asked there, unfortunately. Not much luck." Cae frowned. "You wouldn't have any advice for me off the top of your head, would you?"

"Aside from, 'Don't do this', you mean?" Ven added.

Isi nodded in agreement with the Druid. "Not much," she admitted. "Keep a holy symbol on you, gild your weapons with silver, learn holy magic... Sal'tera should suffice, considering the nature of its enchantment."

Cae glanced down at the mundane sword he wore on his hip and ran a thumb along its pommel. He'd need to take up the Bolt again for a time. "I thought that might be the case, yeah. I don't think I'd be able to just stock up on holy arrows, though. Might there be an easier way to go about that?"

"I could bless your quiver for you," the Cleric said. "It won't have quite the punch of individually hallowed arrows, but each shot from your quiver would sting against Voloki a bit more. I would offer to bless your bow itself, but blessings directly on a weapon take time. Some take months, some take years."

"What about protection?" Ven asked. "Is there some kind of ward you could place on his armor or something? Anything to make him less susceptible to death-magic?"

"Aside from carrying a holy symbol on your person, there's nothing I could do." Isi stroked her chin. "I mean, I could, but it would take at least a year."

"What about my dagger?" Cae drew his shorter mithril blade out of its sheath and presented it to Isi. "What could I do to make it better?"

"Silver its edge," the Priestess replied. "Silver will always serve best against a Voloki."

Venya suddenly leaned in. "Priestess," she started, "is there a way to work holy power into my magic? I need to be able to protect the Dokk if Caeleen fails to stop the spread."

Isi thought for a moment. "It might be possible," she said, her eyes on the table. "I've heard stories of Clerics in the service of Kh'anora wielding nature-magic alongside holy magic. But holy magic adapted by a Druid... Perhaps. But I couldn't help you there."

"I might can help, actually." Cae returned his dagger to its sheath. "There's supposed to be a sacred grove in Tamia just at the foot of the Ías Fuil. I've heard there's a conclave of Druids there, old as Eridan itself. If anyone could do it, it'd be them."

"I can't come to Tamia with you, Cae," Ven replied. "You know I have to be home soon."

"I'm not asking you to come with me. But if I find out anything, I can contact you through the globe and you can come through the trees to learn."

Ven's brow crinkled with worry, but she nodded. "We'll see what happens, then."

* * *

CAELEEN AND VENYA RETURNED TO THE GREY Wood just after midday two days later. When the pair arrived at the Ranger's Cabin, Cae was pleased to find that Leon had settled in just fine; all of Caeleen's belongings had been packed for travel or returned to Viraati Lien, and Leon had already departed for his patrol. The Whisper smiled, knowing that Laithe would be in good hands. He quickly got to loading Tüli up for their trip.

"You're not going to say goodbye to everyone?" Ven asked, her staff following close behind her as she approached her brother.

"Nah, I wouldn't wanna bother everyone," Cae replied. "Besides, they'd probably try to give me some big send-off, and I just... I don't need all that attention, y'know?"

Ven frowned as she laid a hand on her brother's shoulder. "Sparrow... I know you like keeping to yourself. But I don't want you to be all alone. Try to open up some, okay?"

Caeleen sighed. "I'll do my best, Thrushy."

The Druid put her arms around Caeleen's neck. "Stay safe, big brother."

"You, too." The Ranger hugged the Earthspeaker tightly.

With that, Venya approached the same oak she had appeared through, and in a flash of green light, she was gone.

Cae came to the front door where his bag had been left for him. Leaned up against the wall was Sal'tera, the Blade of the Covenant. In the sharp light of the afternoon, the jade embedded in the sword's guard glinted with a brilliant light. Even as he approached, Caeleen could feel the hairs stand up on the back of his neck.

Sal'tera had that strange effect on him, and he suspected it had a similar effect on others; the air surrounding the blade seemed charged with electricity, as if at any moment the weapon might erupt with holy lightning.

The Ranger frowned as he unhooked Gem'shil from his belt. As he picked up the holy weapon and hung it from his hip, a sudden wave of energy rocked through him. He squeezed his eyes shut and shook his head, doing his best to ignore the sensation. It made him jittery and, although he was undoubtedly better on the field with Sal'tera in hand, he was afraid to let himself depend on its power.

He had to be better than that.

He slid Gem'shil into the magic bag. He knew game would be scarce this time of year, but he didn't have time to stock up on any of his own foodstuffs. He knew he had enough for Tüli, he always did. That would be enough.

He went back to his horse and mounted, glancing back at his old home once more. It was a good cabin. Leon would be fine here without him, he was sure of it.

Without a word, Cae and Tüli rode off westward.

5

The road to Fartide was a long one, even for a lone traveler on a swift horse. Caeleen figured that going at a reasonable pace, with no delays, the trip would take at least nine weeks, but he figured he might reach the Tamian border by New Year. It disappointed him a bit to know he'd be missing Frostpeak this year, but there was little he could do about that. Knights don't always have time for holidays, he told himself... and Whispers shouldn't care.

Whatever ill sense he had felt when he set off, Caeleen chalked it up to the gravity of traveling with Sal'tera again. It had been almost a year since the Bolt of Peace came with him on a trip outside of Laithe.

As the Ranger arrived once more at Brookridge, the thought dawned on him that the roads might be crowded for the winter holidays. To make the time he was shooting for, it would be wise to avoid the roads when possible. His eyes turned then to the thick brown canopy of the Widewood, just past Brook's Hill.

Cae smiled as the plan formed in his head; he could remember the forest paths well enough, and no one ever goes into the Widewood for fear of serpents and spiders. Taking the path through the old forest would likely cut down on time. He might make New Year yet. Tüli let out a puff of air through his nose as he turned to ride on toward the woods.

The shade of the trees made the autumn air chillier than usual, but the Ranger and his steed carried on for several weeks though the wood with little interruption, stopping at each little pond they came across to fill up on water and, of course, to drink. Cae was glad he had stocked up on apples and oats before they had left to build Duín Durach, because game was becoming somewhat scarce as the cold crept in closer and closer. But the two of them got by well enough, although Cae was certain they'd both been losing weight during the trip, and soon enough the Ranger could see the silhouette of Highhaven through the trees.

It was just at the start of December by the time they were at last found. Cae had taken to sleeping in the branches of some larger trees, keeping Tüli tied to the trunk during the night next to the fire. Rather than waking on his own, as usual, the Ranger awoke to the sound of distant footsteps coming closer. He was unsure why, but Caeleen found his heart beginning to beat faster; why were there so many, and why were they coming toward them?

He glanced down at his horse with a worried brow. There wasn't much he could do to conceal Tüli, but at least he could slip higher into the crown of the tree he was in, to better hide himself. Perhaps they would leave Tüli be if they didn't know whether or not his rider was nearby. Quickly, the Ranger darted up into the leaves, readied his bow, and nocked an arrow. He kept two more arrows in his draw hand, ready to nock.

Out of the cover of the surrounding trees came six soldiers, all laden in Imperial armor, armed with halberds and tall shields. Caeleen frowned as the soldiers gathered around Tüli, one of them setting down his arms and approaching the young horse. Tüli let out an irritated snort and turned away, and the soldier stepped back.

Shk-shk-shk! Three arrows buried themselves in the ground between the soldier and the horse. All six men looked up to see the brown-and-red-garbed archer descend from the tree by his rope, landing next to his steed with four more arrows ready to fire. "Everyone, get back!" Caeleen shouted. "I am a Knight of Laithe on a diplomatic mission to Tamia! I have no quarrel with you!"

The soldiers all drew back as a seventh figure approached. Caeleen's eyes widened as he recognized the old man with the large gold crown on his brow.

"Unwise to open fire on an Imperial soldier, wouldn't you say?" A sly smile played on the tired lips of Emperor Hail Cestus III as he slowly approached the Ranger.

Caeleen quickly stowed away his arrows and dropped to a knee. "M-my liege!" he stammered.

"Boltwalker," Cestus replied. "Up now, I'd like a word with you."

Caeleen got to his feet and looked into the Emperor's

eyes. For a moment, he was surprised to find Cestus a bit shorter than him. "How might I be of service?"

"I have some questions about your mission to the Diamond Shores, as well as your more recent activities in the Plains," the Emperor replied. "Now, as I understand it, there have been some peculiar happenings in Tamia as of late, yes? Snow and beasts, vagrants and such?"

"Yes, my liege," Caeleen said, trying not to look down at his feet. "According to our sources, some recently recovered documents dating back to the Burned Ages suggest that—"

"Yes, yes, I'm aware," Cestus interrupted. "Lancelot and I have some mutual sources of information, and it so happens that we found these documents not far outside the Tamian capitol. They came along with a few documents regarding Lugosia, so I was inclined to write the lot of it off as fairytale nonsense..."

Cae's brow raised in surprise, but he said nothing. Mull had been clear about Lugosia being real. For the Emperor to deny its existence...

"Either way, we've also had reports of a certain escaped convict being seen around Tamia. Keep an eye out for him, will you? Wears a mask and a shroud, black cowl, black clothes? Carries an axe?"

"The Wild Rose, yes." Cae nodded. "I heard he was loose. I'll do my best to bring him in."

"I'm sure you will," Cestus said with a smile. "And another thing... I'm certain you'll be working closely with Queen Siahra."

"Probably, yes."

"I figured. Well, if you have a chance, give her a

message from me. Tell her she has my utmost sympathies for the loss of her father, and that the hearts of Eridan are with her family."

Caeleen's brow furrowed. "... My liege, King Arian's death was two years ago."

"Yes, well..." Cestus shrugged. "Ruling the Three Kingdoms keeps you busy."

The Ranger's eyes narrowed just a bit, but he nodded. "I'll tell her."

"Excellent!" The Emperor clapped his hands together. "Now, I do have one last question regarding the events following the successful raid of Nighthand Keep."

"What would you like to know?"

"I've been told that after Laithe's recent Festival of Trials, Mull has erected a new settlement in the grasslands between Greyfort and Nighthand." Cestus cocked a brow as he earned in closer. "What exactly does your King have in mind for it?"

Caeleen paused. Cestus had been vocal about his distaste for the Q'leti, and his support for aggressive actions driving them out of existing settlements. If he knew what they'd been planning...

"Hello? Anything?"

Cae blinked as he snapped back to attention. "Uh, actually it's an embassy. Mull thought it would be wise to establish a place for any ambassadors from Gharpasa to take up residence. We hear they're working on some big things."

"Ah! I have to admit, I'm intrigued by what I'm hearing about the ghari. Ships that sail through the air like water! I'd like to see that become a reality, myself."

"My thoughts exactly, my liege!" Cae let a shaky smile spread across his face. It hadn't exactly been a lie, it just wasn't the whole truth.

Cestus stepped back, pulling his coat closer around him. "Well, I believe that's all I needed to hear. Best of luck on your mission, Boltwalker, and give my regards to the Queen!"

"Of course! Safe travels, Your Eminence!" Caeleen bowed low as the Emperor and his retinue turned and made their way back out toward the road.

Once they were safely out of sight, Cae allowed himself a sigh of relief as he collected his arrows and climbed onto Tüli's back, and the two of them headed on westward through the forest.

Caeleen was unsure of the date when he emerged outside of Awanu in Tamia, but he guessed it must have been January. The morning chill was settling in a little deeper in his bones, and he and Tüli were down to the last of their apples. More importantly though, Cae was running low on arrows... which he only noticed when he reached for his quiver upon seeing the panicked towns-folk running through the streets and the tendrils of black smoke rising from a few of the buildings.

The two sped into the town, and Cae leapt off his horse's back onto the overhang of a market stall as Tüli charged into the plaza. Readying what few arrows he had, the Ranger darted across the low-hanging roofs looking for what was causing the chaos.

As he arrived in the plaza, he saw them: a pack of wolves, ebon-furred and massive, bigger even than wargs. Their eyes glowed a strange red, and they had already taken several guardsmen. One was skulking in a circle around Tüli, its yellow teeth bared and dripping with blood and saliva. Volok's pendant grew warm against Cae's chest, and he grimaced.

Caeleen did not hesitate, and he fired an arrow through the beast's eye as he leapt down from the rooftop. A faint golden flash sparked out of the wound as the creature fell, and Tüli darted out of the plaza. Cae rolled over his shoulder and fired two more arrows as he got up, each finding their mark and bringing down another wolf. As he nocked his last arrow, a fourth wolf darted out from behind the plaza's fountain and charged.

The Ranger fired his arrow into the beast's shoulder, but it kept coming and bowled him over. Before it could sink its claws into him, Cae whipped out his dagger and sliced a clean cut across its neck, and the wolf fell down atop him as it poured blood from its sizzling throat. These weren't just wolves, Cae realized; they were *ur-pesu*. Hellhounds.

Cae heaved the twitching body off of him, and looked around desperately for any sort of... There, perfect! A hunter's stall! Caeleen darted over to the abandoned shop and dug into a basket full of arrows, stuffing a handful into his quiver. Taking four more in hand and hopping back out of the stall, Cae grimaced as three more wolves had arrived in the plaza.

Taking a beat to focus, Cae nocked two arrows together and fired, each shot taking a wolf in the eye. Cae looked to the last wolf, now slowly stepping forward. Its black fur was speckled here and there with red, and it was missing one eye, but it was larger even than the others had been. Cae nocked a third arrow and aimed...

A rush of wind blew Caeleen's hair back as two large black-feathered wings burst forth from the wolf's back in a flurry of grey flame and ebon pinion. The Ranger's eyes widened as the creature leapt into the air and began circling overhead, barking and snarling down at him. Caeleen fired an arrow into the sky after it, but missed his mark. He fired again, this shot grazing the beast's snout.

The winged wolf growled, suddenly rocketing downward as swiping with its claws, tossing Caeleen across the plaza.

Caeleen wiped the blood from his eyes and cursed when red stung his vision again. There was a cut on his brow, and it was bleeding badly. He drew his sword and dagger, and the wolf barreled toward him. He knew he didn't have enough strength left for a lightning bolt, so he would have to kill the beast by hand.

The wolf pounced, and Caeleen buried his dagger in its collar. Powerful jaws clamped down on Caeleen's shoulder all the way down to his chest, and the beast shook him like a filthy rag.

Blood poured out of him, and he screamed. He began driving his dagger into its neck again and again, but the wolf refused to yield.

It bit down again, and Caeleen felt his ribs crack under its mighty grip. His vision blurred, and Sal'tera slipped out of his hand and onto the ground.

Weakly, the Ranger grabbed the wolf's mane in his free hand, and he tried, once more, to plunge his dagger into the beast. He could not remove the blade from the beast's neck.

A vicious roar sounded from somewhere above. Suddenly, the hellhound's jaws opened, and Caeleen fell to the dirt. The wolf rolled over on its side, now whining and covered in blue fire. Caeleen tried to focus his vision, and he saw a figure leap over him, followed by a trail of sea-blue mageflame, and drive a shining three-headed weapon into the wolf's belly.

The figure's deep ruby hair, and long blue cape, billowed in the wind behind her, and she ripped the trident out of the beast, slinging it across her back and holding out her hand. Sal'tera suddenly leapt from the ground and into her grasp, and she pointed the weapon at the writhing creature.

"*Uro!*"

The air exploded as a bolt of Sal'tera's white lightning blew the wolf to pieces. Caeleen's vision faded again, and the figure dropped to a knee over him. He smiled as he heard a familiar voice.

"About time you got here, idiot."

Everything went dark.

THE TEMPLE OF BROOKRIDGE WAS QUIET, AND Isiliel sat alone before the mural of Silvia. The visit from Caeleen and his sister had bothered her greatly; if Tamia was under attack by demons, they wouldn't stay in Tamia very long. Even without the vast libraries of Greyfort and Highhaven, Isi knew enough about demons to worry about them spreading. Demons were a plague; they spread and they kill.

She thought back to the Battle for Mistkeep, seeing men, elves, dwarves, and orcs strewn across the field before the Widewood. Torn down by what? Beasts? Animals? Against the legions of Volok, the noble races stood little chance. The White Hammer might hold the line in Krem Zhul-Mkat, and what few Dragoons were left would keep watch over Cidarian for a time, but Tamia? What protections did Tamia have? The Ocean-guard couldn't protect the surface towns, and Omani had no other order of defenders. The Emerald Grove? Isi doubted it; they were absent in the struggle against the Scourge. Tamia needed another line of defense. They needed someone who could make a real stand against the devils.

"Sister Rumoré?" Isi opened her eyes and saw Oskar Offhander at her side. The old dwarf had been instrumental in setting up the Temple here. He and his nephew, Angrim, were excellent smiths, and they had outfitted the clergy of the Temple with arms and armor that rivaled the quality of craft seen in the great monasteries of Lüt'hem.

"Brother Oskar." Isi stood and turned to the dwarf. "I... I have some things that I need to attend to, and I might be gone for some time."

"How long are you thinking?"

"More than a month. Honestly, I can't say for sure."

Oskar's brow furrowed. "That's...that's not good, Sister."

"I know, I know." The older Cleric rested a hand on

Oskar's shoulder. "While I'm gone, I will need you to watch things here."

Oskar took a step back. "Y... you want me to run the Temple?"

Isi nodded. "I know this is asking a lot."

"Indeed, it is... I mean, I've still got m'shop to look after..."

"Oskar, please. People could be in danger."

Oskar frowned hard underneath his beard. "At least tell me why. Is it about the disappearances going on in Tamia?"

Isi nodded. "Dark forces are at work in Tamia. We don't know what it is yet, but there's a chance it might be an incursion from Volok."

"Why is it that everything always happens in Tamia?" Oskar asked suddenly. "They had to deal with the dragon, now this..."

"I wish I had an answer for you, Brother."

Oskar shrugged and reached out a hand. "I'll keep things going for you here while you go do what you need to do."

"Thank you, Brother Oskar." Isi smiled down at her friend, shaking his hand firmly.

Oskar dipped his head before turning to make his way back home. Isi made her way to her quarters and prepared a writ for Oskar before packing her things. Before she headed for Tamia, Isi knew that she would need to head for a larger temple, or at least somewhere where she could brush up and get ready for the upcoming fight. She smiled; it was high time she paid Highhaven a visit.

* * *

CAELEEN JOLTED AWAKE, LETTING OUT A SHRIEK. HE glanced around to find he was no longer on the ground in the plaza, but in what appeared to be a small infirmary. He figured that he was probably still in Awanu, perhaps in their barracks. His traveling gear was cleaned and neatly folded and were resting beside his bed. He looked down at himself to see that someone had healed him; his bare chest now bore deep scars left behind by the hell-hound's teeth, and he could feel another new scar across his forehead, but for the moment he was no longer dying.

"Thank the Gods, you're finally awake." That same familiar voice pricked the Ranger's ears.

Caeleen looked up to see a woman standing there in the doorway. She had Sal'tera strapped to her hip, and across her back was slung a familiar golden trident. Her red hair cascaded down her shoulders, framing her smooth beige visage. Her eyes, that same brilliant amber, now exuded a faint blue glow. She wore a long, thin cape of bold blue that nearly swept the floor behind her, and her armor was made of iridescent-white dragon scales, the scales of Sturamtönn. On her brow was a crown of gold adorned with jewels of blue. Caeleen smiled wide as he recognized her.

"Fates alive," he cried. "Siahra!"

The Diamond Queen laughed, her own grin widening as she moved farther into the room with her arms outstretched.

Caeleen grabbed his coat, flung it on, and leapt out of bed. At once, the Ranger let out a strained groan as he fell to the floor, his shoulder lighting up with pain. He threw a hand onto the scar and quickly spat out his incantation, and the pain subsided, leaving Caeleen gasping for air.

Siahra laughed as she helped her companion slowly get to his feet and threw her arms around his neck.

"It's good to see you, Caeleen!" Siahra said through her laughter as she hugged her old companion tightly. "How've you been?"

"I'm good! I've been..." Caeleen suddenly leaned back as the realization dawned on him. "Wait...are you..."

Siahra cocked an eyebrow and smiled. "Hmm?"

"Are...are you a *Dragoon?*"

Siahra grinned, and she nodded. She flipped her hair back with a hand, and a flicker of blue fire sparked from her fingertips. "Been training ever since you all left for home after the coronation. What about you, hmm? What have you been up to?"

Cae shrugged, his face suddenly red; comparatively, he had accomplished little, especially not compared to taking up a whole new vocation. "Well...I've been teaching a lot. I sort of took over instructing Greyfort's Scout Corps, which... I mean, it makes sense, me being Bowmaster and all that. And, uhhh, I trained a new Ranger, Leon, he's taken over my patrol in the Grey Wood. Other than that... I, uhh... I learned to shoot really fast. Like, almost three arrows a second."

Siahra smiled. "You should give yourself more credit. Being a teacher is a great honor, you ought to be proud."

"I am," Cae replied. "But, yeah, I guess we should get back to the capitol."

"Are you good to travel? We don't have to go until you're ready."

"Oh, yeah, I'm good! Great, actually." He rolled his injured shoulder and winced. So much for that bluff. The shoulder would likely take a few more days to heal fully, even with his healing magic.

Siahra shook her head and smiled. In one swift motion, she unhooked Sal'tera from her belt and handed it back to Caeleen. "alright, then. Get dressed, and we can head on out."

The pair set out for Fartide the sixteenth of January. Caeleen let himself relax as he rode along on Tüli's back again, though for a few days he felt a smidge of apprehension at the creature who served as Siahra's mount. The drake bore shining scales, somewhere between the color of ice and sky, with stripes of a deep indigo here and there. Its eyes were gold, and it wore a harness of dark leather with a gold frame, steel chains serving as its reins. Siahra called him Kéldi. Evidently, the two met not even a week after Caeleen, and his company, had departed after the Battle for Fartide. Cae noted how friendly the two of them were. Siahra's grasp of Udán was almost as strong as Cae's, and Kéldi had more than a bit to contribute to their conversations as they rode. Poor Tüli whined a bit some days, and Caeleen comforted him as best he could. He knew the horse likely had much to say if he could but speak like the other three.

More than once along the road to the City by the Sea, they came upon groups of wandering humans and maotu, covered in filth and wearing tattered rags.

When the Queen and Ranger stopped to offer their

aid, the wanderers just stared at them, their faces blank, and their eyes unblinking. The two would offer from their own food stores, game that Caeleen had killed in the grasslands along the way, fish that Siahra had caught in her river, wild roots and river berries the two had foraged, but the wanderers took nothing from them.

Caeleen shifted uneasily in his saddle at these times; he had been aware of an uneasy feeling in the air ever since he crossed into Tamia. A sense of uncomfortable awareness, like things were normal enough to continue on as usual, yet just off enough to cause concern, but not nearly off enough to determine the cause of worry... well, aside from the hellhounds. But the feeling became stronger still around these wordless vagrants. It was not that they did not want help; it was almost as if they were unable to want help.

They arrived in Fartide on the twenty-ninth. Cae noted that the encampment outside the city walls where King Arian had rallied his armies two years before had been fortified and expanded. The encampment had become a shantytown.

"I like what you've done with the camp," Caeleen said as the two of them trade through the peasantry. "How's construction going inside?"

"Slow, but steady," Siahra mused. "The hardest part has been keeping track of who lived where. We've been keeping files on every citizen who lost their home so they can move back in once we rebuild their homes. It's a lot of paperwork, and we don't have near enough people to go over all of it. I've been doing most of it, myself."

"Sounds rough."

"It is!" Siahra pinched the bridge of her nose. "Gods, it is. But it wouldn't be right to just leave them by the wayside. Anyone who survived the attack deserves to come home."

"Are there still people holed up in the Palace?"

"Only the ones who can't get around." The Dragoon shrugged. "Council's idea. I wanted to keep the Palace open to citizens until rebuilding was done, but they talked me out of it."

"Hmm... y'know, Fartide isn't too far from a Grove of Druids. You could probably ask them to grow a settlement for the survivors."

"I thought about it, but what would we do with it when we're done rebuilding? We can't just leave it to rot."

"Building-tree wood never rots, though. Maybe establish an embassy there? Have King Dravin move some of his dwarves into the mainland, they must be getting cramped in Rey Prele."

Siahra paused and nodded, her brow raised. "That's... actually not bad thinking. I'll bring it up at the next meeting. After the one we're going to, of course."

"So what exactly will I be doing at this meeting?"

"Not much, honestly. You'll be knighted and given a Mareho name."

"*Another* new name? Man, I'm kinda rackin' up these titles!"

"That happens when you're nobility."

"I don't really *feel* like nobility."

"Well, I don't really feel like a Queen. But here we are."

Caeleen smiled and nodded. "Here we are."

As they rode toward the Alabaster Palace, Caeleen looked around at the city, and all the progress that had been made in its reconstruction. Sturamtönn and his horde had done seemingly irreparable damage to the capitol.

In two years' time, however, people once again filled the streets going about their business, and houses Caeleen remembered seeing destroyed now stood firm again, or at least showed signs of repair. The Palace itself now stood tall and proud, restored almost completely to its former splendor. A brilliant white beacon, it stood in the center of the city, between the Surface District and the Ga'ruhe. Caeleen marveled at the structure, in a way he never did with Viraati Líen.

The pair quickly made their way into the throne room, where Siahra took her place on the Diamond Throne. The chamber was enormous, a circular room with its white tile floor bisected by a walkway of blue stone. Massive stone columns stood around the edge of the chamber, and behind them Caeleen stared at the solid wall of translucent crystal that filtered a faintly blue light into the room.

Cutting through the entryway was a deep trench of sorts, filled with still seawater. It didn't take long for Caeleen to realize why it was there; most of Tamia's citizens were merfolk. Of course, they would come through the water. Behind the throne were two large fountains encircled by blue flames, similar to Siahra's magical fires. Caeleen found that their warmth, while not so intense, seemed to spread throughout the chamber, only growing warmer as there approached the Throne.

The Throne itself was fashioned from alabaster, similar to the walls of the palace, laden with diamonds and sapphires in swirling patterns that mirrored the ocean's waves. Leaning against the throne was Arian's glaive, a mithril weapon wielded by the Ruler of Tamia.

Seated in groups on either side of the Throne was a gathering of seven warriors, with one more figure seated on the right. Three of them were clearly Sentinels, their tower shields and halberds indicative of their vocation. One appeared to be some sort of Magus, his iron staff giving off a faint blue glow in his hands. The fifth looked to be some kind of roguish swordswoman, with a cutlass laid across her lap. The two directly beside the Throne were Dragoons, their armor and spears fashioned in the likeness of dragons, one blue and one red. Each of the warriors wore a horn on their belt, likely a sign of their station.

The last figure was a river siren, or so Caeleen surmised from her gently swaying fins. Her long black hair, tied back in a tail running down her shoulder, had roots of silver and blue. Her skin was a lighter shade of brown than Siahra's was, but it was still distinctly beige. Her eyes were a silver so light, they appeared white at first. Her robes were a faint mingling of white and blue lined with patterns of silver thread, and on her brow sat a diadem shaped like a long sea-serpent with a single sapphire clutched in its jaws. Across her lap was a trident, not unlike the one he remembered Siahra wielding. Grand Mistress Suressa, he presumed.

"*Ha maene, kahoe o Tamia,*" Siahra said, her voice ringing out through the chamber. "We have in our midst one who would be named among us. A *Kahoe*, a Knight, of our Diamond Shores." The Mermaid Queen gestured toward Caeleen, who knelt before the gathering with a fist closed over his heart. "Sir Caeleen Percival of House Longwatch, Seventh Whisper of the Dokk Fuil, Bowmaster of Greyfort, and Knight of the Grey Plains of Laithe."

Caeleen bowed his head. "I am honored by your consideration, my Queen," he said. "I will do all I can to serve the Shores. My hands are yours... *Kae tahu ke hina.*"

Siahra nodded. "I have fought beside Sir Longwatch before. He was there when we slew the sea-dragon Sturamtönn, and it was with his blade that the wyrm was vanquished. He aided me himself in hunting the dragon's horde after my father died..."

A beat of quiet spoke as much about the lingering grief over Arian's death as the somber look on Siahra's face. She looked back up with furrowed brow and continued. "Omani, the Sea-Father, has named him my Companion. I can think of few better to serve at our side. *Aha ki koi?*"

"*Ai,*" said the two Dragoons.

"*Ka,*" said one Sentinel.

"*Ai,*" said the siren.

"*Ka,*" said the Magus.

"*Ai,*" said the rest.

Siahra smiled as she rose from her throne, taking her glaive in hand. "*Pare ana,*" she said. "Sir Longwatch, do you pledge your service and your heart to the people of Tamia, to the end of your days?"

"I do."

Siahra gently tapped each of his shoulders with the tip of her glaive. "Then by my right as Queen, I name you Ta Rakau, Knight of the Diamond Shores of Tamia." A moment of quiet passed over the chamber, and she smiled down at the Ranger, presenting him with a horn of his own. "Now, get up. You're one of us."

Caeleen stood up and met Siahra's eyes, hanging the horn from the belt across his chest. "Ta Rakau?"

"Rakau means tree," answered one of the Dragoons. "And Ta is a title, like your 'Sir.' You are a Ranger of the forest, yes?"

"Yeah, I grew up in the Dokk..." Caeleen's brow suddenly crinkled. "Wait, you named me *Sir Tree*?"

The Knights all began to chuckle. Siahra shrugged. "It seemed appropriate."

Caeleen was about to protest as the swordswoman patted an empty seat next to her. "Sit, Rakau. We have things to discuss."

"Right!" Caeleen hurriedly took his seat next to the Knight. "So are we doing introductions, or what?"

"Don't worry about it, you'll pick up everyone's names." She smiled for a moment before her visage turned dark, and she turned to Siahra. "*K'kanu*, I bring grim tidings from the village of Mai."

"I've heard rumors about the events there, Kepa." Siahra frowned. "Is it true what they're saying about the trench?"

"I'm afraid so," Kepa replied. "We lost good folk fighting back the demons coming out of the deep."

Siahra sighed and brought a hand to her brow. "We

need to send more guards out there. Do we have enough to spare?"

"I'm sure we do, K'kanu," answered a Sentinel.

"The Riverhands can lend aid, if need be," added the siren.

"You have my thanks, dear cousin," Siahra replied. She turned to the Sentinel. "Ta Koa'topa, give the order to station a detachment at Mai to monitor the Trench."

"Wait, Mai?" Caeleen asked. "I've never heard of that village. Where is it?"

The Knights all turned and looked at the human in their midst.

Caeleen thought for a moment, then it occurred to him. Red rushed to his cheeks. "It's underwater, isn't it?"

"Yes," replied one of the other Sentinels. "Most of Tamia is in the Diamond Ocean."

"How big *is* Tamia, then?"

"With the surface and the ocean combined? About the size of Q'let and Laithe put together."

Caeleen's eyes widened. "Gods be good!"

Ta Koa'topa laughed. "Shame you'll not be able to see most of it, eh, Rakau?"

"Don't tease him, Koa'topa," Siahra chided. "We'll find a way to bring him along. But for now, Cae, I think it'd be best to have you leading a patrol of the surface. How comfortable are you with drake-riding?"

"Not very... no, not at all," Cae replied. "Sorry, I just... draconids have rubbed me the wrong way ever since my Pa died. But I might have an alternative."

"The griffin?"

"No, not Kaon... Back home in the Dokk, I had

another companion, a Great Eagle named Alahir. He and I grew up together, I learned to ride on his back before I even learned to ride a horse. He didn't accompany me into the mainland before because he had to take care of his hatchlings, but now they're flying and hunting on their own. I might be able to convince him to come down here and join us."

"That would be best," Siahra replied. "We really need you in the air, Cae."

"I'll do what I can."

The Queen nodded. "You'll start your patrols in a week. Until then, I want you to work on familiarizing yourself with the city, and the immediate area. You may not have as much room here as you did in Greyfort, but we should have enough here for you to make yourself at home."

"Do you have a fletcher, and a smith?"

"Of course."

Caeleen smiled. "Then, I'll be just fine."

"We have more to discuss," the Dragoon on Siahra's left said. "*K'kanu*, perhaps the Ranger should take his leave."

"That would be best, Har Burúm," Siahra replied. "Ta Rakau... I'll come find you later."

"Before I go," Cae stammered, "I have urgent news from Davenstead."

"Davenstead?" Koa'topa asked. "What do they want?"

Caeleen frowned. "Apparently, there was an incident at Underlake Prison. One inmate escaped captivity and has been seen here in Tamia..." The Ranger looked to the

Queen. "It's the Wild Rose. Your Grace, we *have* to be on the lookout for him."

Siahra's eyes widened for a moment, and Caeleen saw a similar fear reflected in the blue glow, but her face remained firm. "We'll need you out there looking for him, then. You can track better than anyone I know. But... Cae, please be careful."

"Of course, my Queen." Caeleen stood and, with a quick bow, made his way out of the chamber.

6

*T*he Surface District itself was certainly smaller than Greyfort, which made sense. Most of the maotu would likely prefer to stay in the ocean, closer to the rest of the Kingdom. Still, Caeleen found that Fartide's streets were more than full with all the noble races. The once-crumbled stores and housings were now repaired, and alive with citizenry, sealed cracks still bare on the structures like battle-scars. It took a bit of walking, but Caeleen eventually made his way to Fartide's Market Square, crowded in the middle of the day with common folk and peasantry. Glancing about, the Ranger spotted a sign above one door with a pair of arrows crossed over curved horns on it. *"Lemshak's Hunting Goods,"* it read. With a shrug, Caeleen made his way inside.

The store itself was relatively small. On the wall to Caeleen's right was a display of several shortbows and crossbows, and on the wall to his left were longbows and arbalests. Each weapon was well-crafted and bore a seal similar to the sign outside, a pair of arrows over curved horns. Most of the crossbows and arbalests also bore a different seal, a sword bisecting a horseshoe, showing that they had been crafted in part elsewhere.

Behind the counter was a man with deep blue skin and a pair of blue horns curving back from his forehead over his short black hair. Behind him swished a thin tail, and Caeleen could see he had filed his nails back from their natural, claw-like state. The man had faintly glowing yellow eyes. He blinked, and the glow dissipated. Caeleen was surprised, as he had never met a ghari before, but he had heard of their reputation for wisdom. The Gharpasans were an advanced society; Cestus hadn't been kidding about the stories of Gharpasan airships.

"Oh! Thank the Red Queen, an actual hunter," the shopkeeper muttered, his voice thick with an accent Caeleen figured was native to Gharpasa. "*Acha dan*, friend. Welcome to Lemshak's Hunting Goods, I am Lemshak. How might I be of service?"

"Hello!" Caeleen dipped his head as he approached the counter. "I just got in, and the Queen thought it would be a good idea to get acquainted."

"Ah, I see. A new Knight, are you?" Lemshak nodded with a smile, pointing at the horn hanging from Caeleen's chest. "Things have been strange as of late. I pray you can help make things right."

"I'll certainly try!" Cae replied with a smile. "I'm a bit low on arrows right now, so I was wondering if you had any you could spare."

"But, of course! What kind of fletcher has no arrows?" The shopkeeper gestured to the side wall behind his counter. Row upon row of arrows and bolts of varying sizes and heads rested on display. The ghari grabbed a bundle of arrows tipped with silver and laid them on the counter. "I suspect you'll be needing these the most. Normally, twenty silver-tipped would run you four gold pieces but, for a genuine huntsman such as yourself, I offer you these for two gold and fifty silver. You need more, come back to see me."

"Thank you, sir!" Cae placed three gold in Lemshak's hand and quivered the arrows. A hum, just barely audible, sounded from his back as the quiver's holy magic seeped into the projectiles.

The sound of screams from outside pierced the quiet of the store.

Cae and Lemshak exchanged a wide-eyed glance, and the black feather around Caeleen's neck became warm enough that it burned against his breast.

"Perhaps now would be a good time to test those arrows, yes?" the fletcher asked as he weaved a quick spell with his hands. At once, a pair of wrapped chains appeared on his arms, each attached to its own handaxe.

The two of them ran outside to see the common folk in a panic. The Square was covered in scorch marks, and chunks of the brickwork on the ground had been blasted to pieces. There, in the center of the Square, stood a horrendous sight: the creature looked to have once been a wyrmling silver dragon, five years old at best, but the beast had clearly been long dead. Large chunks of scale and flesh had fallen away to reveal blackened bone underneath, and what meat remained on the creature was rotten and festering, swarming with insects. In the empty sockets where the dragon's eyes should have been, a deep purple glow showed life that should not have been there.

A dracowight. Caeleen had heard of such abominations before only in old tattered books and eerie tales around the campfire with his scouts. He dreaded the thought of facing one, but his disgust gave him more reason to end the vile thing quickly.

The dracowight hunched over a guardsman, the poor soul's half-plate rent apart and his belly cut open. Scattered about were the bodies of two more guards, one male and one female, both torn open in similar fashion. Red slowly pooled on the white stone and brick beneath them, and several more guards stood shaking in a circle around them, their spears pointed inward.

One guard leaned up against his spear, his helm rent open and cast aside at his feet. He turned to Caeleen, wild eyes poking out from between strands of scorched crimson hair, and he spotted the horn on the Ranger's chest. "Y-you! Ta! Can y-augh, g-Gods! *Help!*"

"*Kur bit'düg*," the Seventh Whisper growled under his breath. "Why is it always dragons with this city? What did you do to piss them off so badly?"

"Perhaps you might ask our Queen after we dispose of this..." Lemshak paused for a moment. "This... thing, yes? Please, blow your horn. We may need more Knights."

"Is that what this is for?" Caeleen lifted the horn to his lips and blew as hard as he could. A loud, hollow tone rang out loud and strong across the District, echoing in the air.

At once, the dracowight whipped its ugly head around, its amethystine glow focusing on the Ranger.

In a quick motion, Caeleen pulled out his bow and nocked an arrow.

Lemshak shuddered under the dracowight's gaze. "... I suppose I should have gotten away from you first."

Lemshak and Caeleen dove out of the way as the undead beast charged with an unnatural speed, slamming into the wall of the Hunting Goods Store, and shaking the entire building. Caeleen whirled around and loosed an arrow into its shoulder. A faint wave of holy magic rocked the beast's body as the silver arrowhead sunk into the dracowight's body, causing a wisp of smoke to hiss out of the wound. The dracowight let out a shriek, its rotted voice a cacophony of guttural vibrations that made the Ranger sick to his stomach.

Without thinking, Cae pulled out three more arrows and began darting toward the center of the Square, firing his shots off as quick as he could. Two arrows glanced off the wings of the dead wyrmling, while the other grazed the scales of it snout. The purple light intensified as smoke sizzled from the graze.

As it prepared to launch toward the Ranger, twin axes sunk themselves into the dragon's side. Lemshak gripped his chains fiercely and yanked fiercely, slinging the dragon over his head and into the wall of a neighboring store. The dracowight latched onto the wall and spread its wings, hissing at the ghari hunter. Lemshak grimaced and jerked on his chains again, yanking his axes free. Black blood splattered across the building, and the dracowight leapt toward the fletcher.

Lemshak darted out of the way just in time as Caeleen leapt back in, a blur of brown and red as he dropped his bow. The Ranger drove his heel into the dracowight's jaw and drew Sal'tera, a sound like thunder cracking through the air as the holy blade left its sheath. The creature reared back for a moment, then let out another sickening shriek.

"Back to Volok, *fu thrák kuri!*" the Ranger shouted as he struck. The dracowight reared back on its hind legs, and its left claws struck against holy mithril and burned against the Blade of the Covenant. Caeleen shoved the beast back and took Sal'tera in both hands, swinging as hard as he could at the claw he'd struck, and slicing a large gash into the limb. The dracowight fell forward, pawing at its festering wound. The Ranger raised Kh'ano-ra's blade high over his head and brought it down into the creature's head. A tremor rocked the stone around them as the unholy life burst out of the wyrmling's corpse, wisps of purple haze dissipating into the air.

Caeleen withdrew his blade, cleaned it with his cloak, and sheathed it. Lemshak then approached, his axes and chains now gone.

"Well fought, Sir Boltwalker!" the shopkeeper marveled, clapping slowly as he did so. "I will not lie, I was intrigued when I heard the rumors of the Emperor's sword returning to the land, but you certainly live up to your reputation."

"Thank you, fletcher!" Cae replied. Just then, the sound of wing flaps reached the Ranger's ears as two drakes, one red and one gold, landed in the Square. Off their back came the two Dragoons Cae had seen before.

"About time you got here!" Lemshak shouted with his hands up. "So glad you could join us today, our noble heroes!"

Caeleen inclined his head as one of the drake-masters approached, removing his helmet. His hair, naturally black, was tinted crimson, and his face was very angular. His ears were pointed, but not so tall. A half-elf, likely also half-maotu.

"Forgive us for not arriving sooner, Master Ranger," Har Burúm said. "It is good to see you safe."

"Don't worry about it," Caeleen replied. "I've killed a few dragons before, it's not like I don't know what I'm doing."

The Dragoon nodded, perhaps a bit curtly. "Unfortunately, this is not the first time an incident such as this has occurred. We've seen undead on our patrols before, but never has one come within the walls."

"We need to think about keeping a patrol going here in the City, then. If something else, something *bigger*, were to show up while all the Knights were away..."

"I'll bring it to the Queen's attention." The Dragoon looked back to the remains of the undead wyrmling. Lemshak was already examining it, a small hunting knife in his hand. "Sir! Fletcher! Step back from there; we need to bring that in for—"

"I'll do no such thing!" Lemshak replied. "This creature did significant damage to my store, and the stores of my neighbors! We'll be taking his scales as compensation, thank you very much!"

"Sir, I can't let you—"

"Can't hear you, carving! Good day!"

Caeleen shook his head and laughed. "Hey, I need to get going. I wanna see about getting my dagger silvered, any idea where a good smith would be?"

Burúm sighed and shook his head as he turned away from the ghari huntsman. "For my money," he mused, "I would go with Manshe, the smithy a few blocks that way. Young centaur, her parents came here from Guyanh. I don't think she's in right now, but she's the best in the city."

Cae nodded. "alright. I'm gonna go get a feel for the area."

Burúm nodded, then turned back and mounted his drake. Caeleen made his way out of the Square as the two Dragoons took off.

* * *

THE COAST SOUTH OF FARTIDE WAS SOFTER GROUND than Caeleen would have liked. Tüli had a bit of difficulty maneuvering on the beach as the sun set over the Diamond Ocean, and Ranger and steed rode on warily, eventually turning eastward and heading for the uneven grasses of the mainland. As the two rode on, and dusk settled over the Diamond Shores, Caeleen felt a point of cold touch his nose, and looked up to see the start of snowfall descending from the clouds...clouds that Caeleen swore weren't there a moment ago. The feather pendant around his neck hummed almost inaudibly as the flakes fell, giving off just the faintest warmth.

As the snow came down on them, gathering on Caeleen's cloak and in poor Tüli's mane, they came upon the bones of a town that once stood just outside the Tamian capitol. The settlement that once stood here was tiny and simple, not even a plaza or a town hall, but there still stood, mostly intact, a Temple to Omani. Caeleen dismounted, pulling his hood on, and approached the once-holy site with Tüli's reins in hand. The paint on the threshold, once an intricate pattern of gold, white and turquoise, now had peeled and faded to reveal the grey stone underneath. The walls were solid enough, made of stone rather than wood, like the rest of the town. What remained of the glass windows were carefully stained, and they depicted the Sea-Father in many poses, in accordance to the tales of Creation in which He took part.

Inside, Caeleen found the building almost entirely stripped; no benches or beds remained, and the altar on the back wall was cracked and bereft of any symbols that had once graced its surface. A stone statue of Omani, small but similar in appearance to the one in Highhaven's Temple, gazed down with stern visage at the altar's remains.

The Ranger knelt before the altar and placed a silver piece on the cracked stone. Omani had been kind to the maotu in the aftermath of the Battle for Fartide, and he had earned Caeleen's respect. Looking about, the Ranger could not deny his curiosity at just what happened to this town.

When Caeleen emerged from the Temple, the moon had begun to cast its pale light from the east. Tüli stood just outside the threshold, and the young horse nuzzled into the crook of his master's neck. Caeleen stroked Tüli's mane and glanced out over the dilapidated wooden structures.

"Suppose we can camp here for the night," Cae whispered to his horse. "Think we can head back in the morning, yeah?"

The horse blew out his nose and followed Caeleen inside, lowering himself carefully onto the stone floor. Cae helped the horse down and got to work at making a fire there in the middle of the Temple. Omani wouldn't mind; the church wasn't in use, anyway. Eventually, the flame was large enough to bring warmth to the pair, and Caeleen curled up atop his bedroll and shut his eyes.

"A ways out from Fartide, aren't you, Mister Longwatch?"

Caeleen crept one eye open to see Kh'anora seated by his fire.

"Evening, m'Lord," Caeleen said with a sigh. "A bit far from the forest, aren't You?"

"Perhaps," the Ethereal laughed. "But I am glad to see you safe after what happened with the dracowight today."

"I wish I had been out there before it killed the guards. I'm supposed to keep these people safe, Y'know?"

"You ought not blame yourself, lad," Kh'anora replied. "Even the Gods cannot keep up with everything that occurs in the world, you should not expect to, either."

Cae nodded. "Hey, how's Leon?" he asked.

"He fares well," Kh'anora replied. "He works closely with the other Knights he trained with. I believe they call them the Knights Three?"

The Ranger chuckled. "Yeah. Dunc and Eda. They're good kids. They work really well together."

Kh'anora nodded. "And your family is well, also. Your mother misses you more each day, you know."

"I know," Cae said with a sigh. "I should call home more often. Especially with everything Ma has been through... I just get so busy, Y'know what I mean?"

Kh'anora shrugged. "These things happen... your sister is content as well, as is your Eagle friend."

"Oh! Could You deliver a message to him for me?" Cae asked. "If he can make it down here, I really need his help."

Kh'anora frowned for a moment. "I can," the Ethereal nodded. "But this...this contempt of yours for dragons and their ilk. It is unhealthy."

"W... I mean, it's not like I think they're... I just... I mean, come on. They're dragons. They're dangerous creatures."

"So are humans, I believe you'll find. Do not be so hasty to pass judgment, Mister Longwatch. I think spending time here amongst the Dragoons will do you good."

Cae frowned for a moment before casting his eyes down and nodding. He then reached into his shirt and pulled out the charm given to him by Volok. He looked down at it for a moment before looking back up at the Hunter-God. "Hey, I dunno if it's okay for me to ask this, but... what did Volok mean when She mentioned Her other half before? She said something about a misconception."

Kh'anora looked into the flame for a moment, not

speaking. His eyes shifted down to his feet, and He nodded. "The other half people speak of... She is not... She..." the old God stroked His chin. "... Volok does not have another half."

Caeleen's brow furrowed. "What do you mean?"

Kh'anora sighed. "... This 'other half' the mortals fear so much is Volok's twin Sister."

The archer's eyes widened. "Th... there's another Ethereal King?"

"Yes," Kh'anora answered. The HunterGod shook His head. "I... forgive Me, lad. This is not My story to tell."

Caeleen was about to protest, but he just barely heard footsteps over the sound of the crackling fire. Looking up and out the doorway into the bones of the town, Caeleen could barely make out a figure on the edge of the settlement. The figure was thin, shrouded in a hooded cloak, and stood unmoving.

"Who is that?" Cae asked.

"... I do not know." Kh'anora frowned. "They are... they are hidden from Me."

Caeleen turned and looked at the Tree Father. "Hidden from a God? How?"

"I don't know, Caeleen." Kh'anora frowned. "Something is... wrong."

Caeleen took his bow and moved to string it. Kh'anora raised a hand.

"You need to rest, child," the Ethereal said. "I will keep watch over you this night."

Caeleen narrowed his eyes before nodding. Turning

and nestling into his fur, he shut his eyes, pulled his cloak around him tightly, and tried to sleep.

* * *

THE AXE WHIRLED IN LEON'S HANDS LIKE A hurricane, and he let out a fierce grunt as he slung the blade into the practice dummy in front of him, cleaving the wooden thing in two. He panted for a moment, looking down at the weapon in his hand with a frown. It wasn't his; this was just a practice weapon. Leon's axe was being handled by the Magesmiths. He hadn't bothered to ask what they planned to do to it, as he figured it would be useful either way. This practice axe was... not great. The handle was too heavy, it had no counterweight, and there wasn't enough heft in the head to give it that spin he loved in his own weapon. Still, he knew how to use an axe, it didn't much matter what kind.

Leon let the head of the axe hit the dirt with a *thud* as he shuffled to the fence and grabbed his flask, taking a long draft of the clean water inside. As he wiped his mouth on the back of his hand, he couldn't help but feel a dash of melancholy. Caeleen had left without so much as saying goodbye. It made sense, as he was in a hurry to get to Tamia and help... at least, that's what Baron had told him. Still, it would have been nice to see him off.

Either way, it didn't much matter. That had been months ago. He was the Ranger of the Grey Wood now, he didn't have time to get moody.

"Farrough."

Leon looked up to see King Mull approaching, Leon's

axe in his hand. The Ranger dropped to a knee and bowed his head. "Sire."

"Up, lad." Mull held the axe out for the boy to take. "Here, this belongs to you."

Leon stood and took his axe back from the old King. *Much better*, he thought. His axe was wonderfully balanced, more so than the simple weapons Greyfort kept in its barracks for training. He examined the handle and found new runes alongside the Knights' Creed. He recognized them as Old Eridan, but...

"*Che lanh i meisirnach, aighus-im*," Mull read. "'To my master's hands, I return.'"

Leon cocked a brow. "So... it does... what, exactly?"

"Throw it," Mull said with a grin. "Find out."

Leon looked up at his King, then shrugged. He took a moment to focus on the weapon. There was some kind of magic there, some arcane essence, but... well, magic weaponry was an unexplored field for Leon. He got by well enough on his own. In his mind, he reached out and... took hold of the essence. He couldn't help but snort; he had no idea what he was doing, but he at least figured the enchantment would work.

Leon stepped back, flourishing the axe as he did. He turned away from the King and, with a quick pirouette, he slung the axe in a horizontal spin.

The axe whirled furiously through the air. As it flew farther from Leon, it slowed gradually to a halt in the air, still spinning. Leon's eyes widened.

"D... does it stop?"

"Only when you pull it back."

Leon's face twisted with confusion, but he shook his

head and shrugged. He reached out with a hand, and...
Gods, what was he doing?

As he reached for the axe, it suddenly sped back toward him. Leon shrieked, but he managed to snatch the axe from the air.

"Wh-b... fu-d-wh... *what?*" Leon stammered in excitement. "S-Sire, what did you do?"

Mull chuckled. "Bellam tells me it's a rather simple enchantment. It'll go where you command, and it'll always come right back to you."

Leon marveled at the weapon he held. "This... thank you, Sire, this is amazing."

Mull grinned. "Go on, then. Name your weapon."

Leon gripped the axe in his hands, thinking for a moment. "... I'll call you... Seeker."

"A fine name for an axe. Keep it safe, and care for it well. You may need it."

Leon turned back to Mull. "What do you mean?"

A hefty sigh came from the King's chest. "Lad, you know I have faith in our friend Sir Longwatch. But..."

Leon looked back at Mull grimly. "... He might not be able to do it. He might not be able to find the problem out there."

Mull looked back at his new Ranger with a twinge of gloom in his eyes, and he nodded. "We have to be ready for that darkness to spread this way."

Leon looked back down at Seeker. "... He can do it. I know he can."

Mull nodded. Without another word, the old King turned and left the barracks.

* * *

WHEN CAELEEN AWOKE THE NEXT MORNING, Kh'anora was gone. The snow outside had built up a good few inches, then hardened as it settled in the night. The fire had dwindled to its last smoldering embers, and the cloaked figure was nowhere to be found.

Cae left Tüli sleeping in the Temple and made his way to the edge of town where the figure had been, his boots crunching in the white substance covering the ground. There was no sign of anyone's presence. Cae frowned and scanned the area, looking for any evidence someone had been here. He found nothing. If the figure, whoever it may have been, had left footprints or a trail on the ground, the trail was buried in the snow. But Kh'anora had confirmed the presence of... something.

The Ranger disliked this; first the thing watching him in the new settlement, and now this. He had been doing his best to push back against the unease in the back of his mind, but he could not deny it now. Something was keeping tabs on him, stalking him.

Hunting him.

Tüli whinnied from his place beside the remains of the fire, bringing Caeleen back out of his own head. The Ranger wanted to stay and look for the trail beneath the powder, but the danger was too great. The figure could be a Voloki, or it could be the Wild Rose, neither of which Caeleen was in any position to engage on his own. He would need to bring help, perhaps call in his fellow Knights. Caeleen returned and smothered the embers, strapped his sleeping fur to his saddle, and the two strolled back toward Fartide.

As soon as Cae and his horse were out of the town, the snow seemed to trail off. Caeleen worried his brow as he looked up at the bright expanse above him. Blue skies, not a wisp of cloud to be seen. Down at the ground. No snow outside of the town. It only snowed where he had been... and where that figure was. Maybe it was a stretch to connect them, but coincidences didn't happen that often. Less so in circumstances such as these.

They rode on for about an hour when the Ranger's ears pricked up. Wing flaps. Leathery wings... *Dragon wings*.

Caeleen looked skyward to see a silhouette coming down toward him. A drake! His hand instinctively darted to Sal'tera's hilt, but the sight of a golden trident held by the creature's rider stayed his hand. Siahra landed a few yards away and dismounted her drake, running her hand along Kéldi's wing for a moment. Siahra, herself, was not in her Dragoon armor, but wore instead a short leather surcoat lined with gold and blue with black trousers, her old blue traveling cloak on her back, and her trident in hand. On her brow still rested her father's crown, and a horn much like the one Caeleen wore hung from her neck.

"K'kanu!" Cae called as he drew his dagger and brought it over his heart.

Siahra shook her head, a brow cocked as she slung the trident over onto her back. "Come on, dude. You know how I get about that."

Caeleen tilted his head. "Wh... but all the other Knights do it."

"Only during Council meetings. They all know." Siahra stroked Tüli's mane as Cae dismounted. "You know I can't stand everyone in the... wait, why were you in Creddon?"

Cae turned back to the remnants of the settlement. "Just kinda stumbled on it, honestly. Why?"

Siahra shook her head in surprise. "Nobody has lived here since... well, since the Burned Ages."

Caeleen's brow crinkled with concern. "W... why not?"

"Giant crab."

"Giant cr—*what?* Where?"

Siahra looked back at the ghost town in the distance. Caeleen's eyes followed her line of sight, and his face flushed.

"No. No, no, no! *I slept here last night!*"

"Congratulations," the Mermaid Queen replied. "You're the first person to spend a night in Creddon in recorded history."

"I slept on a giant crab!?"

"And lived!"

Caeleen pushed a hand through his hair. "You can't possibly be serious."

Siahra shook her head. "He hasn't woken up once in all the time we have recorded, but he's down there."

"Is he alive?"

"Nobody knows." Siahra crossed her arms. "But... Cae, are you alright?"

"No, I'm not alright! Giant crab!"

"Forget about the crab for a minute!" Siahra sighed. "Look. We heard something might be out this way. We don't know what exactly, but did you see anything out of the ordinary after you left the capitol yesterday?"

"Yeah, there was some snow right over Creddon and... nowhere else."

Siahra nodded. "That... yeah, that happens nowadays."

"But there was also a... there was someone at the edge of town last night. I couldn't tell if it was a man or a woman or what. I'm honestly not even sure if they were human or not... or maotu, I guess would be more likely."

"Did you see where they went? Where they are now?"

"No, I was on my way back to bring help. If it's a devil, or if it's the Rose, I don't wanna take them on by myself."

Siahra's lips slowly curled into a smirk. "Think you and I could handle 'em?"

Cae tilted his head and smiled. "I think we have a shot."

The two of them turned and made back for Creddon together. The snow still lay thick on the ground, spoiling any chance of them finding good spoor, but the town was small enough to comb over by hand. Tüli and Kéldi remained at the edge of town where the snow had trailed off, and Caeleen and Siahra searched each building carefully. The snow soaked their boots and chilled them to the bone as they trudged about, but eventually they found themselves in a back alley between the bones of four buildings. The snow there, while still definitely built up higher than the rest of the town, had melted and hardened a bit as if it had been there for several days.

Caeleen narrowed his eyes and produced a shovel from his magic bag, then set off at shoveling the snow into the dilapidated remains of a tavern, through a sizable hole in the wall. After several minutes of shoveling, the ground was clear enough that the pair of them could see, to their shock, very large talon prints frozen into the snow, lined with blackened scorch marks.

"A Voloki?" Siahra asked.

Caeleen scratched his chin. "Well...I'm not a hundred percent sure, but it seems likely." He took his shovel in hand and continued clearing the ground. Eventually, he hit something hard buried beneath the snow against the wall of the tavern. Pulling out a pair of thick gloves from his bag, the Ranger set to work at clearing the snow from whatever it was he hit, eventually revealing a thick wooden door. It didn't take much thought to figure that the door led to the inn's cellar... which would bring them closer to the crab. Cae shuddered at the thought, but they were already here, and they had to at least look.

Siahra stepped forward and threw the door open. "Come on, let's just try to be quick about it."

The two descended the stairs and opened the door at the bottom into a dimly lit basement. In contrast to the town above, the basement appeared to be well lived in; crates and barrels in stacks against the walls, a broken bed in the corner with a large chest at its foot, a desk lit by a handful of candles... and a pair of bodies in the middle of the floor.

The Ranger and Queen both stopped to fight back

the urge to retch at the stench and the sight before they entered, but soon got to work at looking over the room. Siahra took to looking at the desk and its contents, while Caeleen began checking the corpses.

The first body was male, a minuscule fellow with wide, pointed ears and curly golden hair, with a bit of groomed and trimmed hair on his chin. He was a gnelf; half-gnome, half-elf. His clothes had been opulent once, rich brown velvet with gold trim, but now they were torn and tattered, stained with reddish-brown from several wounds in his belly now dried up. This poor fellow had been dead for weeks. In his coat pocket was the broken remains of a pan flute, inscribed with intricate letterings in Ishoni, the gnomish tongue. Cae didn't understand what they said, but he could at least identify the swirling glyphs. Fastened to the breast of the gnelf's coat was a brooch in the likeness of a butterfly. Caeleen frowned; this was an ambassador.

Cae turned to the other body. This one was a dwarven female, her brown hair in thick braids and dreadlocks. She bore a vicious stab wound in place of her left eye, and blood from the wound had poured down her cheek and crusted in place. The woman was armed to the teeth, her gambeson lined with knives and daggers. Her right hand still gripped a shortspear of masterful craftsmanship, and in her left was an octagonal buckler bearing the image of a ram's head. She'd died here on the spot... and whoever killed her must have just left her there. In one of her pockets, Caeleen found a scrap of battered parchment. *"Creddon. Tavern basement. 171 gold."* She was a bounty hunter.

Whoever lived here, somebody wanted them dead... and judging by the bodies on their floor, Caeleen could see why.

Cae stood up and began inspecting all the different containers lying about. He found most of them filled with dried foodstuffs and supplies. Eventually, he moved to the chest right at the foot of the bed. Inside, he came upon a sizable targe of black steel, adorned with the stylized symbol of a menacing scarlet eye encircled by black wings. On the back of the shield were solid shackles, dangling from thick chain of the same steel as the shield's surface. The shield hummed with power in Caeleen's hand.

"Hey, Siahra..." the Ranger held the round shield up as he got to his feet. "I found something."

Siahra looked up at Caeleen with wide eyes. "So did I." In her hands, wilted and crumbling, was a rose blossom.

Caeleen eyed the dead flower, and his heart dropped into his stomach. "... Siahra, I don't know if we're ready for this. I know I said we could do it, but I—"

"You're right." the Diamond Queen dropped the bloom back to the surface of the desk. "We need to run."

Caeleen nodded, hastily slinging the targe over his shoulder. The two turned back to leave when they heard the door atop the stairs open.

Footsteps, coming down the stairway.

He was coming.

Without thinking, the both of them dove into hiding. Siahra blew out the candles and slid quietly under the broken bed. She pulled out a small knife and gripped it with trembling hands, trying her best to slink back out of sight.

Caeleen darted back behind the doorway, clutching his dagger with white knuckles and holding his breath. Out of habit, he pulled on his hood, more to make himself feel safer than to conceal his face.

The footsteps came to a stop in the doorway, and Siahra stared, in horror, from beneath the bed at a pair of black boots, accompanied by the head of a bearded axe.

In the sudden silence, the both of them could just barely hear the faintest dripping sound coming through the door. Caeleen's heartbeat slammed in his ears and threatened to deafen him as the black-shrouded figure shuffled into the room, a powerful silhouette in the darkness. The figure was tall, male, unsettlingly thin in the dark and, as he shambled, the sound of his feet and axe scraping the ground pierced the quiet with an eerie combination of hiss and screech.

The man sat down at his desk, his weapon clattering to the stone floor. The sound of wood rubbing against wood came then as he opened a drawer, and several more clatters followed as he dropped handfuls of... *something* inside, then slid the drawer shut. His hands hissed along the desk's surface as he brushed the crumpled blossom aside.

Siahra held her breath and continued to tremble as the man brought his hands together on the desk. His hands glowed a pale pink for a moment, and Caeleen watched as in the light of his palms formed a new rose bloom. He stared at the flower for a moment, his breaths ragged and muffled. He sat there for a long while, staring down at the bloom in his hand as it slowly, but surely, withered in his hands.

Caeleen and Siahra dared not move as the figure stood up from the desk, shuffled over to his bed, and laid down. About a minute after he did so, Siahra inched her head out from underneath the bed and looked up at her Companion in the dim light.

Caeleen shook his head, just barely; the man was definitely still awake. Siahra held in a traitorous sob and slunk back beneath the bed.

Thirty more minutes crept painfully by, and Siahra peered out once more. Caeleen's eyes darted from the figure resting on the bed to the visage of his Queen and back. His keen eyes had been locked on the man's rising and falling form for the past half-hour. The man was breathing shallower now, and his ragged breathing had grown quieter. As far as Cae could tell, he was unconscious. Caeleen jerked his head toward the door.

Siahra inched out as silently as she could, and made her way around the corpses, out the door, and up the stairs.

Caeleen stood in the doorway and looked back over his shoulder.

The man was still asleep. The dagger was still in his hand. For just a moment, he thought he could do it. Then and there, get the problem out of the way. But, if he missed... he had heard the stories of what the Wild Rose was capable of. He knew that, if he missed, there would be no second shot. Turning back, he took to the stone stairs and crept out into the open air to join Siahra.

The Queen of the Mermaids carefully closed the

door behind them, and they made their way as quietly as they could in the falling snow back toward...

Siahra clamped a hand over her own mouth to keep herself from screaming.

Tüli and Kéldi were both dead. Both creatures bore large gashes at the base of their skulls, through which oozed a thick mass of blood and chunks of flesh, red from Tüli and blue from Kéldi. The bellies of both creatures had been cut open down the middle, and their entrails were carefully arranged in a circle around the pair.

Caeleen collapsed in the snow, and crawled toward what was left of his faithful friend, doing his best to suppress his tears. He cradled Tüli's head in his hands, and he nearly shrieked when he looked down at the dead thing.

Tüli's teeth were all gone, as were Kéldi's.

"Siahra!" Caeleen pushed his anguish aside and turned to his companion. "Siahra, we have to go, now!"

Siahra had hit the ground and bent over what remained of her drake, her forehead touched to its bloodied snout. She turned back to Caeleen, and her eyes widened.

Cae turned and looked over his shoulder. His blood froze in his veins as he saw the tall, shrouded figure standing there in the snow just outside the tavern, watching them.

The man did not move as Siahra whipped her horn to her lips and blew as loud as she could. The Ranger joined in, blowing his own horn as he and the Queen broke into a run toward Fartide in the distance.

The pair ran for a good five minutes before the sound

of dragon wings came screaming down as a Dragoon arrived to answer the call.

"Siahra!" the gold-armored warrior called as he dismounted, rushing to Siahra's side. "Siahra, what's happened? What happened to Kéldi?"

Siahra turned to the Dragoon and shook her head, biting back against the moisture building in her eyes. "I'm sorry, Eldur. It's my fault, I left him here alone."

Eldur shook his head. "It's alright. Come on, we need to get back to the Palace." Turning back, the Dragoon helped Caeleen up and got him onto his drake's back.

As Siahra climbed onto the gold drake, she turned back to the remnants of Creddon once more. The man was nowhere to be found. He had not followed them.

7

The three of them alighted on a balcony high in the Alabaster Palace just at dusk. Eldur helped Siahra off the creature's back and gave a slight bow, then swung back into the saddle and took to the air, taking the mysterious targe with him. Caeleen wiped a thick layer of sweat from his brow as Siahra stared out over the waves of the Diamond Ocean. Cae waited for a moment to see if she would say anything, but no words came.

"Siahra..." Caeleen finally broke the silence. "Siahra, look at me. Please."

Siahra turned slowly to look at Caeleen, and the boy blanched as he saw tears running down her face. In a heartbeat his composure shattered, and the two fell forward, crumbling into each other.

Siahra's knees buckled beneath her, and she screamed into the Ranger's shoulder, quivering and clutching his brown coat in trembling fists. Caeleen turned and hid his face in the mermaid's hair, his arms wrapped tightly around her as he clung to her and struggled to stay on his feet.

Caeleen had lost a horse before, but she had only been with him for three months when he was a boy. Tüli had been a faithful friend, and comrade for two years. But Siahra... Siahra had lost her first drake. The bond between a Dragoon and their drake was akin to the death of a Whisper's Wing—closer to the loss of a sibling than the death of a simple steed. Experiencing such a loss for the first time... Siahra had not cried so hard since the death of her father.

The two sunk to the white stone floor and wept for a time.

As quiet fell on the two, and stars appeared twinkling overhead, Siahra finally spoke up. "Caeleen, I want you to live here in the Palace."

Caeleen looked down at the floor and nodded. He needed to be out in the wild for his ranging but, for now... for now. "Where will I stay?"

"We'll figure it out. For tonight... can..." Siahra looked up, her brow worried and her eyes shimmering. "Cae, can you stay here for tonight?"

Cae looked up into her eyes, and he nodded. Slowly, the two of them got to their feet and shuffled inside.

Siahra's bedchamber was larger than Caeleen's cabin in Laithe had been. On one wall was painted a mural depicting many maotu arrayed in shining armor, their tails long and covered in steel scale mail—the Oceanguard, Cae presumed—battling a kraken. *Siahra always said she wanted to be an Oceanguard*, Cae thought. He wondered if she still rode her father's mighty seahorse when she patrolled through the underwater kingdom. He looked back to see her drop her cloak to the floor and step out of her boots. Her bed rested at the bottom of a pool in the center of the room, and she paused for a moment at the water's edge, looking back at Caeleen, her tired eyes rimmed red.

"Umm..." She gestured with an open hand to a large couch on the opposite side of the pool. "I know it's not perfect, but I don't really have anywhere else for—"

"It's alright." Cae offered a weary smile. "Believe me, I've slept on worse."

Siahra stared blankly back at the boy for a moment, then sighed. She shuffled over and put her arms around his waist, resting her head in the crook of his neck. "Thanks... for staying."

Caeleen's smile faded as quickly as it appeared, and he weakly wrapped his arms around her, cradling the back of her head in one hand. "I'm not goin' anywhere."

Siahra stepped back, and she all but fell into the pool, her legs shimmering and vanishing as her long blue tail took form. She swam to the bottom of the pool and curled into the circular bed there at the bottom.

The two looked at each other through the shimmering surface of the water for a moment before Caeleen turned away and dropped onto the couch.

Caeleen's mind drifted back to his horse once more, to the whip of the wind in his hair as he and Tüli tore across the Grey Plains together, and he dozed off.

* * *

THE MEMORIAL CEREMONY FOR A FALLEN DRAKE WAS sacred among the Dragoons. Búrum and Eldur retrieved and prepared Kéldi's remains that night, and the body of the draconid looked almost untouched the next day when they laid him in his nest. His clutch of eggs was moved to the nest of Búrum's drake, and the Diamond Queen buried Kéldi and his nest in streams of flaming breath, until only ashes remained. They then scattered these ashes into the wind over the ocean to be returned to Xanith, Goddess of the Sky and Dominion and Queen of all Dragons.

Caeleen buried Tüli just north of Fartide, in the shadow of the overlook where the drakes roosted. There was no sacred rite for the steed, just a hole in the ground and a pile of stones to mark the place where he lay. Cae buried him facing eastward, toward Laithe. Toward home. He thought Tüli would like that.

Caeleen sat by Tüli's grave alone for some time, looking out at the river flowing eastward into the mainland. The last horse he'd had to bury... old Farmer Mayberry sold them a fine mare when he was six. Her name was Sunbeam. Her coat was a rich chestnut, and her mane was the color of sunshine. She died barely a season after, when a pack of wargs broke into the village. They buried her behind the cottage. Cae frowned and cast his eyes back on the stones. At least they buried her at home.

Eventually, Caeleen wiped his tears away and made his way back to the Palace. There at the gates, he was met by a young maotu fellow in a short blue coat, with a satchel slung over his shoulder. A courier.

"Ta Rakau," he began, "you have our deepest sympathies regarding the events that occurred outside Creddon."

Cae nodded, but remained silent. He was too tired to offer much more than that.

The courier shuffled in his boots. "Considering your loss, Her Majesty wishes to see you in the royal stable. Please, follow me."

Cae sighed, his throat dry and his voice hoarse. "Stables? Why would..." Caeleen's voice trailed off as he realized exactly why. After all, the work had to go on.

The royal stables were a short walk south around the Palace, right at the edge of the Surface District. Half of the stables, again, were aquatic, and housed many of the large devilfish sometimes ridden by the maotu, along with the seahorse once belonging to King Arian, Toire. On the other half were a few horses, though not nearly as numerous as the devilfish. Siahra was waiting there beside Toire's pen with her tail lazily swishing about in the water, her hands running down the sea-stallion's neck, when Caeleen came in.

"Hey." The Queen looked over her shoulder and offered a half-smile.

Cae sat down beside her with his back to the pool and looked back at her. "You holding up alright?"

Siahra nodded. "I think... I think the ceremony helped. Gave me a chance to say goodbye, kind of. I dunno... Are you okay?"

Cae looked at his hands, wrung together and white. "... Not yet. I'm sorry."

Siahra placed a hand on his shoulder. "Cae, what happened out there wasn't your fault."

Cae looked down at her hand and placed his own over it. Her hand was warm, made so by the dragonfire inside her. He nodded, but...

"You need a horse."

Caeleen looked up and met Siahra's eyes. "Hmm?"

"I'm sending you to the Sacred Grove in the Ías."

Caeleen nodded. "Any particular reason? Or just to see if they know what's been up?"

"Just to check in, really. I would go, but I figure they'll probably take to you better. I mean, you... do people know about your relationship with Kh'anora?"

"I don't really talk about it, unless other people bring it up. But, then... the sword helps."

"I can imagine..."

Caeleen shrugged. "Hey, I've been meaning to ask you. When I was attacked by the ur-pesu, you did something I'd never seen done before. You just, like, reached out for Sal'tera, and it jumped into your hand. How did you do that?"

Siahra looked down at her hands. "I... I'm not sure. I didn't even think about it when I did it, it was just... instinctual. Y'know?"

Cae looked down for a moment before shaking his head. "Not...not really, no. But...I dunno, maybe I'll ask them about it when I get to the Grove."

Siahra stood up with a sigh, her tail swiftly shifting and transforming back into legs underneath a long blue skirt. "Uhh, here. I'm giving you our fastest horse. She'll get you there and back, and by then, hopefully, your Eagle will have arrived. Her name is *Katei*."

"What does it mean?"

"... Horse."

"You're not very good at naming things, are you?"

"Shut up."

The Queen had strode over to one of the pens, and was stroking the mane of a tall mare. Caeleen approached and held out a hand, letting the horse come closer and sniff at the open palm. Caeleen could tell that the horse was strong and swift.

But she wasn't Tüli.

"She'll do."

The two of them make their way out of the stable and toward the front gates with Katei in tow, saddled and prepared for travel. Caeleen took oat and apple from the foodstores in the stables, as well as a few large bags of salt for curing meat, and climbed into the saddle. "I'll be back before March. If I go off the roads, cut straight across the hills, I might can make it before Silvishi."

Siahra nodded and took the Ranger's hand once more. "Be careful, Cae. Keep your eyes open."

Cae squeezed the warm hand once, then took Katei's reins in hand and set off.

Normally, the ride to the Grove would be about twenty days, but that would have been riding along the road east to Gilgal and then north toward the Ías. Instead, Caeleen elected to ride straight for the Grove from Fartide, across the rolling hills of grass directly toward the pass into which folk made for the Maple Mountains. He stopped on his way out of the city to restock at

Lemshak's, picking up plenty of arrows to last on him his... was it a pilgrimage? Technically, he figured.

Five days went by without incident, Caeleen taking just enough from the game in the hills to get by on his own and taking care not to tire out the horse lent to him by his Queen. Over those few days, Siahra took up much of Caeleen's thought. He'd nodded in agreement with her when she assured him that Tüli and Kéldi hadn't been his fault, but that was for her. She didn't need to worry about him; she had enough going on being a Queen. But honestly, who else was there to blame? The Rose, yes, but Caeleen had made the decision to confront him. What happened to them was on his head.

Then, came the sixth day.

Caeleen had been tracking a group of three deer from a distance for the past two days. This had been no small feat on the back of a horse like Katei; large and powerful, but not built for quiet travel, Katei was obviously meant to bear an armored warrior rather than a huntsman. But Cae had keen eyes, and he stayed on the trail of his game without giving himself away.

On the sixth day, Cae had finally closed the distance and brought the deer within range of his bow. The three of them were on their way up a small incline, just on the side of a little hill. Two bucks, one doe. The doe had swollen a fair amount and was clearly about to give birth. Caeleen had his eyes on the larger of the two bucks. He thanked Kh'anora that he remembered to bring salt for curing with him; if he could take the buck, it would be enough to keep him fed until he reached the Grove.

He had done well preserving and retrieving his

arrows, and his quiver was stocked well enough. The Ranger stood up in his saddle, drew his bow and readied two arrows. He drew, stilling his breath as he focused in and aimed for the buck's head.

The deer turned his head, exposing an eye as it looked off toward the west.

Caeleen loosed his first arrow. It took the buck through the neck, and the beast dropped. Cae nocked his other arrow and fired right away, putting the shot right up through its heart. The deer fell still, and Cae lowered his bow. The other two deer started as Cae gripped Katei's reins.

Three more arrows flew in from the right. Two sunk into the doe, dropping her quickly. The last took the other buck through his back leg, bringing him scrambling and crying to the ground. Cae whipped his head eastward to see the source of the shot. Seven people, three armed with shortbows, stood spread out in the flat land between this hill and another. Among them were three beasts—two brown hyenas, and one black-furred war hound—all large for their breed. Gods above, where did they even get hyenas?

All ten of them looked thin, sickly, as if they'd not eaten in days. Cae frowned; these folk were likely among the vagabonds reported throughout the Kingdom. "Stay your weapons!" he called as he rode closer. "I'm a friend!" He leaned in close to Katei's ear and whispered a low command for the horse to stay close before he leapt off. Katei rounded the hill and disappeared from sight as the vagrants gathered in a half-circle around the Ranger.

One vagabond, a large, bald human with a thick grey-

speckled beard, leaned forward as he shuffled closer. "...
Knight."

Cae brought a hand instinctively to the pauldron over
his shoulder, then to the horn hanging from his chest. "I
am," he said. "Are you all alright? Do you need help
getting back to town?"

The bald man shook his head slowly. "Knight...
noble. You are rich."

Cae furrowed his brow as he shook his head, more
quickly than the bald man had. "Afraid not, friend. But I
can help."

"No...you are a noble." The bald man's eyes darted to
the bag on Caeleen's hip, then back to his face. "You have
food."

The bald man raised an open hand, and the circling
vagrants stopped.

Slowly, Cae's hand closed around Sal'tera's hilt.
"That buck I killed will be the first food I've had all day."
Cae kept his voice low and calm as he spoke. "My
pockets are just as empty as yours."

"Lies," the bald man growled. He pulled a shortsword quickly out from under his ragged cloak. "Your
bag. Give it to me."

Cae gritted his teeth and whipped his holy blade out
of its sheath, a clap of thunder obliterating the quiet and
rocking the air around him as he did so. "Stay back."

The group of vagrants fell back several steps with the
thunder, but quickly recovered their feet. The bald man
did not falter, but stood with his open hand raised for a
moment, unmoving. All at once, the hand clenched into a
fist.

The beasts launched forward.

In a breath, they were upon the Ranger. Cae swept broad to his right, sparks crackling off of Sal'tera as he swung, and the two on his right stumbled over each other to evade the mithril edge. With a sudden twirl, Cae turned about and ran the blade into the collar of one hyena, which had been just about to leap onto him. The beast collapsed to the ground at Caeleen's feet, a deep gash seeping red into the dead grass. Cae took the blade in both hands and stood poised to strike the other two. His eyes darted around. The other vagabonds had drawn their weapons.

Chnnk! Caeleen flicked his blade up just in time to parry an incoming arrow before it buried itself in his temple. He swept to the right again, this time leaving a nasty cut across the black dog's face. The hound scrambled back as the other hyena pounced. Cae caught it in the face with an elbow, knocking it to the ground. He ducked out of the way of another arrow coming from his left. He darted to the right, throwing his elbow into the nose of an old man with long grey hair holding a club. He struck the old man in the temple with Sal'tera's pommel, and he went down.

Klinnng! A third arrow glanced off his pauldron. The shot came from the bowman right in front of him.

Another vagrant slipped in from behind the old man. This one was a gangly long-limbed woman, and she held a small handaxe. She swung it wildly at Cae, who shifted just past each strike. With a flick of his sword, the axe flew from the woman's hand. Cae butted her in the nose with his forehead, and she dropped.

The hyena he'd elbowed jumped onto his back. Cae rolled it off him just as another arrow came in, *shhk!* putting the beast down.

Cae leapt forward and quickly slung a dagger at the bowman before him. The white blade slid across the man's thumb, and his shortbow fell to the ground. Cae dropped the boy with a boot across his jaw.

The bald man had closed in now, and he brought his two swords down hard. Cae took the hit with Sal'tera, but the block brought the Ranger to his knees. Another arrow whizzed by. Cae bent back under a swipe from the left, then brought himself back up to parry a swipe from the right.

The two remaining archers inched closer as one last vagabond, a large woman wielding a battered greatsword, began to charge. Cae clocked the bald man in the chin with Sal'tera's guard, then dropped the sword. Closing his fists, the Ranger put two jabs from the right into the bald man's nose, then dropped him with a solid left hook.

Ducking just under another arrow, Cae recovered his blade just in time to deflect another. The woman with the greatsword was upon him now. She whirled her blade once over her head, then swung into Caeleen's blade with incredible might. Cae let her bowl him over, and he rolled over his shoulder to the right as he fell. Shooting back up to his full height, Cae reeled back and cracked the flat of his blade across the back of her head. She fell down atop the bald man.

An arrow grazed across Cae's cheek. The bowman was at close range, he should have had a killing shot. Must have been the hunger. Caeleen didn't care. A quick dart forward, and a wide clock from Sal'tera's pommel, put the bowman down. That left only one archer, directly behind Cae. She was young, with short black hair. Cae spun around and charged without thinking.

Shk!

Cae let out a ragged cry as an arrow sunk into his leg. Luckily, the shaft went all the way through, but it hurt like hells. Cae glared up at the girl, who was already reaching for another arrow. Not happening, Cae decided. Taking Sal'tera in both hands by the center of the blade, he closed the distance in a heartbeat and cracked the hilt across the girl's temple, like a club. She dropped.

Cae let the holy blade fall from his hands as he dropped to his knees. Carefully, to avoid tearing the wound open further, he reached beneath his thigh and snapped the tip off the arrow. He could pull the shaft out safely, try to close the wound with a spell, but he needed to get to the Grove quickly. The spell would stop the bleeding for a time but, without proper healing, his right leg would be useless soon enough. He swore under his breath; he let himself get careless. He was blowing off steam. He should have been able to dodge that arrow. He should have—

The dog, the one he'd cut across the face, was on him then. Teeth sank into his shoulder.

Cae yelled out, more in frustration than pain. He reached over his shoulder and grabbed the hound, slinging it over his head and slamming it to the grass. His fingers tightened around the dog's neck.

The beast thrashed and writhed, struggling and

growling and snarling. Caeleen's grip tightened, his tired fingers becoming iron.

Cae shut his eyes, blood running freely from his shoulder, and he roared.

Snap.

The dog went limp under his fingers. Caeleen fell to the ground on his other shoulder, squeezed his eyes shut, and screamed.

When he opened his eyes, the world was a blur. He wasn't fading, or anything, but he needed to act quickly. His hands darted to the shaft still protruding from his leg, and he jerked it out. He cried out again as a gout of blood spurted forth. He closed his hands around the holes in his leg.

"Amon Äti, t'visti da hävi!"

The hole in his thigh closed, but it still throbbed with pain. He did the same for his shoulder. It healed better than the leg, but it was still sore. Cae was no Cleric. He needed proper healing magic. He needed to get to the Grove. He glanced around. Seven attackers, all unconscious. Two dead hyenas, from Gods-know-where. And there, at his feet, a dog. A dead dog.

Gods help him, he killed a dog.

Carefully, Caeleen got back up to his feet, shuffled toward the three dead deer on the hillside, and whistled. Katei trotted back around the hill. Cae stood still for a moment, just trying to breathe, to pull himself together.

After a moment, he just couldn't. He bent over and vomited. As he retched and tried to rid his mouth of the bile, the pain in his thigh brought him toppling to the ground, inches from a face full of his own sick. Caeleen scrambled away from the mess, got his feet back under him, and made his way to the buck he'd struck down. Dragging a sleeve across his mouth as salty frustration stung his eyes, the Ranger pulled out his hunting knife and went to work on his game, trying to put the attack out of his mind. He would leave the doe and the other buck for the vagrants when they awoke. He only needed the one.

After carving as much as he could off the buck and stowing it away in his bag, Cae dragged himself back onto Katei's back and urged the horse on north and eastward. He salted and dried the lot of it that night by the light of his fire and curled up in his cloak beside Katei. His thigh still throbbed with pain. With some effort, he cast his healing spell on it once more. It stopped throbbing, but the whole leg tingled with numbness. Until he reached the Grove, he was in no condition to be fighting.

By his estimate, he would reach the Grove in another five days. He prayed that he wouldn't need to fight until then.

Isiliel stood before the mural of Silvia just before the dawn, her bag packed and hanging from her shoulder. She thumbed through the pages of an older tome, looking for a specific passage. She didn't use this spell too often, but she'd done it enough now that she could summon up the strength to open the Gateway, herself. She certainly wasn't powerful enough to do so when the Temple was first established, but her connection to Silvia's light had grown significantly in the last two years... and she found, to her great surprise, that her training with Brother Offhander helped greatly. Training her body had aided in emboldening her spirit.

"*Silvia, mina Vaeli di mina Lieli... palëa si páka!*"

As the incantation hung in the air, a crackle of light danced from the painted hands of the mural. The holy light gathered together, and into the air before Isiliel erupted a shimmering, radiant portal. Isi fell to a knee and drew in a harsh breath. The spell was still hard on her. Wiping a bit of sweat from her brow, the Priestess stepped into the golden light.

When she emerged, Isi found herself right where she meant to go: the Temple of the Seven in Highhaven. She remembered how in awe of herself she was the first time she had made the portal; weeks of travel achieved in seconds! She knew it wasn't much compared to the feats of many other members of the clergy, or even compared to the Magi at the Institute here in the city, but it was still a big step for her.

Isi stepped out of Silvia's Shrine to find the High Priestess gliding through the foyer. The old woman had always mystified the Cleric; though Isi was older than the High Priestess by at least seven hundred years, the elderly human possessed a wealth of wisdom the likes of which Isiliel had seen in very few mortals.

"*Reilan ko*, High-Mother." Isi offered a small bow as she passed the High Priestess.

"Oh! Good evening, Miss Rumoré," the lady replied. "I'm afraid I wasn't expecting you at this hour. It is wonderful to see you in good health."

"Thank you," Isi said. "Have you had many visitors since I last came through?"

"I'm afraid not," the old woman said with a sigh. "With everything happening these days, it seems people don't have as much time for the Gods."

Isi's brow creased with worry. "Perhaps things will get better soon. We'll just have to wait and see, hmm?"

The High Priestess chuckled. "Oh, I'm not too worried about it, child. The Gods will keep their vigil whether or not we give them their due."

Isi offered a sad smile. "I suppose you're right."

"Will you be needing your chambers here during your stay?"

"No, I don't think so this time. Think I'll just take a room at Cecil's."

"Very well. Give my regards to your friend at the school, won't you?"

"I will. Good morning, High Mother!" Isi bowed once more and walked out the door.

Across the street, she quietly crept into Cecil's inn and made her way to the bar. A human was standing there at the counter, a fellow by the name of Stephen. As the Cleric sat down at the bar, Stephen gave her a tired smile. "Good to see ya again, Miss Rumoré," he mumbled. "Checkin' in?"

"Yes, sir," she replied, a bit of pity clear on her face. The bags under the barkeep's eyes told her how long his night must have been.

"Sounds good, we got your usual room ready. Ya need anything up there? Might be a little early for breakfast, but it couldn't hurt."

"No, I think I'll be alright. Figured I'd try to grab a few hours of sleep before I go see Iómi."

"Any idea how long you'll be in town?" Stephen asked as he slid Isi her room key.

"Just depends, honestly. Need to do some research, but I might be heading off to Tamia in the coming days."

"Ohhhh..." the barkeep's weary eyes narrowed. "This about all those rumors?"

"Afraid so," Isi replied. "But it should be fine. I'll see you around, Stephen. And do get some rest. You look exhausted."

"Hey, we all gotta pay our dues somehow!" Stephen grinned as Isi dropped a gold piece on the counter and stood to make her way up to her room. There the weary Cleric practically collapsed onto her bed. As she drifted off to sleep, a smile played on her lips. She was here on business, of course, but it was always good to see Iómi.

After a few hours of solid sleep, Isi made her way to the eastern edge of the city and approached the gates of the Arcane Institute. There, at his little desk atop the wall, sat Kreek the goblin, his fingertips rubbing at his crystal ball.

The critter looked up as Isi approached, and he grinned with his sharp little teeth.

"Mornin', Priestess!" Kreek called down. "Here to see Lady Amilë?"

"I am!" Isi shouted. "Is she awake yet?"

Kreek peered into his crystal ball and chuckled. "Fell asleep at her table in the Archives. Hall V!"

"Thank you, Kreek!" Isi headed through the gates,

letting the peering arcane powers of High Magus Pah'-drim settle over her for a moment.

Soon enough, his spell retreated; Pah'drim liked to know who was on present on Institute grounds, but he was no stalker. Respect for privacy was a bit of an uncommon trait for an Oracle, but Isi was thankful for Pah'drim's discretion. She didn't like the idea of peering eyes watching her, especially during her visits here.

The Arcane Institute was home to the greatest collection of written word in all the Three Kingdoms, the Grand Archive. The building itself was tall enough, a tower reaching almost as high as the tallest spire of Castle Cestus. Each floor represented a hall corresponding to a letter, and each floor had six doors. Those doors led into, from what Isi could best gather, a sort of pocket plane containing that floor's hall. Isi couldn't begin to imagine how difficult (and expensive, no doubt) those planes must have been to manifest!

As Isiliel approached the enormous archway leading into the tower, a bluish haze began to seep forth from the entrance. Out of the mist emerged the spectral form of a dog, slender and graceful, with long fur that seemed to trail behind her. The phantom hound looked back at Isiliel with a familiarity in her pale eyes.

"Kaesel." Isi bowed her head in respect to the guardian spirit.

Kaesel inclined her head in response. The ghostly form spoke no words. Isi wasn't sure she *could* speak, but she certainly understood, and the aura of intelligence the hound put forth encouraged respect.

"Hall V, if it please you," Isi said.

Kaesel nodded and turned slowly back into the tower.

Isi followed, and she stepped into the arcane circle in the center of the room. The whole tower was illuminated by spheres of flame floating against the walls between each door, casting dancing flits of orange light across the floor. Though the magic circle was a bright violet, it did not cast any light into the chamber.

Kaesel let out a howl that echoed upward into the tower, and Isiliel began to rise rapidly through the tower.

After but a few seconds, the Priestess came up through the floor of a chamber near the top of the tower, nearly identical to all the rooms below. A bold V was engraved over each doorway.

Isiliel stepped through the door and found herself in an endless library, rows upon rows of bookshelves loaded down with pristine tomes of every size and shade. Sunlight poured in from the glass ceiling in this far-flung plane, illuminating the hall in a warm golden light. Just outside the doorway Isiliel had stepped through sat a collection of tables, and here and there sat individuals pouring over notes and books and inscriptions.

It was at one of these tables Isi's eyes came to rest upon a slumped over form in black and purple robes, their hood pulled up concealing their face. The robe's colors were important for a magus's identification; purple told those around that this Wizard had been studying at the Institute for long enough to earn their Initiate's papers, and the black indicated the Wizard's focus in the Art of Necromancy.

There were a few other Initiate Necromancers at the

Institute, but Isi spotted a string of worn-and-weathered trinkets and charms around the figure's pale wrist. Isi smiled as she crept up from behind, kneeling down beside the Wizard and placing a hand softly on their back.

"Iómi," she cooed. "Wake up, darling. It's morning."

The slumped-over figured stirred for a moment, then curled further into the bundles of its robe. A muffled groan came from somewhere underneath their hood.

Isi shook her head and leaned in closer. "*Pïli a raki, Paiasidé...*" the Cleric sang softly. "*Addane mina në ká'su?*"

As the sweet tones left Isiliel's lips, the figure beneath the robe uncurled, and soon enough the folds of their hood fell back. The pale blue eyes of Iómi Amilë looked back blearily at Isi through strands of tangled black hair. The Wizard smiled. "Hey, you."

Isi leaned in closer and pressed her lips against Iómi's cheek. "Hello," she replied.

Iómi sat up and stretched her arms out wide, letting out another groan as she did so, then pulled her hood back off of her head. The pointed tips of her short ears just barely poked out from underneath the muss of raven locks running down her back. It was getting long now, all the way to her lower back. The sleepy Wizard looked again at her Cleric with a smile. "Mm... whatcha doin' here?" she asked. "I, uhh... I mean, I know we had plans for Silvishi, but aren't you a little early?"

Isi shook her head. "No, it's not that," she replied. "I need your help with a few things."

Iómi nodded then leaned forward and nestled her

head into the crook of Isi's neck. "M'kay. But gimme five more minutes."

Isiliel's cheeks turned red, and she brought her arm around Iómi and pulled her in close. "Alright," she said, "but after that, we're getting breakfast. Sound good?"

Iómi nodded, wrapping her arms around Isi's waist and burying her face in the Priestess's hair. Isi hummed contently as she looked over the notes over which the Initiate had fallen asleep. It seemed Iómi had taken an interest in her matron deity; her little space at the table was littered with notes on the worship and lore of Volok. Burial rites for Necromancers, traditional offerings of incense and herbs said to be pleasing to the Grave-Mother, stories of the creation of the Four Hells, the birth of the orcs and... *Voloki and the Like: a Flamewalker's Guide to the Hells*, by Lord Gavrinn Stormfall.

Isi's brow furrowed. "Iómi, why are you studying Demonology?"

Iómi let out a snore in response. The poor girl was out cold.

Isi rolled her eyes and kept reading. Much of what Iómi had found on demons, Isi already knew; salt, blessed water, holy magic. As expected, however, the shelves of the Grand Archive yielded a wealth of information Isi had never heard before.

"The flames of a gold or mithril draconid are believed to greatly weaken a demon or a devil, perhaps even force them back to their home plane. Some studies suggest that, should the pits in the darkness where demons are born be snuffed out, their numbers would dwindle to an eventual extinction. But to do so would be

an affront to Volok, who created the demons to guard her domain.

"Devils, however, are another story; though they inhabit the Hells alongside their demonic counterparts, Priests and Clerics of Volok deny the Grave Mother's involvement in creating the devils. Their origins are unknown, but they maintain many similarities with the demons, primarily their weakness to Silvian magic.

"Many devils embody a symbol in their very forms, often from the material in the Hells from which they were birthed; chains, fire, stone, gold, thunder. Unlike the demons, who boast incredible power and capacity for destruction, devils often possess a great level of cunning, as well as the ability to make their servants more powerful. Men, beasts, even dragons have been known to bind themselves to the service of a devil to achieve vile and calamitous powers."

Isi tore through the pages of the hefty tome, admittedly astounded by the information before her. For eight hundred years had Isi walked the world; for six hundred years had she served the All Mother. How did she miss so much information? She'd fought beings from the Four Hells plenty of times before, but there was so much information here about them she'd never heard!

Isi looked down at Iómi, still asleep in her arm. The young Wizard had been apprehensive about joining the Institute at first, but Isi was so glad to see her leaning into her studies. She would make a wonderful Wizard... for as long as she could last. The corners of Isi's mouth twitched down just a bit. She didn't like thinking about it, but... well, half-elves weren't as long-lived as elves.

Iómi might live to see four hundred someday, but that was about as far as her body could carry her. Certainly, she could extend her life through magic, but then what? There was no such thing as perfect immortality. What, would Iómi shed her flesh and wander the realms as a spirit to be hunted? Create a phylactery and let the world fear and hate her as a lich? No. Iómi would follow her Goddess into the grave, and there was nothing either of them could do to prevent it. Isi knew Iómi hadn't given it any thought, but the idea of her, Caeleen, or Baron dying had been eating at the back of Isiliel's mind since the day they lost King Arian.

Iómi stirred against Isiliel's neck and sluggishly brought her hands up against the Cleric's chest and pushed herself upright. She sighed, her tired breath warm on Isi's face. She pushed the tangled ebon hair out of her face as her eyes crept back open. "M'kay, I'm up. I'm... uhhh... hi."

Isi smiled again, putting her worries aside. "Hi."

Iómi rubbed the tiredness away from her eyes. "Shmuh... mm... so what, what did... what did you need help with?"

Isi closed the book and turned in her seat. "Actually, I found a lot of what I was looking for here," she said. "This book you had here about the Voloki is helpful for what I..."

Iómi tilted her head as Isi's voice trailed off. "Helpful for... what?"

Isi looked back at the Wizard, her eyes suddenly stern. "Iómi, why are you studying the Voloki? Were you..."

"Was I what?"

"... Iómi, are you planning on making for Tamia?"

Iómi frowned as she looked down at the heavy book on the table, and she shrugged. "I mean, I was thinkin' about it. The signs are pointing toward Voloki magic of *some* kind out there. I figured I might be able to help."

Isi sat quiet for a moment. "W... well, were you planning on going alone?"

"Yeah, honestly." Iómi waved a hand and conjured her oak-and-onyx staff. "I mean, most of the other Necromancers here are worried about it, but they're focused on their studies right now. It's... I dunno. Why? What are you thinkin'?"

"Caeleen came to the Temple a while back," Isi replied. "He's there now with Queen Siahra, they're trying to find the root of it all."

"Oh, boy..." Iómi rubbed her eyes. "Look, I know Cae is, like, a great tracker and hunter and whatever, but I just... I'm sorry, but he's not that great at fighting. He's just not. He needs somebody to look after him."

Isi nodded. "Maybe Her Majesty will let us join him when we get to Fartide."

"They might not be in Fartide by now, though. Think about it, why would you keep the best hunter in the land cooped up behind city walls? Knowing Cae, he probably wants to go out and build a hut somewhere."

"Actually, I think he prefers cabins."

"Isi, that is not *remotely* the point!"

Isi laughed as Iómi threw her hands in the air. The Priestess stood then, and she took Iómi's hand. "Come on.

Let's get some food, then maybe we can talk about getting out of here."

"Wait, wait..." Iómi frowned. "We can't leave without..."

Isi's brow crinkled. She was hoping Iómi wouldn't say that. "Do we really need to?"

Iómi nodded. "I just need to check in on it, I'm not bringing it along. I'm not."

Isi's mouth pressed into a flat line, but she nodded. "After breakfast, then."

After leaving the library, and stopping off at the kitchens for a quick bite (which was an adventure all in itself, as the kitchens were deliciously magical and run by a wildly clever gnome chef), the pair made their way to the great vaults, wherein the Institute studied and safeguarded all their most dangerous artifacts.

The vault itself was a large triangular structure hewn from an ancient mass of black stoneglass (some folk throughout the realms called this stone "obsidian," but those people were usually stuffy, shut-in, and had never seen stoneglass themselves), still laden with veins of pure mithril.

With permission to enter from the old dwarven vault-keeper, Iómi and Isi made their way down winding stairs of blue light, as Iómi grumbled quietly about how these magical stairs should just carry them like the library. Isi just squeezed the Wizard's hand and ushered her along into the dimly lit vault.

Eventually, the two reached the twenty-third floor, Iómi now leaning heavily on Isi's shoulder, and shuffled into the chamber therein. Inside was a chamber void of any solid object save one: a short sword with a blade forged of pure vothril and lived with platinum. Graadrog, the Flame of the Lord of the Dead. The sword had been buried in the cemetery at Brookridge, where it was given to Iómi by... someone. The blade was suspended tightly in the air by chains of that same blue light, chains that faded to nowhere before they reached an anchor.

Standing there examining the weapon was an older elvish man, his skin a pale gold, with hair of silver-white worn now in an elaborate braid. The robe he wore had no sleeves, leaving the extensive burns on his right arm exposed. Iómi asked once where those burns came from, but Pah'drim just shook his head and said that no one alive now remembers.

The High Magus turned and nodded to the two as they approached. "I had a feeling you would make your way here," he said. "Your friend is in over his head."

"Heard about that, did you?" Iómi replied. She bowed before the older mage, and he bowed in like fashion.

Pah'drim turned and inclined his head to Isi before turning back to the blade. "I'm afraid we've not learned much in the last two years," he sighed. "The riddle of Graadrog is as baffling to me as it has ever been."

"We understand its function well enough," Iómi added, "but that's about it."

Isi's brow crinkled as she stepped forward. "What can you tell me of its origin?"

"Little more than I could glean upon first examining it," Pah'drim replied. "Crafted by a dragon, as I said then.

But I do not believe the dragon was this 'Lord of the Dead.'"

"There aren't any records of any Necromancer with that title in our library," Iómi said. "Whoever he was, he must have been stricken from history in the Great Fire."

"So what was the sword doing in your cemetery?" Isi asked.

Iómi crossed her arms. "I... don't think it was."

Isi lifted an eyebrow. "... You brought it with you from your cave beneath the cemetery."

"I know, but... I don't think it was always there."

Pah'drim frowned. "What do you mean?"

Iómi shook her head. "Look, I knew that graveyard. I would have noticed it before. It wasn't there until the night it presented itself to me."

"Presented itself?"

"Someone took one of my skeletons... well, not *my* skeletons, but one of the ones I lived with in the... you know what I mean. But, whoever they were... they were a long, *long* way out."

Pah'drim stroked his chin. "It is entirely possible that this 'Lord of the Dead' is an elf, or an elatu, something with a great lifespan..."

Or a lich, Isi thought. She stared at the sword for a moment longer. Somewhere in the back of her head, the priestess nursed an uncomfortable suspicion. Whatever presented Iómi with Graadrog, it was probably watching them. Perhaps, even now, in this chamber, it could perceive. Could it see through the Institute's defenses? Maybe. But with all the word coming from Tamia right now, all the reports of death-magic... who better to gain from it than a "Lord of the Dead"?

"We have to bring it with us," said the Cleric.

Iómi whipped her head around, eyes wide. "What??"

Pah'drim crinkled his brow further. "Are you sure, Priestess?"

Isi nodded. "Whatever is there, it might give us a lead. Besides... I don't think it's safe for us to keep it here. Not in the vault."

The High Magus' eyes widened. "... You think it's watching us?"

"Maybe..." Isi inclined her head toward Iómi. "Take the weapon. You know how to use it better than me."

Iómi nodded and approached. She wrapped her fingers around the hilt of the short sword as the chains dissipated.

A heart...

Iómi froze. Did they hear that, too? She turned to Isi. No reaction. Perhaps not. Perhaps it was just her.

Yes. I can feel it in her chest... A Silvian heart.

Wh... what about it? Iómi thought.

Silence.

Iómi looked back up at Isi. "Are you sure this is a good idea?"

Isi offered a wary smile. "Don't worry. It won't hurt you. Not while I'm around."

Iómi nodded and smiled back, and she did her best to put her unease aside. It would be fine.

The two bid farewell to Pah'drim and made their way up the stairs.

* * *

Siahra stared at the spear in her hands, her tail absent-mindedly twisted around its base. She had rarely used the spear itself, always relying on her trident, but she had always kept the weapon here by her bed as a reminder of the bond she shared with Kéldi. The Dragoon's spear, when crafted for a drake-rider, was crafted in the drake's image, forged with magic drawn from the rider's spirit, and tempered with the drake's own breath. Through the spear, the rider and their drake were made one.

The death of a rider's drake was not necessarily uncommon, but it wasn't something that usually happened so soon in a Dragoon's service. Both Eldur and Burúm had lost drakes before, but the both of them had been Dragoons longer than Siahra had been alive. Most Dragoons had their first drake for at least five years. Siahra hadn't even been with Kéldi for two yet. To lose a friend so close so soon...

"Siahra."

The Mermaid Queen looked up to see Har Burúm standing at the edge of her pool. She sighed and made her way up to the surface, her tail shimmering and vanishing as her legs took form on the floor before her teacher. "Sorry, how long... how long were you standing there?"

"Not long," the older Dragoon replied. "I just... I know the hurt is fresh in your mind. But, with everything happening in the Kingdom right now..."

Siahra turned her face away, her eyes dim. "I... I don't know, Burúm."

Her Burúm lighted a hand on the Queen's arm. "K'kanu, I know you're hurting right now. But... you need to think about it. You're a symbol of hope for your people. If you step out of the skies now..."

"Burúm, I'm just not ready right now. I don't..." Truth be told, Siahra didn't know when, or even if, she would ever be ready. For how little time they had together, Siahra had imprinted on Kéldi. Perhaps it had been to help her cope with the loss of her father... she had spent countless nights burying her tears in Kéldi's scales thinking about Arian. She couldn't be seen weeping over him, she had to be strong. She had to be the Queen. She...

"I understand." Burúm stepped back. "Should the time come that you decide to take up the spear again, we have drakes ready for you."

Siahra nodded as Burúm walked out of the room. She stood there for a moment, then she fell back into her pool and sank down to the bottom. Her tail curled around the bottom of her spear again, and she clutched the mighty weapon tightly, letting her eyes sting with salt as she squeezed them shut.

Perhaps she would take a new drake in time. Or perhaps she would never fly again. For now, she just wanted to sleep.

8

*C*aeleen drew closer and closer to the Ías Fuil; the clouds overhead began to gather, and snow began to fall once more. This time, though, the snow did not quite surprise Cae; everyone knew the Maple Mountains were cold year-round. Katei whined a bit at the sudden chill, but Caeleen urged her on. She complied, but Caeleen felt a pit in his stomach. In a Kingdom of merfolk, a horse probably didn't see much use, even a prize beast like Katei. She probably wasn't accustomed to riding so far and in such cold weather.

The closer the Ranger rode to the mountains, the thicker the trees became. Huge, towering maples, many of them more than twice the size of any others of their kind he'd seen, stood bare and powerful against the grey skies, their bases surrounded with the crumbled remnants of their foliage half-buried under the white dusting.

Caeleen was pleased with how well Katei handled the terrain as the ground gradually became rough with the trees' thick roots. At a certain point though, the density of the trees became too much for her, and the mare could go no farther. Cae had cast his spell on his wound a few more times over the past few days, but the leg was still numb.

By his estimate, Cae knew he was a half a day's ride from where the Grove supposedly was. He gently urged Katei to continue, to please just keep it up a little longer, but the poor thing just couldn't handle the woods without a path.

Caeleen sighed and dismounted, bringing Katei to a nearby tree and tying her to it. He looked farther into the approaching forest with grit teeth; even just walking on his own pricked at the nerves in his leg. The arrow that struck him had done some kind of damage that he didn't know how to treat. He needed to stay off his leg, but he also needed to get to that Grove.

Cae slowly brought himself to the ground and sat against the tree beside Katei. His hand played at the feather pendant around his neck, and he sighed. He could try to ride around, find the road into the mountains and see if there was an actual path to the Grove from there, but he doubted there would be. And even if there was a path, would he have enough food for him and Katei to make that ride there and back? Cae doubted it. He only had enough venison left for... Gods, he didn't know.

A screech struck Caeleen's ears from above. Wincing, The Ranger lifted his eyes to see a sizable white-feathered bird, not much smaller than an eagle, perched in the maple against which he sat, lean body and sharp beak with a decently long pointed tail, with a thick halo of downlike white feathers around its shoulders and neck. A snurvin falcon.

Cae screeched in response, asking for help. He figured that, if the snurvin nested in the area, it might could relay word to the Druids. He wasn't particularly good at speaking to falcons, but he was good enough.

The falcon cocked its head. No response.

"Oh, Fates alive..." Cae moaned. He reached into his bag and pulled out a slab of his venison and used his hunting knife to cut off a strip. The snurvin fluttered down and landed on his knee, and he held the strip up to its beak.

The snurvin pecked at it for a moment, then shook its head. "Not very good, is it?" it asked, in flawless Eridian.

Caeleen reeled back, his eyes widening. "Umm... sorry, I... didn't have time to... y'know. Cook it. Or anything."

The bird shrugged. "Well, thanks, anyway. It's a nice gesture, but you better keep it. No offense, but you look rough."

Caeleen furrowed his brow. "L... look, I'm sorry, I just... I've never met a bird that spoke Eridian before."

"Well, you still haven't! Ha!" The snurvin flapped back into the air and erupted into green light. Caeleen shielded his eyes and turned away. When the light died down and he looked back, standing before him was an old man with a short grey beard and dull blue eyes. He was garbed in tattered green robes covered in moss, and the cloak and hood that covered his head and back were woven out of large leaves of a dark green. In his hand was a large wooden staff whose head seemed to branch and form a canopy of tiny green leaves. The old man reached into the canopy and pulled out what appeared to be the tiniest apple Caeleen had ever seen and popped it into his mouth.

Caeleen's eyes widened. "You're from the Grove! You're one of the Druids from the—hi! I'm so glad you found me!" Caeleen stuck out his hand for a shake.

The old man chuckled and grabbed the hand, shaking it solidly. "Sagan Witherwillow, pleased to meet ya!" The Druid pulled Caeleen up to his feet.

"Sir Caeleen Longw-*uff!*" Caeleen winced and groaned as his numb leg lit up with pain as he tried to stand. "Ah, *skrí!* Sorry, I got sh-*ugh*... I got shot about five days back, my leg's been acting up since..."

Sagan cocked a brow as he looked down at the hole in Caeleen's trousers. Leaning forward, the old Druid stuck the base of his staff into the hole and ripped it open.

"H-hey!" Cae stammered. "What are you doing? I only have a couple sets of pants on me..."

"That's your own fault. Buy more clothes." Sagan knelt down and inspected the wound in the Ranger's thigh, humming thoughtfully as he poked at it. "You treated this yourself?"

"Yeah, I did," Cae replied. "A Cleric taught me a healing spell when I was a kid."

"A Cleric of Silvia?"

"Yeah, why?"

"Don't use that spell anymore." Sagan let go of his staff and rubbed his hands together over Cae's wound. A bit of dirt fell from his palms and onto Cae's thigh. "If you're gonna do healing magic, pray to your own patron. I'm assuming you pray mostly to Kh'anora?"

Cae nodded. "How could you tell?"

"You tried to talk to a bird. Kind of a dead giveaway." Sagan closed his eyes, and a green light emanated from his open palms. *"Nasa-Taed, oshtell hur kriip."* The green light showered down over Caeleen's leg, seeming to soak into his flesh. Almost right away, the leg regained feeling. Good as new.

Caeleen looked down at his leg in awe, then looked back to the old man. "Th...thank you."

Sagan winked at the boy. "On your feet, kid. You're almost there." Standing up, Sagan took hold of his strange tree-staff and turned to Katei. "Poor girl can't handle the woods, huh?"

Cae nodded. "She's from Fartide. Guess merfolk don't train their horses for much besides quick trips."

"Well, we can't just leave her here." Sagan clicked his staff to the ground and held out his hand. *"Bel mis!"* In another green flash, Katei vanished, and in her place was a little brown mouse.

"Whooooa!" Caeleen dropped to his knees and scooped up the little critter, tucking her into his coat pocket. "That was amazing! How did you *do* that?"

"The Tree Father offers many gifts to those who..." The Druid's voice trailed off as he looked down at Sal'tera, his eyes fixing on the holy sword on Caeleen's belt for a moment. He looked back up and met Caeleen's eyes again, his expression suddenly stern. "Come on, we have a lot to talk about." With that, another flash of green burst forth as Sagan took his snurvin form once more.

Caeleen looked down for a moment before turning back to the skies.

"Hey, hold on! At least let me change my pants!"

It surprised Caeleen to note how quickly he and the Druid made their way through the forest (once he changed out of his torn trousers). Following the snurvin as best he could as it hopped from tree to tree, he found that his leg truly was right as rain, much to his relief. He darted between the trees fast as he ever did before, faster even. He suspected that old Sagan had worked some kind of magic into his body because the two were making remarkable time. He was sure this unnatural speed would leave him when he turned to go back to Fartide, but by then he would at least have Katei again. But he had no time to think about the return trip. He had so much he wanted to ask, so many things he hoped to learn from the Druids of the Grove.

Caeleen noted something peculiar as they traveled deeper and deeper into the woods: the trees surrounding them, where they really should have been bare and grey-ish-brown in the biting chill of February, now seemed to keep not just their foliage, but their vivid green color. Even the ground beneath them was coated with thick moss, and bits of grass stood defiantly here and there in the dirt. This forest was more than just living. It was thriving, steadfast against the cold. The Ranger knew it to be nature-magic, a testament to the power of Kh'anora, but he could not contain his wonder at the sight.

As the sun set behind the trees and sent beams of gold light down through the branches, the two of them reached a clearing amidst the mighty maples. In the canopy of the great trees was a smattering of large, flat stones overlooking a round ridge. Inside that ridge was a little pond, though not one that had always been there. In the center of the pond was one more flat stone, out of which seemed to flow a constant stream of crystal-clear water. Atop this stone was an enormous emerald, the largest Caeleen had ever seen. From the surface of the water, there seemed to rise a fine mist tinted ever so slightly green in the emerald's light and, around the whole pond, was a circle of arcane writing that slowly turned in the air. Just past this pond sat another mundane stone, atop which there rested a bowl glowing the same brilliant green, filled with some kind of piping hot soup.

Sagan descended before the pond and transformed back into his human state. "Here we are, kid!" The old Druid turned back to Caeleen. "Welcome to the Emerald Grove! Our own little slice of the Great Green Mountain."

Caeleen marveled at the wondrous Grove, his mouth agape. In his very bones, the Ranger could feel some kind of wondrous magic in this clearing. He felt it seeping into the surrounding trees, feeding them.

Sagan smiled at Caeleen as he gawked. "Like it, do ya?"

The Ranger nodded as a question formed in his head. "How is it all still so green?"

"How, indeed." Caeleen turned to his left. Out of one of the trees came a familiar, shimmering light. He'd seen this spell before, when his sister came to visit. Out of the light had stepped a broad-shouldered half-orc, with wilted hair of silver-white and skin of a faded brown mottled with green. His right arm appeared to be made of stone, and it glowed with green runes all along where his veins would have been. He leaned into a tall staff fashioned entirely of jade, and in his left hand was a large scimitar, the back of its curved blade covered with orcish markings. The robe draped over his body was made entirely of brown moss. "It's simple magic, really. I sense you have that power in your blood somewhere as well, friend."

Sagan dropped to his knees and bowed low before the half-orc. "Shiz'ame."

Caeleen looked down at the old man with one brow raised, then back up to the half-orc. "Shiz'ame?"

The other Druid nodded. "It means 'Earth Lord.' I am Shiz'ame Bakh, Archdruid of the Emerald Grove and Archpriest of our mighty Wood-Father."

"Ah. Sounds fanc-uh... wuh... *whoa.*" Caeleen dropped to a knee as the sensation washed over him. This Druid radiated fathoms on fathoms of power from his form. "Y-uh, y-you humble me with your presence, sir! Or, or I guess, maybe, 'my lord?' Or uhh..."

"Just 'Bakh' will do." The old half-orc smiled. With a wave of his hand, Bakh beckoned Sagan to stand, and the Druid obeyed. "I've been having dreams of Sal'tera's arrival for many moons. Thank you for bringing the Bolt of Peace into our home."

Caeleen looked down at the holy blade on his hip, then back up to the Archdruid. "... I'm not... I'm not leaving it here. I kinda need it, there's a *lot* going on in Tamia right now."

"Oh, no! I could never ask such a thing." Bakh chuckled. "No, but it is fated that Kh'anora's Blade bathe in the light of the Grove."

"There was a prophecy about it," Sagan continued, "but none of us can remember the words. Shame, too, it was a nice little rhyme."

Caeleen gave Sagan a quizzical look before turning back to Bakh. "So what exactly is supposed to happen?"

"I am not sure," Bakh replied. "We believe the blade will drink in some of the power instilled here in the Grove, and its enchantment will increase in potency."

"Whatever happens, it should help," Sagan added.

Cae nodded, stroking his chin. "Well, while that's going on, I'll have time to fill you guys in on what's been happening."

"No need," Sagan replied. "We have eyes all over Solvaar. We've been watching the situation in Tamia pretty closely since things started getting weird."

Cae stopped for a moment. His brow furrowed as a frown settled onto his face. "W... well, can you guys *help?* I mean... no offense but, like, when was the last time anybody heard from you?"

"What do you mean?" Sagan's brow crinkled as he looked to the Archdruid. "The Shiz'ame maintains a steady communication with High Magus Pah'drim in Highhaven."

Cae turned to Bakh with widening eyes. The Archdruid nodded. "It... has been sometime since he and I last spoke, I will admit."

Caeleen balled his fists without thinking. "So, so what? You just, you just aren't gonna *do* anything? We're just on our own?"

"The Emerald Grove are not battlemages," Bakh answered. "We are watchers, not warriors."

Caeleen stuttered with exasperation. "B-wh-a-whuh —g-guys! *Guys!* I got mauled by a hellhound, and my horse got carved oven by a murderer! You can't just *not* help when people need you!"

"Calm down, kid." Sagan clapped a heavy hand onto Caeleen's shoulder. "You're not helping anyone by freaking out."

"Well, then, help me understand!" Caeleen pushed the old man's hand away. "Please! I'm not, I'm not *getting* it! Kh'anora is out here helping us, why aren't you? What's keeping you in here?"

"The Druids of the Emerald Grove serve the realm of Kh'anora," Bakh explained. "We do not serve the Empire, nor do we serve the Clans."

"People are dying!"

"Death is a natural part of life, child." The Archdruid held up a hand. "Please, try to understand. This is the way things have always been done."

Caeleen took several deep breaths then unclenched his fists. He reached down, unsheathed Sal'tera, and pushed it into Bakh's hands. "Look, just...just do what you need to do so I can get back to Queen Siahra. They need my help, and I have to get back out there." Without another word, the Ranger turned and approached one of the enormous maples, darting his way up into its branches.

Sagan shook his head and frowned. The kid was young, he would come to understand in time... If he was to be a servant of Kh'anora, he'd have to.

Bakh gripped Sal'tera tightly in his flesh hand, and he stood for a moment in reverence of the blade. Standing up straight and letting go of his jade staff, the Archdruid looked up at the emerald. He shuffled over to the edge of the pond, and extended the blade toward the stone. Just as the tip of the sword touched the gem, a low rumble of thunder rolled across the sky far overhead.

Slowly, the blade drifted out of Bakh's hand and twisted through the air until it hovered over the emerald, its tip pointing downward toward it. It spun slowly there, the green light coming from the emerald slowly drifting up into the white metal. The sword began to spin faster, and faster, and faster still. Thunder shook the air once more, this time louder and closer, the sword itself shining that brilliant green light now.

The Druids fell back as a bolt of lightning crashed down into the weapon from above, the air around them exploding as thunder rocked the Emerald Grove. Caeleen nearly tumbled out of his tree, but he caught himself on a lower branch. The sword arced through the air, exuding its blinding white light once more, brighter now than Caeleen had ever seen it. The emerald regained its brilliant green shine, and the sword swirled through the air, then shot down and buried itself in the ground at Bakh's feet in the blink of an eye. Bakh inched forward, his stony fingers creeping around the hilt of the weapon. Sparks arced into his hand, and he just barely winced as he drew the blade from the ground and held it aloft. Caeleen dropped back to the ground silently and stared up at the shining weapon.

"Tree Father bless us," Bakh whispered. "The Blade lives."

Sagan stared in awe, the aura of the holy sword washing over him. "Shiz'ame, I... I don't know what to say. It's beautiful."

Caeleen hid his amazement under a grimace. Before he could think, the Ranger stretched his hand out toward his sword. In a flash of lightning, the blade leapt into his grip. The two Druids turned to look at the Ranger.

"I'm sorry we can't stay," Caeleen said flatly, "but I have to get going." He turned and was off the way he had come.

Sagan stumbled forward. "Hey, kid, hold on—"

"I *have* to go."

Caeleen tore back through the woods, vaulting and darting through the trees with his jaw clenched. This voyage was a complete waste of time; not only did the Druids of the Grove already know that Tamia was in crisis, they refused to do anything about it. All that power, power greater than any other Druid in all the world, and they won't even use it to help people? What was even the point then?

Caeleen was back at the edge of the forest by nightfall, the glowing sword in his hand lighting his way. He had gone just as swiftly as he'd arrived, this time without the use of Sagan's magic. The Ranger stared out at the open hills before him and groaned as he felt Katei stirring in his coat pocket. He wished he'd kept his composure long enough for the mouse to be turned back into a horse, but something in him just boiled over. He pulled the little critter out of his pocket and stared at it for a moment.

"Don't suppose you know how to transform on your own, do ya?" the Ranger asked.

Katei tilted her head at him, curiously.

He sighed.

"Having trouble?"

Caeleen turned to see Kh'anora standing beside him, His shimmering green hood pulled over His head.

Cae shrugged. "One of the Druids in there turned my horse into a mouse. Don't suppose You'd be willing to help turn her back, huh?"

The old God laughed under His breath and took the mouse in hand. "I can," He said, placing Katei on the ground and snapping His fingers. As if Caeleen had blinked, though his eyes never closed, there stood the mare in her true form, though still with a bit of a frazzled look in her eyes.

"Thanks," Cae said as he came down to his knee before the Hunter God. "Listen, the way I acted back there..."

"Think nothing of it, lad," Kh'anora said with a sigh. "I've always thought the ways of the Emerald Grove peculiar, but they mean well. They will not hold your anger against you."

"That's good..." Cae kept his eyes down as he got back to his feet. "Is everything okay in Fartide?"

"All is well as far as I can see," the Tree Father replied. "But, after what happened in Creddon... You'd best get back to the Alabaster Palace. Besides, Alahir is well on his way, and may even get there before you do."

Cae smirked. "Don't suppose You could get me there a little quicker, could Ya?"

"Not this time, my friend." Kh'anora winked. "You'll just have to take the long way."

Cae nodded, looking back at Katei. "Say, Kh'anora... why don't the Druids ever fight?"

"It is not in the nature of their vocation to take up arms," the Ethereal replied. "Becoming a Druid means devoting your life to the realm of nature. While there is an inherent violence to the natural order of things, the path of the Druid is one that requires an acceptance of the tides of time, and all that comes with it. It's not that they cannot fight, it's just... not in their nature to do so."

"But what about... ha!" Caeleen grinned suddenly. "In their *nature*. Nice."

Kh'anora shook His head with a little smile.

"But, uhh... but what about the Earthspeakers? Lord Koromaer always told me Earthspeaker Ophelia was vital in beating the Wyrm of Ruin's Peak."

"Well, I never said all Druids were the same, now, did I?" Kh'anora replied with a chuckle.

Caeleen rolled his eyes. "Well, whatever... still. I wish it didn't have to be this way."

"So do some Druids of the Grove," Kh'anora replied. "They've prayed to Me several times, asking Me to bring a change of heart to old Bakh. I would love to do so but, well... I'm afraid it just doesn't work like that."

Caeleen shrugged. "At least we do what we can, yeah?"

Kh'anora nodded. "Indeed..." He lighted a hand on Caeleen's shoulder. "I do hope you know I'm proud of you, Mister Longwatch. You've served your people well."

Cae smiled. "Thank you, my Lord. I just... I feel like I should be able to do more, Y'know?"

The Tree Father looked down at His feet. "I know. I feel the same more and more these days."

Caeleen frowned as he looked back south and westward. "Hey, did You see where I did that thing? I reached out for the sword and it just like, jumped into..." He turned back to where the Ethereal had been standing, but He was gone.

Caeleen sighed. "Gods' sake, why does He always do that?"

* * *

SIAHRA DRIFTED INTO THE ARMORY, HER SPEAR slung across her back as her tail slowly pushed her through the waters. For some time, the supply of armaments in the Palace had been dwindling, but things had been slowly improving since the forges lit back up when the Dragoons arrived. The Diamond Queen glanced around at the rows of carefully crafted Tamian half-plate and chain suits. Her smiths worked tirelessly to rebuild their stocks, and she was proud of them. *Perhaps they're due a raise,* she thought. She'd run it by Suressa, see what she thought.

In the center of the large dome-shaped chamber was the *Makao-Toai*—the Mageforge. Similar forges existed in Viraati Lien and Rey Prele, but their forges were much smaller. The Makao-Toai itself had been fashioned long ago before the Great Burning, built out of the skull of an ur-kaula, a devil in the form of an enormous red shark. In its jaws was a bright sphere of light, into which the mighty magesmiths of the maotu fed materials to be melded into a more malleable state. They would then draw the broken-down remnants of their materials out and shape them into tools, trinkets, and armaments. This was how the iridescent-white scales of the mighty Sturamtönn had been shaped into the armor she now wore.

Overseeing the magesmiths now was her Court Magus, one of her Council of Eight Knights... well, Nine Knights now. His name was Temui. He had been Court Magus to her father, and his mother before him. Siahra believed the old fellow was growing weary of his service, but she hadn't spoken to him about it yet. Perhaps once things calmed down, the two of them could have that conversation.

"Temui!" Siahra called. "You wanted to speak with me?"

Temui turned and bowed deeply, his silver hair swishing through the water as he did so. "My Queen," he said with a sigh. "I'm glad you've come. We've been..." his voice trailed off as he saw the mighty spear on her back, and his eyes turned aside. "Forgive me, my Queen. I did not mean to interrupt your grieving."

"No, no! It's totally fine." Siahra held up an open hand. "I don't think Kéldi would want me to be moping around."

Temui nodded. "Very well..." with a flick of his wrist and a spark from his fingertips, a light flashed between the two merfolk, and there appeared the strange targe from Creddon. "I've been looking over this artifact as you requested, and I have some concerns."

"What did you find out?"

"Well, first and foremost, I must say I've never dealt with a magic of this nature before. The very core of its enchantment seems undeniably malignant. The magic feels as if its source is rooted in a measure of pain inflicted by—or perhaps on—the shield's crafter."

Siahra cocked a brow. "'Pain-magic'? That's a little disconcerting."

Temui nodded. "More specifically, I'd call it blood-magic."

"And that's definitely worse."

"I'd suggest not handling it with your hands. I'm not finished examining it, but I suspect the enchantment to be a powerful curse."

"Do we know what it does?"

"Well...on the surface, it's clear that the shield is imbued with a potent ward. Its wielder would likely be nigh-on immune to fire, magical, or otherwise."

"Even hellfire?"

Temui shrugged. "Couldn't say. We don't have any to test it with."

"That's fair. So it's, what, just a fire-ward? What're the shackles for, then?"

Temui brought the targe closer to himself with a wave of his hand. "It's more than just a ward... it has another effect that worries me." Temui turned his eyes up toward the surface. "It... we had a volunteer agree to test the shield."

The Queen's eyes widened. She knew Temui's habits

when it came to testing magic. "Temui, did you throw a fireball at one of my soldiers?"

"Yes," the Wizard replied, "and not only did it not harm him at all, he deflected it and blasted a hole in my tower."

"Is that what that was?"

Temui frowned. "Yes...and when that hole let the sun into the chamber, he said something that put me off."

Siahra tilted her head curiously.

" 'I can't feel it,' he said. 'It's like it's nighttime,' he said to me."

Siahra's eyes narrowed. "He couldn't, what...? He couldn't feel the sun?"

Temui nodded. "Indeed. And, then, he attacked me."

A few of the nearby magesmiths turned to look back at the pair. Temui waved them off and beckoned for Siahra to follow. The two of them left the forge and drifted among the rows of armor, along with the targe.

"He attacked you?" Siahra asked in a hiss.

Temui's frown deepened. "It was a quick change. Not immediate but, when I asked him to remove the shield, he hesitated. I asked again, and he refused." He paused, then looked right into Siahra's eyes. "He came at me with his spear. Grazed me in the leg."

"Are you okay?"

"I'm fine, but he didn't give me any choice but to put him down."

Siahra shook her head. "D-don't, don't say it like that. They're soldiers, not sick old seahorses."

Temui dipped his head. "Apologies, my Queen."

Siahra winced again at his grating pronunciation.

Temui had a way of making Mareho sound more like the harsh Orc-Tongue.

"I never saw him fasten them," Temui went on, "but he was wearing the shield's shackles when he died."

Siahra shook her head. "So what do you think made him attack you?"

"I'll need some time to study the shield further," said the Wizard, "but... I believe the shield is either meant to force the wearer into aggression, or... more likely, it is designed to ensure the wearer's allegiance."

"Allegiance to whom?" Siahra asked. "Temui, do...do you think whoever made the shield was watching?"

"Your Majesty, I don't know what to think." Temui flicked his hand, and the targe vanished. "I'll keep it sealed away in the tower for now, when I'm not examining it. But I suggest we all be more on the alert. That detachment for Mai may need to stay here for a time to guard the Palace, just in case."

"Absolutely not," Siahra replied. "We might need those hands here later, but Mai needs them now."

Temui nodded. "As you wish, my Queen."

* * *

THE RIDE BACK TO FARTIDE TOOK ABOUT TEN DAYS. Caeleen rode back through the gates of Fartide just as dusk fell on February the twenty-sixth, the eve of Silvishi. The Ranger smiled through his exhaustion; he hadn't expected to make it back in time for the holiday, but here he was. He figured Siahra would probably want a report of how his trip had gone (and also probably want her horse back), so he and Katei cantered on through the streets. Even in the scarred bones of the destroyed capitol, the people were alive with excitement over festival preparations. Glowing strings of white light hung from the rooftops, lanterns hung in the air that gave off a golden glow. Children ran about with little sparklers, and troupes of minstrels wandered the streets, playing their jovial tunes. It warmed Caeleen's heart to see the people going strong after everything that had happened there.

Caeleen found the Alabaster Palace wreathed in yellow and white, the very air around the structure filled with holy light. As the young Knight approached, a deep, hollow tone filled the air as maotu horns heralded his return. The sound caught Caeleen off guard, but he found it better than the blaring brass that rang out in Greyfort. The Ranger and his steed crossed the bridge leading to the palace's front gate, and Cae slowed Katei to a stop as a few handlers came up to take her reins.

"We're glad to see you back safe, Ta Rakau!" one of the handlers said as she looked over Katei carefully. "I trust our mare lived up to your standards?"

"She did good," Cae said as he hopped down from the horse. "But she got turned into a mouse for a little bit... so, y'know, I'd keep an eye on her for a while. Just make sure she's alright in the head."

Another handler frowned at him, her eyes wide. "Wh... *how*? What happened out there?"

Cae shrugged. "Look... things happen when I'm around. I don't even know anymore."

"Caeleen!"

Cae turned and smiled wide as Siahra approached,

garbed in a tunic of white and gold, a long red cape trailing behind her. She wore her hair in a long tail over one shoulder, tied in a golden ribbon, with a smaller circlet on her brow in place of her larger finned crown. She looked radiant, she really did. But Caeleen spotted the faintest bags beneath her eyes. It must have been a long few days preparing for tonight, especially with everything else going on. Cae felt a pang of guilt sting his chest. He wished he could have been here to help with everything but... honestly, would he really have been all that much help? He was a hunter, not a party planner.

Flanking Siahra were two younger girls, likely the Queen's own handmaidens, dressed in similar fashion. "I'm glad you're back," the Queen said. "You were right, you made it just in time!"

"Looks that way, yeah!" Cae replied, dipping his head. "Gimme a minute to get settled in, then I'll give you my report."

"Actually, if you're not too winded, I was hoping you might come down to the festival with me." Siahra nodded toward the town. "The Surface District always puts on a great party. Wanna come?"

"Oh! Yeah, totally!" Cae offered a weary smile as he reached up to tie his hair. "Although I'm a little worse for wear right now. Don't suppose you have anyone around who knows how to prestidigitate, do you?"

Siahra looked down at one of her handmaidens. The little one waved a finger at the Ranger, and in a flash of twinkling white light, he was sparkling clean. He let out a little laugh; the little one had caught him quite by surprise! The handmaiden gave a little curtsy, her blue-tinted curls bouncing as she did so.

"That's Iki. She's training to be a Sorceress." Siahra held out her arm with a little smirk. "We don't quite know where her gift comes from, but she's hoping the Institute in Highhaven accepts her."

"Maybe we can see if Iómi can out in a good word?" Cae suggested, taking the Queen's arm as they started along the bridge.

"How is she, by the way? I remember her mentioning a daughter in Han'kiri."

"Han-what?"

Siahra blinked for a moment before her eyebrows popped up. "Oh, no, it's, uhh... Grey-something? Grey-fort!" she said, her voice trailing into a laugh.

Caeleen chuckled. "I really need to take a class or something, I'm just not picking the language up fast enough!"

"Cae, you've been here for like, a month! Don't worry about it, you'll get there!"

The two of them carried on all the way into town. Again and again, the two were stopped by folks on the street who would bow deep before the Diamond Queen and ask little questions about how life was at the Palace: Has she thought about taking a groom? Who this home-less man was on her arm? Oh, he's a Knight? Terribly sorry, he doesn't look very knightly!

Cae would laugh. They were right, he wished he could have at least gotten out of his traveling clothes first, but oh well.

As the evening wore on, the pair made their way out

of the city walls and into an open field just past the shanties, where vendors and merchants and all different folks had set up a sizable carnival.

Cae found himself a bit dizzied by the scale of it all; Silvishi in Evenwood was certainly smaller by comparison. He hadn't seen Silvishi in Greyfort, as he had elected to spend the holiday both years working on his archery... like most days when he wasn't working with Leon or the scouts, honestly. Gods, he *really* needed to get out more.

"Oh! Oh, man, *yeah!* Cae, come on!" Siahra grabbed Caeleen's wrist and took off, dragging the poor Ranger behind her toward a raucous gathering of people. In the center of the crowd was a haphazard circular fence. Inside was a pair of maotu, the both of them stout fellows. One of them was lying face-first in the dirt, a bit of blood pooling under his nose. The other hopped around roaring excitedly, as members of the audience tossed purses of coin amongst one another.

"Come on, now!" shouted the man in the ring. "One of you has to be able to take Makala!"

Caeleen cocked his brow. A fighting pit for Silvishi? What a wild celebration! "They do this every year?"

"Yes, yes we do." Siahra grinned as she unclasped her cape and tossed it to one of her handmaidens. "I won't be long."

"What?? Siahra, wha—"

The audience came alive with cheers as the Diamond Queen vaulted into the pit. "Blessed Silvishi, Makala!"

"Ahhhh, K'kanu!" Makala made a show of taking an elaborate bow. "Was just wondering when you'd get your pampered butt out here! These appetizers just ain't doin' it anymore!"

"Well, I'm here now," Siahra replied. "Think you can take me this year?"

"Oh, I think I'm man enough." Makala pounded his fists against his chest. "Let's go!"

Siahra cracked her knuckles and looked back over her shoulder. "Cae, care to do the honors?"

Cae shook his head and laughed as he leaned in against the fence. "Alright, alright. Back against the ring."

Both fighters stepped back and leaned against the wooden fence.

"Uhh... can we get the sleeper outta there, right quick?"

A couple of bystanders hopped in and retrieved the unconscious challenger, carefully bearing him out of the ring.

"Thanks! Okay... fighters ready?"

Makala offered a thumbs up, not taking his eyes off of Siahra. The Queen looked back at her Ranger and nodded.

"Fight!"

Siahra and Makala launched themselves toward the center of the ring.

Makala threw an enormous right hook up into Siahra's side. Or at least, where her side should have been; planting a foot firmly as she dipped into the pugilist's range, Siahra spun around his punch and leapt up. Her shin cracked against his neck and dropped him to a knee.

"I got sixty-four on the Queen!" one spectator cried.

Makala caught a second kick before it connected with his nose, and he threw Siahra up into the air. When she landed, a fist rocketed into her gut, doubling her over as Makala chuckled.

"*Kaniha i Makala!*" someone else shouted.

Makala brought his fists together over his head and brought them down in a furious hammer. Siahra threw her arms up and barely caught the blow. Makala grabbed her by the shoulders and threw a knee into her chin, sending her flying back against the fence.

"No, no, ninety on Makala!" barked an elf leaning against the pen next to Caeleen. The corners of his coal-black eyes crinkled under the breadth of his grin.

Cae's brow cocked. "I'll take that bet."

Makala danced his way over to the fence and shot a fist toward Siahra's nose, intending to drop her.

In a blur of motion, the mermaid batted the fist off to the side and cracked an elbow into Makala's mouth. Wiping a bit of blood from her mouth and winking, she quickly followed up with a fierce headbutt into his nose. Makala fell back for a moment, and Siahra leapt up onto the fence and threw herself onto her opponent's shoulders. Her legs locked around his head and, with a furious twist she slammed the bigger maotu into the ground.

"*Koku!*"

Siahra stood tall over Makala and cracked her neck with a grin. Makala roared once more and threw a vicious uppercut toward the Queen, but Siahra was out of the way long before the attack could reach her. Darting back into range, she drove a back heel right into Makala's temple, and the merman was out cold before he hit the dirt.

Siahra spun on her toes with her arms out wide. "And a Blessed Silvishi to the rest of you!"

Everyone around lit up with cheers. Cae smirked as the elf beside him dropped a purse of gold into his hand and shuffled off. Siahra leapt over the fence and donned her cape. Her handmaidens smiled up at her, each holding a coin purse of their own.

"That a yearly occurrence?" Cae asked.

Siahra shrugged. "Been kickin' Makala's tail since I was thirteen."

"You guys get kinda crazy for Silvishi out here, don't ya?" Cae asked.

Siahra cocked a brow. "What, do you not have a pit in the Dokk?"

Cae laughed and shook his head. "In Evenwood, Silvishi is a little quieter. We like to curl up inside by the fire. You and your Silvishen just sorta hang out for the day. Nobody works, or anything, it's just like one big day off for everybody."

Siahra tilted her head, the corner of her lip just barely twitching into a hint of a smile. "I think I'd like that."

Cae nodded. "It's really great! But you have to make sure to get your shopping done a day or so in advance. Nobody opens their stores, or anything so, if you have to go out and get food, folks tend to get miffed."

Siahra laughed. "I don't think we need to worry about that here. I think we're good on groceries at the *Palace*."

One handmaiden snorted.

Cae shot her a grin, but his face went blank as it clicked. "Wait, we?"

The Diamond Queen shrugged as she locked arms with her new Knight. "Will you be my Silvishen, Ta Rakau?"

Cae's cheeks turned red as his eyes darted off to the side. "I'd uhh, buhhhh... I'd, I'd be honored! I, y-would, I, you..."

Siahra laughed and slapped at the Ranger's chest. "Gods, you're such a dork! Just say yes!"

Cae let out something between a cough and a laugh, and said yes.

THAT NIGHT, CAELEEN WAS BROUGHT TO HIS ROOM in the Alabaster Palace, at the base of a short tower set aside for the Palace Guard. Even despite the relatively small size of the tower, Caeleen's bedchamber was nearly twice the size of the bedroom in his cabin back in Laithe.

It seemed Siahra had spared no expense in setting him up here; there were racks on the walls for him to hang his weapons, a fine table in the corner for his little shrine to Kh'anora, and a soft bed with sheets of fine satin. The wardrobe on the far wall was filled with different outfits, most in more modern Tamian fashion, long coats of navy and marine with silver bars, white shirts with frills and billowy sleeves, blue velvet trousers with sashes of silver, black boots of supple leather, at least a dozen capes of bold blue with silver trim and tassels, all of them of exceptional craft and material.

These were noblemen's clothes, they must have cost a small fortune.

Caeleen didn't know what to think; on one hand, this was generous on the Queen's part. But, on the other hand... why? Why give him all this wonderful stuff when he was just going to leave? Siahra had to know he couldn't stay. He would need to be out in the field. Once he got into his patrols, he likely wouldn't even be back in Fartide often.

Cae sat on his bed and pulled off his boots and coat, having hung his cloak on the rack by the door, and let out a deep breath. At least, until after tomorrow, he would allow himself to relax. It was Silvishi, a day of rest. Even Pa had taken Silvishi off to gather his strength.

He allowed himself a little smile as he pulled back the sheets and crawled into bed.

9

*I*siliel clutched onto Iómi's robes tightly on the back of the shadow-wreathed creature sailing through the sky high over Siahra's river. Despite her not having any problem with Iómi's Voloki magic personally, the... *thing* underneath them still set off all sorts of red flags in her head as a Silvian Priestess. Iómi had called it a *pizuri-ditke*, a lesser wraith, assuming the form of a large raven. The giant corvid seemed almost made of smoke, and a strange haze billowed out of its wings as it flew.

Isi was unsure how they were even flying on its back, as the bird didn't seem to have a physical form, but she didn't ask questions. Iómi seemed happy enough. Still, Isi would occasionally glance down at her amulet, reassuring herself that everything would be fine.

In the clear night sky, under a spectacularly bright moon, the city of Fartide stood barely visible in the distance. On the horizon, the swirling spires of the Alabaster Palace were just barely visible, and the City by the Sea looked more like a children's diorama than a bustling capitol. The wraith... Whiskey, Iómi called it, pulled its wings in closer to its body, and the creature seemed to propel itself forward with magic. Mystical darkness billowed out behind it as it tore through the air.

"How much farther?" Isi shouted over the screaming winds.

"A few hours, maybe?" Iómi replied, her voice clear in Isi's mind. "Whiskey can get pretty fast, but I don't wanna push her too far."

"Why's that?"

Iómi looked back over her shoulder with a sly little smirk. "Because I don't wanna fall off."

If not for her overwhelming dread, Isi would have rolled her eyes. Instead, she clutched the Wizard's robes tighter. "Iómi, have you actually done this before?"

"Not out this way, but we've made it to Davenstead before!" Iómi paused for a moment, biting her lip. "I mean, we kind of crash-landed in Forever Lake, but..."

Isi groaned and buried her face in Iómi's neck, and she heard the Necromancer laugh. Iómi knew about Isi's anxiety regarding her magic. Voloki mages and the Silvian clergy have long clashed with one another, perhaps ever since the feud between their Matrons in the tales from before the world. Only recently, when Necromancy had become recognized by the Church of the Seven as holy magic, did the Silvians relent in their aggression. But poor Isi had been brought up believing that Necromancers were dangerous. She did her best to ignore that impulse, and it meant so much to Iómi that she did, but the Wizard understood that Isi couldn't help feeling—

"Back to the Hells with you!!"

Iómi and Isi barely had time to turn their heads before a swirling mass of muscle and feathers came crashing down onto Whiskey's back, scattering the raven's form into a whirling haze of black. Isi barely clasped her fist onto an enormous yellow talon, her other hand an iron vice around Iómi's wrist.

The haze tore in frantic circles around the attacker, an enormous eagle, as Isi's hefty plate flashed into existence on her form. The eagle beat its massive wings in a fury, dispersing the haze about it. The wisps of black regathered into their bird form, and Whiskey descended onto the eagle, screeching as her black claws dug into its forehead.

Isi shrieked as she heaved Iómi onto the attacking bird just as her hand slipped, and she plummeted toward the river.

"*Isi!*" Iómi screamed, her fingers sinking into the eagle's feathers as she reached out in vain toward her falling companion.

Whiskey wrenched her claws upward, and she closed her beak tightly into a pinch of the eagle's flesh on the side of its neck. The eagle swore and grunted as it spun about, a bit of meat tearing away from it as it broke away from the wraith. In a beat, the raptor darted back in, catching one black claw in its own talon and sending the two birds into a mad spiral toward the ground. Isi crashed into the waters with a great splash.

"Stop it! *Stop it!*" Iómi screamed over the howling winds whipping about them. "We're not here to hurt anybody! Let *go!*"

Whiskey pried herself free from the eagle's grasp just in time for the birds to both crash down into the running waters below. When the spray of water vanished, the two birds stood firm in the river, their eyes never leaving each other.

"*Ushvizna min Vilshe!*" Whiskey hissed, her voice thin and vicious. "*Ushvizna yi!*"

"Save your words, vile creature!" The eagle grimaced as he slowly began to circle the corvid. "Return to the Abyss from whence you came!"

Had it not been for the blessing of the All-Mother, Isiliel would likely not be able to stand. But stand she did, and a sudden burst of sunlight from her shield pushed the eagle back.

"By my authority as Priestess of the All-Mother," Isi roared, "I *order* you to stand down!"

The eagle shirked away at first, but slowly it turned to face the Cleric. "What business has a Silvian with a wraith? In these times, no less!"

"The wraith is a servant of my companion!" Isi replied. "You will do no harm to either of them!"

"And what authority have you over the Wing of the Dokk Fuil?" The eagle spread its wings and prepared to strike.

Iómi dropped into the water and coughed, her eyes widening. "Wing of th...hold on, *hold on!* Are you from the Shadowed Mountains?"

The eagle looked down at the Wizard at his feet. "I am."

Isi lowered her shield for a moment, and the light dimmed and faded from her shield. "Wait... there's a

Ranger in the capitol here. His name is Caeleen. You've met him, haven't you?"

"Gods, what did he say—Alahir!" Iómi cried. "That, that's your name! Right? Alahir?"

The eagle cocked its head. "H...have we met?"

Isi let out a sigh, and her armor shimmered and vanished, leaving her traveling robe in its place. "My name is Isiliel Rumoré. We accompanied Caeleen back to Evenwood two years ago."

Alahir's eyes widened. "Wait...wait, wait! It was you! You're the one who saved Miss Allysia!"

Isi smiled, her breath still ragged. "I did."

Alahir gasped, drawing his wings in and bowing his head low. "M-my lady! Please, *please* forgive my aggression! I did not realize—"

"It's fine, Alahir." Isi turned back to Whiskey. "Are you alright?"

"*Mi trushku,*" Whiskey replied.

Isi blinked. "I... I actually don't know what that means."

"She's fine," Iómi said, still wading her way toward Isi. "Are *you* okay? You fell, like... a *long* way."

"I'm alright." Isi pulled her hair back into a thick tail over her shoulder.

Alahir shook his feathers out. "If I might be so direct... and with my apologies to you as well, Miss...?"

"Iómi."

"Yes, Iómi. If I might say so, perhaps it would be best if the two of you joined me on my way to the capitol. I assume this wraith of yours is a conjuration of yours, Lady Wizard?"

"Yeah, but I think I'll stick with her. I'm comfortable riding her anyway, and... yeah, no. I don't know you."

Alahir nodded. "Still, I would take care using your magic in this Kingdom. It *is* Voloki magic that..."

"Yeah, I got it."

Alahir turned back to Isi. "Good Priestess, I leave it to you. Will you fly with me, or would you rather stay with your friend the Wizard?"

Isi paused. She looked back at Iómi and gave a half-frown. "Iómi, don't take this the wrong—"

"Get on the eagle, Isi." Iómi waved off her partner's concern with a smile. "You've been freakin' out since we took off."

Isi scratched the back of her head awkwardly as she approached Alahir. "If you'll have me, friend, I will fly with you."

Alahir bent low to the ground and allowed the Cleric to mount his back. "Hold tight," the Great Eagle said, spreading his wings out wide. All at once, he leapt into the air, and with several great beats of his wings the eagle was off, Isi in tow, followed closely behind by Whiskey and Iómi.

CAELEEN AWOKE BEFORE THE DAWN, WHEN THE SKY was all a purplish-bluish haze. Though he was awake, he had trouble crawling out of his new bed. But he did, and he went to put on his traveling clothes... then stopped. He'd just gotten back into town. Would Siahra want him here in the city for a while? Would... no. No, he needed to be out there. At least ranging outside the city. He pulled on his gear and slid Sal'tera into his bag, taking out Gem'shil and strapping it to his hip. There would be time to test the Blade's new power later, but he didn't want to become overly reliant on its magic.

Once he dressed, Caeleen made his way down to the tower's kitchen. The guards were already awake and seated around their tables, practically diving into their bowls of hot fish soup. Cae ladled out a bowl for himself and grabbed a bit of bread, sitting at the end of a long table. The guard greeted him stiffly (albeit a bit sluggishly, as they were mostly still half-asleep) and went on eating.

One of the guards slid Cae a stein. "Ale?"

Cae cocked a brow. "This early?"

The guard shrugged. "It helps. What do you do when you see things out there?"

Cae looked down at his soup. "... I mean... I just kinda... keep working. Makes it easier to put the bodies out of my mind if I've got a bow in my hand."

"But what do you do when they pile up, hmm?"

"Well, I... uhh... I guess I make my peace in my downtime. Deal with the pain before you go back out, before you have time to lose anybody else. Y'know?"

The guard nodded, looking down at his drink. "Hmm...well. Guess we both have our methods, eh?"

"Does the Queen know you're drinking on the job?"

The guard shook his head. "She don't care. Too busy runnin' the ocean."

Cae frowned, but said nothing. He'd have time to say something to Siahra about all this later. He ate his soup quietly, and the guard chattered on, occasionally one of them offering the Knight a comment. It was nice, a chance to relax before the work went on, but Cae couldn't quite shake off the discomfort.

Eventually Cae finished up his bowl and headed out of the kitchen, stuffing the last of his soup-sopped bread in his mouth as he went. Outside the tower, Caeleen cut across a courtyard filled with gorgeous underwater plants, all suspended in floating spheres of water that gave off a faint blue glow, and made his way through the castle and out to the main gatehouse.

"Ta Rakau!" Cae turned to see a young courier, the same one he'd met before he left for the Grove, coming out of the gatehouse and running toward him. "I have a... *hoo!* I have a letter for you!"

Cae stopped and waited for the lad to catch his breath. "From who?"

"Fruh...from Laithe. Someone nah... someone named Leon? Leon Farrough?"

"Why are you out of breath, where were you running from?"

"The coast, Ta. There's...there's something coming."

"Something c..." Cae sighed. "Did you also need to come find me?"

"Yes, Ta."

Cae shook his head and laughed a little as he took the letter. Sure enough, Leon's scratchy handwriting was on the front, with Mull's own seal keeping the message shut tight. "I'll be down in just a minute, alright."

"Yes, Ta. Thank you, Ta." Without another word, the

courier darted off, stumbling. Cae shrugged as he broke the seal and read his former Squire's letter.

CAE,

I SENT THIS LETTER THROUGH THAT NEW MAGIC POST thing, so it should get there around the end of February. Cost me two whole gold, which is just ridiculous for a letter, but, whatever. Happy Silvishi, by the way!

Things are alright here in the Plains. People are getting a little antsy about the rumors coming out of Tamia. I heard some people in the Fixin's say they're starting to get sightings of ghosts and stuff in Haven. Have you guys heard anything about that?

Dunc and Eda are doing good. Dunc moved into the cabin with me. He's in my old room, and I moved into your old room. Eda still lives in the city, but she got a great deal on an apartment in that one tower out by the coast, the one where we found the baby biyagi. (She adopted him. Called him Croak, taught him to be kind of a guard-dog... or guard-frog. He has a little sword now!)

Your sister came by a few weeks ago. Said she wanted to see how I was adjusting without you around. She was here for a couple days. She worries about you, y'know. You oughta write home more often.

Anyway, hope to hear from you soon. Stay safe out there!

.   .   .

- Leon

Cae smiled and pocketed the letter. Leon had a point, and Kh'anora had tried to make it before. He needed to check in on his mother sometime.

Cae was the first Knight to answer the call on the coast. There were a handful of guards already there, and they filled him in on what happened. The "something" coming was, in fact, refugees. Cae concealed his frustration for a moment; another refugee crisis for Tamia would raise more concerns... and frankly, would open up an opportunity for Cestus to make Siahra look like a weak leader. Not to say that's the first thing the Emperor would do, but Cae wouldn't put it past him.

The village of Mai was gone. So was the city of Kuari. A whole city, overrun. Apparently, there were more Voloki in the trench they were built on the edge of than anyone anticipated. Fortunately, the city of Weiru was able to bolster their defenses and fight of the waves of fiends, and even house some victims from the other two settlements, but there were just too many in need. The refugees on their way to the surface had been traveling for two days. Cae considered it a blessing that Fartide had reached a point in its reconstruction where they'd be able to hold several homeless, but still. Word had been sent to Siahra and the other Knights, presumably by more than just the one courier, and Cae was the first to arrive.

Sure enough, it took Siahra mere moments to join him, riding with Har Burúm on the back of his drake. A company of guards and servants followed close behind with food and blankets and supplies. It wasn't long before a steady line of battered, weary merfolk crawled out of the ocean, stumbling awkwardly as some of them assumed their bipedal forms for the first time.

Caeleen did the best he could to be of some small service, handing out blankets and food as quick as he could. Many of the people greeted him in Mareho, and he would smile and nod politely, unable to offer a response. This went on for about an hour, just handing out food and tending to the wounded, which was made easier by Caeleen's new incantation.

About midday, the train of refugees made their way slowly and carefully up into the city. The maotu had built safe houses within the walls for this specific purpose, and there was plenty of room in the shanties. Things went far smoother than they had before, and soon enough Siahra was on her way back into the Palace with Caeleen in tow.

The two sat in Siahra's chambers, Caeleen oiling Gem'shil's blade as Siahra went over papers on papers. This situation with Mai opened up a whole new slew of problems. The detachment she had sent out to the village hadn't reported back. She'd need to station a company of Oceanguard out there, which she really didn't want to do. Deploying the Guard outside Twipari was practically a declaration of martial law; despite the Guard's best intentions, people feared them for their sheer deadliness. While rumors were certainly flying about what was going on in Tamia now, putting the Oceanguard in motion would blow the lid on things entirely, and all Eridan would know the Diamond Shores were in crisis again.

Cestus would use that to shake faith in Siahra's rule. Caeleen didn't say it aloud, but Siahra did.

"Cae, I don't know what I'm gonna do..." Siahra buried her face in her hands. "Why is everything happening to us right now?"

Cae shook his head. "Maybe we could seal the trenches? Place wards over them to keep whatever's down there from getting out?"

"We already have wards on the trenches," Siahra replied, "but they're not strong enough. We might consider bolstering them, but with what mages? We'd need permission from Cestus to bring in anyone from the Institute."

"That doesn't make sense," Cae said. "High Magus Pah'drim is an Oracle. Aren't the Oracles supposed to have some kind of autonomy over their organizations?"

"They're supposed to, but Cestus has Pah'drim backed into a corner. Pah'drim might have command of the laws of physics, but he can't just create funding for the Institute."

"You'd think he'd be able to do that. Y'know, create gold."

"Creating gold and creating currency are two different things."

"How does that make any sense? They're just coins."

"It doesn't. None of this makes sense." Siahra stood up abruptly from her desk. "Look, the bottom line remains the same. We're on our own out here."

"I'm not so sure." Cae reached into his coat and pulled out Leon's letter. "Here, have a look at this. My old Squire sent it to me."

Siahra took the letter and read over it. "You really should send word to your mother."

"Not the point!" Cae rolled his eyes as he sheathed Gem'shil. "The point is, people are worried about Tamia. Laithe is worried about us. Hells, why do you think they sent me?"

"Because we know each other?"

"Because I'm a good hunter. Mull wants to help you. If you call on Laithe for aid, they'll answer. If you can have your forces out protecting the people, then I can get together a hunting party to find the source of all this and bring it down. Let me bring in Leon, maybe call for Isi. If I can get together a solid crew, we can find the root."

"Do you really think Leon will come?"

"No doubt." Cae managed half a smile. "He's a Ranger. Tracking down monsters is what we do."

Siahra looked back at Caeleen for a moment longer without a word, and the Knight could see a familiar twinge of fear in the amber of his Queen's eyes. "Okay...okay. Write to Mull. Get your team together. I'll handle the rest."

Caeleen nodded. "We can do this."

"We can... we can."

Cae stopped for a moment. "S... Siahra, are you alright?"

Siahra opened her mouth to speak, but then sighed. "I just... I, I wanna be there. Y'know? I can't stand not being out there, not working."

"I know." Cae took Siahra's hand in his. "I know you do. Believe me, I want you out there with me. But... you have to be there for your people right now. They need to know you've got a handle on things."

Siahra squeezed her eyes shut and took a deep breath. "I know... I know." Squeezing the Ranger's hand for just a moment longer, she turned and looked out toward her balcony. "You and your team will have room and board at any of the barracks and forts across Tamia. Find whatever's doing this to my people, Caeleen."

Caeleen offered her the archer's salute. "I will. You have my word."

* * *

Leon sat at the bar in the Fort's Fixin's when the illusory globe flickered to life. He looked up from his cider, Duncan seated beside him and Eda sitting on the bar with Croak in her lap. Winni and Cici were cleaning glasses behind the bar when the globe began to play its message.

"Good people of this great Empire." Cestus's face was grim and tired, more so than usual. "I stand before you today with grim tidings."

"Oh, Gods, what now?" Eda groaned, petting her little biyagi.

"As I'm sure you've heard, there are rumors going around that our friends in the Diamond Shores have found themselves in another crisis." The Emperor grimaced. "I stand before you, unfortunately, to confirm those rumors."

Leon's brow furrowed as the old man spoke.

"We know not why and we know not how, but there

appears to be some dark magic at work in Tamia. Ghosts and evils have spread across the West. Dark auras and living shades seem attached to the empty-hearted vagrants now roaming the Tamian roads and wilds. And it pains me to say that... there have been sightings of the Wild Rose killer across the Western Kingdom."

Leon's mouth fell agape. What was he doing? Was he trying to cause mass panic?

"Recently, some vagrants traveling the Kingdom have crossed over into Haven Kingdom. This, I cannot allow."

So the rumors were true, Leon thought. The troubles were spreading. How long then before they reached Laithe? How long before all of Solvaar was fighting demons?

"... It is with heavy heart, then, that I must declare the Kingdom of the Diamond Shores under total quarantine."

Duncan's ale splashed to the floor.

"The only persons in or out of Tamia will be those of my own choosing and permission. Anyone else found crossing into the Shores will face Imperial justice." The Emperor pinched the bridge of his nose before looking back up. "Pray for your brothers and sisters in the West. May the Sky Mother and all the Gods beside Her carry swift aid to the Tamian people."

The globe's haze enveloped the image of the Emperor as the light faded. Almost immediately, the murmurs began all across the tavern. Leon stared down into his mug, his face blank. A quarantine of the entire Kingdom... Caeleen was out there. Innocent people were out there. How is anyone going to help now?

Leon stood up and shuffled his way out of the tavern. His axe weighed just a little heavier on his back as he made his way out of the city gate and toward the stables.

"Farrough."

Leon looked up to see Spymaster Baron by his side. His approach had been silent.

"How did you do that?" the young Ranger asked.

"Same way you do. I'm just better at it." Baron reached into his coat and pulled out a note bearing the seal of the Tamian Royal Family. "This arrived today, postmarked one week ago." Leon took the note and began reading.

Your Highness,

Things are worse than we thought here in Tamia. The demons have invaded the underwater settlements, and we can't keep an eye on everything in the Kingdom.

Tüli died. I'm sorry, it was my fault. I brought him with me into dangerous territory, and he paid the price for my mistake. He was killed by the Wild Rose, as was Siahra's companion drake, Kéldi. Investigating the Rose's hideout was my decision.

Things are getting worse out here, and we can't protect everyone. I need a team out here to help me find the source. I need you to send Leon out here to help me track down whatever is doing this. I've sent for Isiliel as well, and I'm planning on reaching out to Iómi, too. I would also ask for Baron, but I know you need him there right now. We need to work faster, or this curse might hit all of Eridan, or worse.

I hope to hear back from you soon, Lion.

- SIR LONGWATCH

LEON FROWNED. "HE NEEDS US."

"He does."

"But the quarantine..."

"To Hell with the quarantine. You're a Plains Knight, we don't abandon people in need."

Leon frowned, but he nodded. "How will we get me over there? I'm sure Cestus is gonna be cracking down on patrols, keeping everything real tight."

"Sir Bellam will handle it," Baron replied. "Take a day to gather your things, then be at the Palace tomorrow night. It's difficult for him, but we can send you there without you ever crossing a border."

Leon cocked a brow. "Why didn't we send Cae over there like that?"

"Teleportation is expensive. We don't have easy access to a fairy sanctuary, and none of the Clerics in the Cradle can do it yet, so Bellam has to craft his own magic dust for the circle. The materials he needs for that usually run us about two thousand gold each time."

Leon threw his brows up. "Gods...alright, I get that."

"Tomorrow night. I'll meet you at the palace gate. Try not to draw too much attention until then."

* * *

"Welcome to Gilgal, Ta Rakau."

Caeleen kept his hood pulled over his face as he nodded curtly to the guardsman who greeted him at the edge of town. Perhaps the hood gave him an aura of mystique or solemnity, but really he just didn't want everyone to see the dark circles under his bloodshot eyes. He hadn't slept in three days.

The Ranger-Knight did his best to look graceful as he slunk down off Katei's back. "How are things out here? Everything alright?"

The guard shrugged. "We've been lucky. We've had a few bats, a bit of snow, but nothing we can't handle with some blankets and a few crossbows."

"Good. I'm gonna be here for a few days scouting out the area before I head north. Any ideas about where I oughta start?"

"No...no, not particularly. But perhaps the fellow from Dane will know something?"

"A Danesman, all the way down here?"

"Nah, not a Danesman. Says he's a Daven, left just before they shut the gates. He should be at the Temple to Dioth toward the middle of town if you're interested."

Cae nodded his thanks as he led Katei to the barracks' stables, wrapping his cloak tightly around himself as he did. Even in his new winter clothes—a thick, padded coat of grey and a white cloak lined with wolfbear fur—the chill in the air was getting to him. The cold seemed to make his eyelids heavier, the extra effort in getting around making his every movement just a bit slower. Gods, he was so *tired*.

After ensuring Katei was secure with the stable master, Caeleen shuffled around to the back of the building. It seemed the snow, while it had certainly melted, had frozen over against the wall, leaving a thin layer of frost at the base of the back wall. Caeleen ignored this, and he laid down on his pack. He curled further into his cloak, feebly trying to fight off the chill as his eyes slowly crept shut. He had no dreams as he slept.

He woke to a familiar sensation tickling the back of his mind, one he'd not felt since the day he left home. A tired smile touched the corners of his mouth as he opened one eye.

"You look tired, Whisper."

Standing before him was an enormous brown bird, a Great Eagle of the Dokk. The bird looked down at him with silver eyes that spoke relief and concern both at once.

"I feel tired." Caeleen stretched his legs out, his boots poking out of the edge of his cloak, and straightened himself up against the wall. Standing next to his Eagle, Cae noticed, were Iómi and Isi.

"Why didn't you go inside and use one of the beds?" Isi asked as she knelt down beside the tired Ranger.

Cae shrugged, reaching up and rubbing the tiredness from his eyes. "Didn't want anybody to know I was so beat, so I just hid back here to get some shuteye..." He looked up to see that the sky had grown dark in the time he had been asleep. "How long have I been out, by the way?"

"We just got here, dude. Your guess is as good as ours." Iómi reached a hand out to Cae. He took it, and she pulled him up to his feet. Once he had regained his balance, Iómi threw her arms around his neck. Cae let out a tired laugh as he pulled her close.

Alahir slowly stepped forward, pressing his forehead to Caeleen's. "It is good to see you again, old friend."

Cae returned the gesture, stroking the eagle's beak. "You too, pal... I've missed you."

"And I you," Alahir replied. "I received word that you needed aid. What happened to your horse?"

Cae opened his eyes suddenly, his mouth dropping into a subtle frown. "Tüli, uhh... he..."

Alahir nodded with a sigh. "I understand. Forgive me, I did not mean to open an old wound."

"It's okay. I'm just glad you're here."

Isi crossed her arms with a measure of discomfort as she looked around at the open field of stark-white grain-like crops. "What are they growing here? Some kind of winter-wheat?"

"Valkospi," Cae replied. "Looks like wheat when you're growing it, but those are actually just the sprigs. The meat itself is a kind of clove, like garlic."

"Yeesh..." Iómi's brow raised. "That's a *lot* of valkospi. Who needs that much?"

"Perhaps it is a common ingredient in Tamian dishes?" Alahir asked.

Cae shook his head. "It's an old superstition. Valkospi is said to have warding properties. Keeps ghosts away and stuff."

"Where did you learn that from?" asked Isi.

"Ven loves plants."

"... That makes sense, she's a Druid."

Cae stroked his chin. "Ió's right that it's a lot of valkospi though... the guard said they hadn't been hit too harshly yet. Maybe it actually worked?"

"Do you think the valkospi might truly be magic?" Alahir asked.

"Wouldn't surprise me," Iómi replied. "Magic is everywhere. It's in the air we breathe, it's in the ground, it's in the stars..."

"If that were the case, then most of the townships should have similar crops growing already," Cae said. "Tamia ought to be covered in the stuff. But, still... just planting valkospi? That seems too easy. If crops could resolve this mess, then Tamia wouldn't be under quarantine."

Iómi's eyes widened. "What did... what? What do you mean quarantine?"

Cae sighed. "Yeah, y'all picked a pretty bad time to come. Cestus just put Tamia on lockdown."

"W... hold on, but... what, what do I..." The Wizard's face drained of color. "But I need to get home. I need to see my daughter."

Alahir grimaced. "Is there not a way to travel across borders outside of a physical crossing?"

"Teleportation spells are stupid expensive," Iómi said. "I could never pull it off."

"I can open gateways between Silvian temples," Isi replied, "but I have to be at a Silvian temple to do it."

"No good," said Cae. "Closest one we can get to is gonna be in Dane, up in the Ías."

"Ooh, that's...that's a ways." Isi grimaced. "I could erect a temporary shrine, see if that works. Ive never tried it before, but..."

"I don't think it'd work," Cae replied. "There's a difference between hallowed ground and a place of worship."

"So if I want to see Wini, then we have to end the quarantine." Iómi wrung her hands together as she nodded. "Yeah, okay. I mean, we, we were out here to do that anyway, right? We're here to, y'know, find the thing that's, uhh, that's messing with the Kingdom. Yeah, we can do that."

Isi put a hand on Iómi's face. "Iómi. Look at me. *Kase mina, Kutamé.*"

A pale hand lighted atop Isi's as Iómi looked back into the Priestess's eyes and nodded, though her brow still showed her worry.

Cae looked back to his Eagle friend, and with a nod, the two started walking. Isi turned and followed, taking Iómi by the hand and leading her along.

The Temple of Dioth was simple in structure. A compact, pentagonal building painted in the red and grey of the Lord of Balance and Justice, the interior consisted of little more than a shrine in the center, desks with clerks to allot payment for Slayers' jobs, and a board on each wall where those jobs could be posted. What few folk milled about in the temple were all armed, and bore pendants in the shape of a scale, the holy symbol of Dioth. Baron wore their same pendant sometimes around his neck; though it was not an official badge of office, it was safe to assume that anyone wearing the scales was a Beastslayer.

At first glance, it looked more akin to a guild hall than a place of worship, but the Diothi priesthood hadn't been struck dead for blasphemy yet, so such sparsities were seen as appropriate. An older fellow in robes of red and grey greeted the company at the door (except Alahir, of course, who waited outside) with a collection plate, asking for a donation to help play the Slayers' Way. The Ranger gave a pair of gold pieces.

"Good Father," Cae asked in a low tone, "I was told there was a fellow here from Dane in the north. Is he here now?"

The old man nodded, his grey beard rustling against his robes. "There, at the altar. The one with the red hair." He pointed a crooked finger to the center of the chamber where stood an elven man with crimson locks, donned in a black surcoat underneath a cloak of black fur. His ears were ghostly pale, and his shoulders were broad under sleeves of blackened chain, but he was not quite as meaty as the Slayers thereabout.

Isi grabbed Caeleen's arm. When he turned, the Cleric's brow was creased and furrowed, her mouth bent into a frown. His eyes widened as he felt a piercing heat from the pendant on his chest.

The Ranger and Cleric made their way outside. Alahir and Iómi were already there, the Wizard's eyes wide as she stared out into the fields outside the settlement.

The valkospi didn't work.

The corpses stood swaying along with the wheat-like

plants outside the settlement, the hiss of their ragged breaths just barely making it back to the town. Among them, Caeleen could see an enormous winged creature, its body seemingly translucent. The creature looked similar in shape to an altóg or a feral vampire, but a gaping maw holding rows on rows of glistening teeth took the place of the creature's face. For all his knowledge of beasts and monsters, Caeleen had never seen the likes of it before... but he remembered. It had seen him.

He'd shot it before, at Duin Durach. It had been watching him.

Isi turned back to the town. "Guards! Slayers!" she shouted. "Mount up, we've got trouble!"

The barracks opened up and yielded a company of soldiers and, out of the temple, came a handful of Beast-slayers. Among them was the cloaked elven man, his hood now drawn.

"The dead walk your fields!" Isi called, her morn-ingstar erupting with holy light. "They come for your families, they come for your houses! Stand now, and protect your own!"

The Slayers all took up their arms, many with cross-bows and many more with blades. The hooded man drew a gleaming rapier and a long black whip from beneath his cloak.

Caeleen held up a hand. "Hold on. I need to... I need to see something." Cae grimaced as he turned back to the winged creature.

"And who are you to give us orders?" came a call from one of the Slayers.

"Ranking officer," Cae replied over his shoulder,

holding his horn aloft. "Stand ready."

As Caeleen walked out into the fields of valkospi, he slowly drew Sal'tera from its sheath. The sky rumbled with distant thunder as the mithril blade gleamed in the open air. The winged beast strode forward, the dead parting for it as it seemed to glide through the field, until it stood before the Ranger.

"I..." Caeleen trailed off as he looked at the sea of bodies around him. "... I have to admit, I'm impressed. From what I gather, Necromancy on this scale is pretty taxing."

"Your words are kind," came a voice from somewhere in the maw of undulating teeth, "but you hide behind them. Be not ashamed of your fear, bowman."

"I'm not afraid," said Cae. "Not for myself, at least."

"No, indeed, you are not." The translucent creature leaned forward. "But you fear for them... your people. Do you not?"

Cae gritted his teeth. "You won't hurt them."

"No, not yet."

"Not ever."

The creature pulled away, standing tall over the young archer. It cocked its head, and its strange horns, or perhaps they were its ears, seemed to twitch.

"I won't allow it."

The air fell quiet for a moment. The dead all around turned their heads, and a sea of empty eyes focused on the Ranger.

Isi gripped her morningstar tightly, the weapon beginning to give off a subtler golden glow. Iómi summoned up Whiskey, who assumed her avian form.

Alahir lifted his wings and prepared to make for his companion.

"Amusing," replied the creature. "My Emperor was right to monitor you."

"I assume that's been your job all along, then?" Cae asked. "You've been keeping tabs on me?"

"I have. I began my watch over you after your blade felled the Serpent of the Trench."

"Sturamtönn?" Cae cocked a brow. "I didn't kill him. All I did was bring the sword, and someone else killed him. The sword isn't even mine."

"Perhaps you believe so," said the creature, "but the Tree has used you. You are an instrument of his will. Your actions have shaped events in this world."

The Tree... the creature must have seen him with Kh'anora. Cae frowned. "Anybody could have done what I did. I'm not special."

From somewhere deep within the creature, there came a chuckle. "Perhaps you'll not see your merit until the end."

"He has no merit."

Cae whipped around to see the cloaked elven man standing by his side. When did he get there?

"You have no power here, devil." The stranger spoke in a voice both commanding and weary. "Leave. And take your dead with you."

The dead looked to the stranger now, as did Cae and the creature. The stranger sighed, took a step forward, and cracked his whip out wide. The whip lashed across three of the cadavers nearby, scattering them to dust and fire. The surrounding corpses stepped back, and the whip seemed to retract of its own accord, coiling itself back into the stranger's hand.

"Begone. I won't ask again."

The creature looked down at the elven man for a moment longer. Cae's eyes widened as he stared down at the smoldering remnants of the three bodies.

The creature turned then, spread his wings out wide, and took flight, heading south toward the River. The dead followed suit, quickly moving from a shamble to a run in an effort to keep up with the thing. After a moment of flight, the creature's body shimmered for a moment, and then vanished.

As the soldiers and Slayers retreated into town, Cae's eyes stayed fixed on the waves of bodies speeding away from them. "So... that wasn't an altóg."

"No," said the stranger. "It was a *letchya*. A moon devil."

Cae nodded. "How do you go about tracking them?"

The elven man shrugged. "Haven't figured that part out yet."

Cae chuckled as Alahir came up beside him, and he stroked his feathers with a shaky hand. "Funny. I've spent twenty years learning to be the best I can at hunting. I'm not used to being hunted." He smiled as he turned to look the stranger in the face.

For a moment, a wisp of cold brushed across Caeleen's face as coal-black eyes looked back at him. The chill passed, but in its place came a realization. "H...haven't we met?"

The elf's brow rose. "I... yes, I think so. You were at the fighting pit on Silvishi, weren't you?"

Caeleen cracked a smile. "We had a bet on Queen Siahra's fight! What are you doing out here?"

"Same as you, I would imagine." The stranger shrugged. "I have certain gifts, and I thought I'd use them to do some good."

Isi and Iómi reached them now, and the priestess stepped forward with a furrowed brow. "How did you do what you did with the whip? That looked like holy magic."

The stranger held out his leather weapon for Isi to inspect. "The whip and the sword are consecrated. Blessed by Xanith."

"You're a Xanithan?"

The stranger shook his head. "I pick up what I need to, but, no. I am a *viltar*."

"A magic swordsman," Iómi mused aloud. "Do you have any affiliations? Are you with a school, or anything?"

"No," the stranger replied. "I suppose you would call me self-taught."

Cae nodded and clapped the elven man on the shoulder. "Well, we could use your help, if you're not busy, since we kinda have to take out those bodies. You got a name?"

The elven man smiled. "You can call me Alec."

10

"*A*gain."

Siahra swirled her spear over her head and brought the weapon down across Eldur's chest. The shaft of his own weapon deflected her strike, and the blade flew back. Spinning with the weapon's momentum, Siahra made a quick pirouette and swung for her opponent's body. He blocked again, and she quickly brought the back end of her spear around and cracked it against his helmet. The Dragoon stumbled, and Siahra swept her weapon toward his feet. Eldur dropped to the floor, and Siahra tapped the back of his helm with the tip of her spear.

From the side, Burúm flew in with two scimitars. Siahra barely managed to bring her spear up to deflect his whirling blades, shoving him back with her shaft. Burum countered with a swing from both swords, and the spear flew from the Queen's hands.

Siahra dove back, twirling through the air in a spiral of blue sparks as a longsword leapt into her hand. Eldur was back on his feet now, holding one of Burúm's scimitars. Siahra darted forward, batting Eldur's blade out of the way before twisting past a swipe from Burúm. A flash of blue erupted from her eyes, and a whirl of phantom swords surrounded her.

The two Dragoons leapt just out of the way of them, and Siahra lunged toward Burúm, tapping twice against his blade to open his defense before cracking her elbow into his chin. His helmet flew off as he dropped, and Siahra whirled around just in time to parry a strike from the other Dragoon.

Eldur snagged the other scimitar, and began throwing quick sweeping attacks wildly at the Queen, which she danced around expertly. She threw her free hand open into his face and, out of it, came a flash of brilliant light. Dazed, the Dragoon fumbled back, and Siahra twirled once and dashed him across the face with her shin. Catching one scimitar before it could clatter to the ground, the Queen now pointed a blade at each of her teachers, her breath heavy and ragged.

"Good! Good..." Burúm stood slowly, his hands up. "You're getting better."

Siahra grimaced, dropping her blades and taking up her dragonspear. "Not good enough. You got too close. If this happened in the field, whoever I'm fighting won't be holding back."

"If this ever happened in the field, we'll be there to back you up," replied Eldur as he got his feet back under him.

Siahra smirked. "Not if they kill you first."

Burúm chuckled. "They won't."

"Your Grace!"

The three Dragoons whipped around as the Wizard Temui stumbled into the room.

"Your Grace, a message from Highhaven..." the magus offered Siahra a scroll, the Imperial seal still unbroken. Siahra took the message and read over it.

As she read, her eyes widened and her face drained of color. "... w... we're under quarantine," she stammered. "The Empire is shutting us out."

The room fell quiet for a moment. Two years of recovery, with little to no help from the humans, had planted doubt in each of their minds. Now, it seemed, their suspicions had been confirmed; Cestus had abandoned them.

Siahra's jaw clenched. "... I'll kill him." Before her advisors could protest, the Diamond Queen marched down from the top of the guard tower, tailed all the way by the mage and Dragoons. As she made her way across the courtyard, and through passageways toward the Great Hall, her footsteps began smoldering with azure cinders.

"Your Grace, wait a moment!" Temui called. "We can't afford an altercation with the Empire with everything else—"

"The Empire owes us. We've guarded their shores for generations, I refuse to be discarded like a worn dishrag. I need a word with Cestus, and I need it now."

Siahra burst into her throne room and strode for the Alabaster Throne. Temui followed close behind, with Burúm and Eldur on his flank. The Queen had enough going on, but this? Quarantine? That was the line. Cestus never made much attempt to hide his contempt, but this open disdain was unprecedented. Siahra would not have it. One man's hate could not be the death of her people.

"I want a cast to the Emperor, *immediately*." Siahra's knuckles turned white as she gripped the arms of her throne. Temui whipped out the caster crystal as the crystal globe descended from the ceiling, suspended by simple sigils inscribed above. The crystal floated forward out of Temui's hand, giving off a faint pink glow as it drifted toward the Queen on her Throne.

The haze swirled in the floating globe for a moment. Siahra's brow furrowed.

Another moment of swirling.

The globe floated back upward, and the pink crystal returned to Temui's hand.

"It seems the Emperor is ignoring us," said the mage.

"Like Hells he is!" Siahra slammed her fist onto her Throne. Shooting up out of her seat, the Queen spun toward her attendants. "My armor, *now*. I'll take one of the solo drakes, fly down there myself, and beat some sense into that fool." As she stormed down the steps from her Throne, she reached out and clutched the dragon-spear that flew into her hand.

"Your Grace!" Burúm stepped forward, his own spear clacking against the white tile. "I beg you to reconsider! If the Emperor's forces see you crossing the border, they could attack you!"

"Come with me, then." Siahra spat back. "If the Legionnaires want a skirmish against three Dragoons, then let them taste dragonfire."

"The Udári are not tools for intimidation, Your

Grace!" This time, it was Eldur who spoke. "This is not who we are, not who *you* are!"

"Don't presume to tell me how to handle threats to my people." Siahra pointed her spear toward her advisor. Blue flames swirled at her feet as her eyes began to glow. "Last I checked, the Diamond Crown was on *my* brow, not yours."

On instinct, Eldur flourished his spear and took a defensive stance, yellow flames licking his armor as he did so. "Your Grace!"

At once, a blinding white light burst forth from the center of the chamber. After shielding their eyes from the flash, the three Dragoons turned and stood firm, their spears poised to strike. As the light faded, there now stood in the room a blond-haired fellow garbed in green, an axe and a longbow strapped to his back, astride a lean brown horse. Siahra recognized the lion-head shape of the pauldron on the boy's shoulder; he was a Knight of Laithe.

The boy looked about timidly. "... Is this a bad time?"

"N... no?" Siahra straightened out, her flames dying down as she whirled her dragonspear back behind her. "We weren't expecting anyone, though... are you from Laithe?"

"Yes, Your Grace," said the lad as he dismounted and dropped to a knee. "Sir Leon Farrough, Guardian Ranger of the Grey Wood and Knight in Service to His Majesty King Mull."

"You're Leon!" exclaimed Siahra. "So Mull received Caeleen's message, then?"

"He did," Leon replied, quickly getting back to his

feet. "Forgive me, Your Grace, but I have to ask you keep this mission under wraps. With the quarantine going on, my being here..."

"Your presence is technically treason, yes," said Eldur. "But, honestly, who's complaining? We need you here."

Leon bowed his head toward the Dragoon. "Thank you, Sir."

Siahra nodded. "Caeleen needs you. He was headed north toward Gilgal last I knew. Will you be able to catch up to him?"

Leon nodded, patting his horse. "I learned everything I know about tracking by learning to track him. And whatever horse you put him on, Buck and I can chase him down."

"Good." Siahra beckoned him forward. "Come on, we have a lot to fill you in on... and we also need to get your horse out of my throne room."

THE CHASE AFTER THE HORDE LASTED ABOUT A DAY. Though Caeleen and his company kept a solid pace, something about these dead, perhaps some kind of magic from the letchya at their head, gave them a speed that the company could not match. Though they kept out of range, Caeleen and Alahir were able to keep track of them from the air. The letchya itself was nowhere to be found, save for the wisp of a shadow that would occasionally pass around and behind the scrambling sea of bodies.

Iómi and Isi kept pace on the ground atop Whiskey,

who had taken the form of a large wolf striding across the grassland in a whirl of smoke. Alec had mounted Katei and taken up the rear. Though the rider and horse were unacquainted, something about the viltar had inspired something in Katei to hold a greater speed than Caeleen was able to achieve with her. Still, she wasn't as swift as a Great Eagle, or a wraith.

The chase after the dead ended at the banks of Siahra's River that night. Almost like a warding spell had struck them, the horde slammed to a halt at the water's edge. Caeleen and company slowed and regrouped as they saw this sudden halt. The Whisper and Wing swooped down to the earth, meeting their companions for a moment as they eyed their quarry.

"I don't understand," said Alahir. "Why are they not crossing?"

"Running water has a particular effect on those who are dead," said Alec. "Water creates life. It has a similar effect on them to Silvian magic... but not quite as deadly."

"That's good," Cae added. "We don't want those bodies running downstream and contaminating the water."

As they watched, the horrid form of the letchya reappeared on the other side of the River. Rearing back on its legs, and spreading its wings out wide, the gaping hole of a maw spread open ever wider, and the devil let out a sickening screech into the night air. Cae and Iómi clapped their hands over their ears, and Isi and Alec threw up light warding spells. Poor Alahir, however, dropped to the ground, unable to shield himself from the screech.

As the company watched, the corpses began to push into the waters, bodies toppling over one another and piling up to form a macabre bridge.

Alec shook his head. "Well...I never said it would stop them."

"Spread out!" Cae shouted as he drew his bow. "Isi, I want you on the water, we need to stop that contamination from spreading! Iómi, see if you can get those guys to turn around!"

"On it!"

"Alec, Alahir, you're with me. We're taking the devil out, here and now!"

Alec nodded, and he whipped Katei into a sprint. The company fanned out, and the letchya twisted its head toward the approaching crew. With another series of shorter screeches, the corpses turned and began shambling out of the water.

Cae and Alahir screamed over the water and rocketed toward the winged horror. Three arrows whistled through the air and grazed the letchya's wing, and Cae launched himself from Alahir's back, Sal'tera drawn and singing through the air as lightning exploded across the sky.

As Katei skidded to a halt at the water's edge, Alec sprung from the horse's back, his form scattering and swirling into a mist as he soared across the river, reforming at the letchya's flank.

A flash, and a tearing sound, and Alec's rapier had pieced the skin of the devil's wing, drawing a shriek from the creature. Sal'tera swirled around Caeleen's form as he leapt up onto the beast's back, Alahir screeching and pushing from overhead. The letchya dug its claws into the dirt and, out of its maw, shot a bolt of white light, dashing across the eagle's chest, and bringing him crashing to the ground.

Iómi and Whiskey advanced on the incoming horde, and Iómi spread her hands out wide. A blackish-greenish haze poured out from her hands as she growled, and the fog washed over the first waves of undead. The bodies stopped for a moment, the bodies behind them pushing and moaning against the barrier of rotting flesh. After a moment, the halted bodies began to glow ever-so-faintly silver for just a moment, and they at once turned, and began clawing at the rest of the horde.

Iómi screamed, forcing her will into the bodies as they fought. Her gaze lingered on the fringe of the horde, picking up any of the letchya's bodies as they fell. Whiskey swirled all round the Necromancer, a cyclone of smoke as Iómi wielded her magic. Dozens, then hundreds, of bodies under her command.

Never before had she worked on this scale, even in the graveyard outside of Brookridge. Her mind spread across the riverside, hundreds of her fingers and teeth tearing into noxious flesh, a sickly groan spilling and sputtering out of hundreds of her throats as she clawed back at her enemy. For each body she tore down, she felt the agony of rotted hands rend another body of hers to pieces. The letchya's corpses were clever, clever enough to identify her hosts before they attacked.

Kill, Iómi ordered through a haze of pain. *Take them all until there is only you.*

Isi splashed into the waters downstream from the

fighting and clutched her amulet. Squeezing her eyes shut, she poured her magic out into the water, felt it spread like fire across the expanse from bank to bank around her. Already, the fetid blood of countless bodies was streaming toward her. At once, the priestess set to burning the plague away as it came, leaving the waters clear and clean. More and more blood came, and more and more she destroyed it. Her eyes squeezed shut as she recited her prayer faster and faster.

The letchya thrashed its tail against Caeleen, the holy blade in the Ranger's hands tracing a line of red across the appendage. Alec cracked his whip across the creature's face, scattering a handful of teeth across the ground. Alahir tore at the devil's shoulder with his beak, latching onto its body with his talons. The letchya screeched again and scattered its assailants with a mighty beat from its bleeding wings. Caeleen bound back onto the creature, a trail of electricity dancing off of Sal'tera as he ran. The letchya slashed at him with its claws, its leathery wings sending waves of wind around as it attacked. Caeleen dipped and dove around each swing, and he aimed his blade for the beast's chest.

"Uro!!"

The sound of thunder deafened the company for a moment as white light blinded both them and the horde. When sight returned to them, the letchya had fallen about twenty yards away. Its chest was blistered and smoking, and it trembled as it rose to its feet, but its eyes fixed then upon the Ranger.

"That blade... Its magic does not belong in your hands." Despite the mangled state of its face, the devil's voice was as clear as it ever was. "It shall please my Emperor when I present it to him... Along with your head."

"Oh, for Seven's sake," Cae groaned, his knees shaking. "Why aren't you dead yet?"

"Cae, look out!"

Cae turned at the sound of Iómi's call just in time to see a wave of undead streaming toward him.

He threw his sword back up, attempting to hold back the tide of bodies with broad swipes, but his strength was spent. The sheer force of the dead bowled him over, and a sea of festering hands clawed at him, tearing his coat and clawing at his skin. He could just barely hear the screams of his companions over the cacophony of moans and hisses.

Caeleen clawed desperately at the rotted bodies weighing him down, trying to lift himself up high enough to escape or at least breathe, but the dead held him down as rotten teeth attempted to sink into his flesh.

Sal'tera fell from his hand.

Krak.

Caeleen felt a bit of weight on his chest dissipate as a few of the bodies atop him crumbled to dust.

Krak.

The whip. Alec. He was there now, dashing the bodies asunder, trying to free him.

Krak.

It would not be enough. So many dead were already upon him.

Krak.

He could feel tears upon tears in his skin, seeping hot fluid into the earth beneath him.

Krak.

Sal'tera leapt back into his hand.

Krak.

"*Kän.*"

Boom.

In an instant, Caeleen was on his feet again, the dead scattered yards away, all around, clawing back onto their feet. The air around sizzled with electricity, sparks of it, dancing about the Ranger's body. Lightning. He'd been struck by lightning. No, more than that, he had *summoned* it. Not from his own strength, but from the air. Whatever Shizame Bakh had done to Sal'tera, it had opened up a wealth of possibilities. Caeleen could feel it all, brushing the very edge of his imagination. How much more could he do with this power?

The dead were advancing again, tearing forth on hand and foot. Cae was still losing blood fast. He clenched his teeth; he wouldn't have time to heal himself before they were upon him. He would have to deal with them first and seal up his wounds after the dead were gone. He reached out in his mind for something, anything, to help him beat the horde back...

"*Tuu'lákra!*"

Caeleen felt the electricity light up his veins. His eyes widened; all at once, the waves of bodies seemed to slow to a crawl. He looked into the air and saw Alec creeping inch-by-inch through the air, his whip slowly trailing behind him. The Ranger gripped the holy blade in both hands and charged. With one swing, a clap of thunder scattered five bodies into the air. He swung again, sending another two spraying into the sea of dead. Caeleen lashed out like a gale, swinging his blade harder and faster than he had ever done before.

Soon enough, the world slowly crept back to its normal speed. Cae had done well enough thinning the number of corpses, but he was overrun once more. Back under the bodies he went but, this time he was charged, full of thunder and life. Caeleen scrambled his way out of the pile and gasped fresh air as Alec whirled about, his long whip swirling and glowing bright orange like a tongue of flame. The dead flocked for Alec then, trying to overwhelm him with sheer numbers. They could not; the swordsman's own magical speed kept the dead from ever touching him.

Caeleen drew his bow and set his sight on the letchya. He had to kill this devil, here and now, before it could gather another army. He took ten arrows in hand, more than he'd ever held at once, and opened fire, roaring out his frustration as he fired. The arrows let out white light as they streaked through the air, discharging the lightning in Caeleen's body as he fired. The solid *thk-thk-thk* of arrows filled the air as the archer pelted the winged thing with shots. One shot took out an eye, one shot pinned an ear to its head, and several shots pierced the melting flesh of its chest.

The letchya growled. "Another day, then." Without another word, the beast beat hard with its leathery, blood-soaked wings, wheeled northward into the sky, and vanished. What corpses remained untaken by Iómi dropped then, cold and unmoving, to the ground.

Cae sucked down several ragged breaths. With the sudden burst of magic strength spent, Caeleen holstered his bow and leaned heavily on Sal'tera, using the holy longsword like a cane as he hobbled over to where the letchya had just been standing.

"We can't follow him now," Alec called. "You're in no condition to be working."

"I'll be fine."

"Oh, come here." Isi trudged out of the water, her robes soaking wet. "You're bleeding everywhere, those corpses probably gave you hand-rot."

"... Yeah, okay."

Caeleen sank to his knees and fell into the Cleric's arms. The Priestess's hands hovered over Caeleen's body, bathing him in golden light and sealing up the holes and bite marks covering his arms and legs. One particularly nasty tear on his right breast took longer to seal, and it left a gnarly scar.

"How did you do that?" Iómi asked, her and Whiskey lighting down from across the river. "You were moving fast. Like, stupid-fast."

Cae shook his head, the absence of magic (and blood, frankly) leaving him dizzy. "I took the sword to these Druids up in the Ías. They... I dunno, they did something to it."

Alec peered down at the Ranger, his eyes narrowed. "We should take a day, rest up. Nightsister, I'm sure you're probably tired after taking that many bodies."

"Nah, I'm good, I'm..." Iómi looked back to the other side of the river where a sizable mob of undead stood quietly, awaiting her mental orders. With a wave of her hand, the bodies dropped to the ground, once more at rest. With her other hand, she wiped a thin layer of sweat from her brow, only then noticing the wet hair matted to her forehead. "... Yeah, you might be right, actually."

Cae sat up from Isi's arms and sniffed at the air, wincing as he picked up an odd scent. Looking down at the grass, he could see in the crushed and clawed ground where the letchya had been, there were blackened spots in the grass like scorch-marks around the indent of its prints. Reaching out and running a finger along them, Cae found the scorch marks ice-cold.

Alec cocked a brow. "What do you smell?"

"It... stinks. It smells like..." Cae sniffed again, and he frowned. "It's faint, but it smells like sulfur."

"Most demons do," Alec replied. "It's unfortunate you're not a bloodhound, we might be able to tail it."

"We don't need a bloodhound. I can track a hydra by the smell of its venom, I'll be able to track the letchya."

"Oh? Well...that's impressive." Alec let out a short laugh. "If that's the case, we... actually do need to get back on the move soon before the scent fades."

"I agree," said Alahir, stepping forward. "I can carry us in the scent's direction, if need be. Have the wraith and the horse follow me, and Caeleen and I can lead the way."

"Will you be able to hold the scent like that?" asked Isi.

"I imagine it will be similar to following the trail of a draconid," said the eagle. "A creature of that size with a scent that particular will leave spoor in the air as it flies."

"We used to do it all the time back in the Dokk," said Cae. "We can..."

Alec held up a finger. A single flake of snow dropped down onto Alahir's beak.

As the Great Eagle shook the frost from his face, more snow began to drift down upon them.

Alec frowned as he stared up into the sky.

"Can you track the scent through snow?" asked the stranger.

Cae grimaced. "Not so easy, not by itself..." he mumbled. "But we roughed him up pretty well. He's still bleeding. If we can catch scent of the blood trail before the snow covers it, we might have a chance."

"Cae, you're in no condition to be chasing after anything right now," said Isi.

"On foot, of course not. But I can ride. If we work quick, I can tail it."

"I'm with Cae, actually," Iómi said. "We want to catch it before it can patch itself up and pull more bodies."

Cae pushed himself up onto his feet and shuffled back toward the water. Katei waited on the other bank, lapping at the water. Out of his bag, the Ranger produced a strip of dried meat, tearing at it with his teeth. He was still dizzy, but he couldn't let that matter right now. At the moment, that devil was the only lead he had. He would find it, stop the incursion, lead a company into Creddon to take the Rose, and then go home to Laithe... to Evenwood. Ven was right, he needed to see his mother.

11

*L*eon nursed his wine, the mix of cinnamon and warm drink almost too sweet in his mouth. *Perhaps,* he thought, *this is why Caeleen doesn't drink.*

His eyes darted about to the other patrons in the Blue Cup. There were quite a few folks in the tavern, even for the time of day, and they all seemed... shaken. Most of them, Leon noted, looked to be maotu. The distinctions between the merfolk and humans were barely noticeable, but Leon's eyes picked up the way they seemed to glide across the room as if drifting through invisible water, and the way they rubbed and scratched at their skin.

They looked scared, and they had every reason to be; the young Ranger had heard about what happened when Caeleen came through a few days ago. He'd heard about the strange bat-creature and its horde of dead, how they spilled their rot all over the fields of valkospi just outside the edge of town. Leon turned his nose when he smelled the stench on his way in, and saw where the villagers had been digging up the crops and burning them.

Leon didn't like just up and leaving the town, but there would be time to return and help out later. All he needed for now was a heading, and he had one. Truth be told, he didn't even need to ask; on his way into town, he saw the broad trail of trampled grass headed southwest. That was enough for him, but he had to be sure that was where Cae was going.

Sure enough, the old man in the Temple confirmed it. "The man in white with the sword of thunder," he'd said, "followed the dead and their wings." Leon wondered to himself what it was about sages and their like that made them speak in that sing-song voice, but he wasn't going to risk offending the priest by asking. Besides, surely someone had written a book on it somewhere, it was only a matter of time before it wound up in one of the dusty old bookshops in Greyfort.

Leon didn't finish his drink before he left the Cup, mounted Buck and took off after the trail. Buck wasn't as fast as Tüli had been, but he could still make excellent time. Before the sun had set, and the snow began piling onto the ground, Leon could see where the trail of crushed earth halted at the banks of Siahra's River. Leon rode closer to the water's edge and looked closely. It surprised him to find that, though the ground all around the water was full of dried and rotted flesh, the water ran clear as crystal. He'd seen this kind of purification before; Isi kept the Grey River free of contaminants with her holy magic. With any luck, she was there as well.

Leon ran his hands over his coat, and he could feel

tiny sparks of static tickle his palm. Like the thunderous breath of a blue draconid, Sal'tera's magic often left the surrounding air charged with electricity. It was a subtle tell, not one that would be easy to pick up on if you didn't know to look for it, but Leon had used this trail to find his way back to Caeleen when they got separated during some of their more harrowing hunts.

Sweeping the area, Leon found a faint trail of that static heading north. Leon frowned as he thought through what might have happened. Perhaps Cae and his company hadn't brought down their prey yet.

Why were Cae and his company headed north, though? What would be waiting for them in the Ías? Leon mulled over this question grumpily as he shivered on Buck's back, riding hard after the trail northward.

SIAHRA GRIMACED ON HER ALABASTER THRONE, HER eyes focused on the targe suspended in the air before her. Her Knights had gathered around her, and they also kept their eyes on the cursed shield before them. Even now, contained by Temui's magic, it exuded an air that made the warriors gathered in the throne room shift uncomfortably in their seats.

Ta Pohaka, one of the Council's Sentinels, stood up from his seat. "It's uh... it's a little small, isn't it?"

"Small for one of your vocation, certainly," said Temui, not taking his eyes from the shield. "But for a common soldier or commander, it's fairly average."

"Why does it have shackles?" Kepa asked.

"It's part of the curse," Siahra answered. "You try to use the shield, the shackles latch onto your arm."

"Then what?"

"Well...last time someone tried it, Temui nearly got himself killed."

"Ah..." Kepa frowned. "Well, I assume this person is..."

"Very dead, yes," said Temui. "Unfortunate business, but it was him or me."

Pohaka crept closer, leaning in and peering intently at the eye emblazoned on the targe's surface. "I've never seen this crest. Who do we think made it?"

"We don't know," said Siahra.

"All we know is their magic is especially powerful," said Temui. "We suspect the use of blood magic, but I don't want to jump to any conclusions."

Burúm's hands gripped his spear a little tighter. "Blood magic...disgusting."

Eldur looked uneasily at his fellow Dragoon, seeing faint sparks of electricity dance along his weapon. "Easy, *veno*..."

Siahra stood, taking her father's glaive in hand. "Let's go over everything else we know so far... Rakau and I found this shield in Creddon, in the remnants of an old basement."

"If it was in Creddon, it must not be too much trouble," Kepa suggested. "No one has lived in Creddon for generations."

"One person has." Siahra frowned as she turned to Kepa. "We discovered that that's where the Wild Rose has been hiding."

Kua'topa shot up from his seat then, his hefty plate rattling as he did so. "We've had his location this whole time?"

Siahra nodded. "We're taking a legion down that way to deal with him."

"Why haven't we just handled it already?" asked Pohaka. "He might be famous, but he's one man. He can't possibly be that powerful."

Siahra shook her head. "He killed Kéldi before we even realized he was nearby. He couldn't even cry out to warn us... I kept this from you all because I need you all alive. I'm sorry for not telling you everything, but this is where we're at right now."

The room fell quiet at the mention of the fallen drake. Kéldi had been widely respected throughout Twipari since forming his bond with Siahra. He'd become a symbol for the city, a testament to their resilience against the more dangerous forces they contended with. It was sobering to remember that he had fallen, but moreso jarring to know just how it had happened.

One man. That had been all it took.

"So..." Temui broke the silence as he waved a hand, sending the shield off to the side. "What is our next move, my Queen?"

Siahra looked down at the King's glaive. It would need to accompany her, but... it was not her weapon. She furrowed her brow as she looked to her Dragoons. "If I am to lead this attack, I will need a new drake."

Eldur's brow rose. "Are you certain?"

"No, not about anything," said the Queen. "But that's

not important. What matters is the work."

Eldur nodded. "I will ready the thunder for your ceremony."

"Thank you, Har Eldur." Siahra sat back down on the Alabaster Throne. "If it's all the same to you, friends, I need some time alone now. I have a lot to think about."

One by one, each of the Knights gathered there stood, bowed before their Queen, and made their way out of the room.

Siahra waited until all of them had left, then bent over in her seat and buried her face in her hands. Gods help her, how was she going to do this? Taking another drake seemed an impossible task by itself. But leading this attack? So soon after Kéldi's fall? It was laughable. She was just a child, for Seven's sake, she knew she couldn't.

And yet, it seemed, she had to. What choice did she have? Siahra was a queen, the great defender of the Tamian people, of all the maotu. That had to take precedence. The people come first, always. And this is what the people need right now.

Alone there on her throne, Siahra let herself weep for a while.

* * *

A murder of crows called out from the snow-blanketed trees as the company rode up to the first rocks and hills of the Ías Fuil. Cae pulled his cloak tighter around him on Alahir's back as they stood atop a large boulder, waiting for their companions. Whiskey could check her speed and keep pace with Katei, but Alahir did not have quite as much control over the speed at which the wind carried him. As such, the Whisper and Wing took on a familiar role, scouting ahead for their companions.

Aside from the occasional vagrants they could avoid, and the game they were able to swoop down and take with Alahir's claws, the rolling hills of northern Tamia were quiet in the few days they had been traveling. Even the animals had grown scarce, as if something were telling them to hide from the coming darkness. Only the largest of creatures still roamed the wilds, save for the occasional deer. Cae found it suspicious, in fact, seeing wild game about at a time like this. Was Kh'anora watching over them, placing food in their path? Maybe.

After a time, the others caught up to the Ranger and his Eagle. Cae hopped down from Alahir's back and curled further into his cloak, the snow having piled up high enough to reach his ankles. "We'll be in the Maples pretty soon," he said through his shivers. "Show of hands, how many of us have actually been up here before?"

Alec raised his hand, and Isi shrugged, wiggling her hand in the air for a moment. "I was here for a bit back in the day, don't really remember too much of it. I helped the Biesann orcs tend to their wounds after the War."

"I heard about them," said Cae. "They were at the Battle of Dane. Baron told me Clover was there, heard he did a real number on 'em."

"You've met one," Isi added. "He was at the Battle for Fartide. Chieftain Brok'kan."

"The leader?"

"All the orcs there were Biesann."

"Huh. Well...now I feel a little ignorant."

Isi shrugged. "But yes, Clover offered his aid in rebuilding as well, as a way of making amends for his role in their suffering. He did what he could, but..."

"But the Empire left a lot of bodies behind," said Alec. "So did the Clans, though. Kind of how war works, I suppose. Everyone is a villain to someone."

Cae frowned. "Either way, there may be some Biesann up ahead. With any luck, we might can get them to help us."

"Worth a shot," Alec replied. "Shall we get going?"

Cae nodded, mounting Alahir once more and taking to the air. The smell of sulfur was faint, but he still had it. Gently steering his avian brother with hands and knees buried in his feathers, Caeleen allowed his nose to guide him higher and northward toward the frost-covered Ías Fuil. He could see Frostdrake Mountain looming ahead, a titan of earth and ice splitting the western end of the continent the same way Ruin's Peak did in the east.

Legend held that Frostdrake was home to the Udásíaki, one of the most powerful silver dragons in all the realms. Stories said that the Udásíaki's ancestors were so great and terrible in their might, their bodies turned to frost and stone, forming the mountains themselves. Cae read the story time and again growing up... mostly out of spite. He dreamt of being the one to slay the Udásíaki when he was grown.

Cae looked toward the peak of Frostdrake and grimaced. Circling the peak were two-winged shapes. "Alahir, heads up. Those things..."

"One is the letchya," the Eagle said. "The other... the other is..."

"What?"

"... I'm not sure. It's too small to be a roc, but... it's fairly large. Larger than me."

"You're right. We've seen dragons that size..." Cae frowned. "Should we close the distance? See if we can catch them off-guard?"

"No, we shouldn't go in alone. We don't know what it is, so we don't know how best to approach it."

Cae grinned. "I missed you, Alahir. I needed you to be my impulse control."

Alahir chuckled quietly as he turned in the air, making his way back toward their companions.

In a moment, the company had found themselves in something of a light forest at the base of the mountains. The snow was falling harder than it had before. They knew it would be a danger to take to the air at this point. Until it let up, Alahir was grounded. The great eagle grumbled as he trudged along. The poor thing was slow on his feet, and he wasn't particularly fond of the cold on his talons.

The trail into the mountains would have been long and trying even were it not covered in a sheet of white. More than once, Caeleen wandered from the path for a moment before he realized the snow beneath him had reached nearly to the tops of his boots. He did his best to conceal his violent shivering, but every now and again he could see Alec the stranger glancing over at him from the corner of his eye.

Cae grimaced, and his curiosity about this viltar

continued to eat at him through the numbness the cold brought to his head. The frost was clearly setting into all of their bones... but not Alec's. Not even his teeth chattered, from what Cae could see in the thickening snowfall.

After a few more hours, it seemed the heavy powder that battered Caeleen's body had left him tired. No, more than tired. He was drained. It frustrated him to no end. Though they all slowed in the harsh weather, each of them had something to keep them moving. Isi had the light of Silvia to hold her up, Iómi had her sorcery and her wraith protecting her from the elements, and Alec still seemed somehow immune to the cold. Only Caeleen and Alahir seemed to take the full weight of the frost. Cae needed desperately to lie down, to take a moment to just rest his bones. His muscles ached with every stumbling step, and it was a fight to keep his sight from fading into a complete blur.

Another step, and Cae felt himself lurch forward, the snow rushing up to break his fall. Instead, he felt an arm catch him and haul him back to his feet. Isi frowned at him and slipped his arm across her shoulders. As he turned to look, Iómi and Alahir both watched intently, their eyes displaying an intense worry. Had they been calling for him? He couldn't be sure; even Isi's voice seemed distant. Alec watched as well, but his gaze wasn't so much concerned as it was curious. Caeleen meant to ask what he was so curious about, but the words didn't come.

At some point, the company hunkered down and made a fire. Caeleen rested in the warm cover of Alahir's feathers, and weakly nibbled at a bit of salted deer. All of them huddled together in the eagle's side, with Iómi and Alec taking shifts on the fire. They kept it low enough that Iómi could hide their smoke with her magic and hopefully keep their quarry, or any other unfriendly eyes, unaware of their presence. Unfortunately, this also kept the warmth of the fire from doing as much good as it could.

Dark settled in oppressively around them that night. Caeleen passed into sleep soon after they settled. He woke twice in the night. The first time had been when the warmth of Volok's pendant alerted him to... something nearby. The fire had died out, leaving the Whisper in total darkness. He couldn't see, or smell, anything out of the ordinary near them, and there was little he could hear at all under the winds that had picked up in the night. He felt Alahir stir over him, and he knew the eagle had woken up with him. With a tired hand, Caeleen reached over and pressed a message into the thick of Alahir's feathers with their ancestor's code: *danger?*

Alahir rustled the feathers of his neck in response: *unsure.*

Caeleen furrowed his brow. *Eyes out.*

Alahir rustled. *No. Rest.*

Cae sighed. He knew the great bird was right. *Alert?*

Another rustle. *Alert.*

Cae nestled into Isi's back and shut his eyes. Alahir would wake him if an enemy came.

The next time he woke, Cae knew he was the only one awake. Someone had rekindled the fire in the night. He knew not how at first, considering no one had stirred enough to rouse him, but his answer sat on the other side of the fire. A familiar brown horse, with a green cloak huddled up beside it.

Thank Seven, Leon had made it. That meant Mull had received his letter. The boy had probably come by way of magic, sent by Magus Bellam straight to Siahra...

Siahra. Gods, he missed her. He prayed that she was staying strong in the face of everything happening, especially this confounded quarantine. Fartide seemed a world away now. The dark seemed to cut him off from every realm there ever was. Would he ever make it back to Fartide? Would he ever see Evenwood again?

Would the sun even come up in the morning?

Cae tried to put these worries out of his mind, curling back up into sleep.

He awoke the next morning to the sound of clashing steel.

He jolted up, his strength restored. Leon had out a pair of shortswords, and Alec flourished his rapier. The viltar lunged forward, all thrusts and flash, and Leon ducked and batted each swipe aside. Alec melted into mist and swept around, appearing behind the young Ranger. Before Leon could turn to face him, a boot of supple black leather kicked the boy to the ground. Alec chuckled, his blade poised to pierce the boy's heart.

Caeleen reached for his bow and tried to draw a shot, but his fingers were still numb with cold. "S-stop..." he moaned, the bow falling from his hands.

Alec and Leon turned to the weak voice, halting at once.

"Morning, Rakau," said Alec. "Good to see you're awake."

"What...what are you d-doing...?" Caeleen asked.

"It's okay, Cae!" said Leon. "We were just sparring. It's fine, everything's fine."

Cae looked over at Leon, blinked a few times, and at last let out a sigh. "Don't scare me like that when I first wake up... Gods..." the older Ranger hauled himself to his feet, shuffled across the little camp, and threw his arms around his old squire. "Bless you, kid. Thank f-Fates you made it."

Leon squeezed his old teacher tight. "Anytime you need me, Sir."

Cae pulled away and frowned. "Hey, look... I'm sorry I skipped out without saying goodbye. It's been... it's been a confusing few months."

"Don't worry about it," Leon replied. "You've had a lot going on... Sorry to hear about Tüli, by the way."

"Thanks... it's been rough."

Alahir stirred awake then, rising up to his feet and shaking off the snow from his form. "Seems the weather is letting up." Through the trees, the eagle could see dark clouds still covered the sky, but the snow had finally ceased. "Whisper, perhaps we could take back to the air? Do some proper scouting ahead?"

"Let me, uhh... let me warm up a little first." Cae shuffled back over to the great bird, but then stopped. "Where are the girls?"

"The Cleric went off to find firewood, and the Necromancer went along with her." Alec shook out his cloak. "... those two are awfully close."

Cae nodded. "They h... they hit it off pretty well back in the day. When we all first met." The Ranger squatted down before the remnants of Leon's fire and produced a flint and firesteel from his bag.

Alec held up a hand to stop him, and with a snap of the viltar's fingers, the fire sparked back to life. Cae let out a sigh and rubbed his hands together before the flame, letting the warmth spread feeling back into his fingers and joints. As the chill lifted from him, his muscles began to ache, at which he smiled; the pain was preferable to the numbness, especially in this cold.

Alec watched the flames with a curious look in his eye. "The Silvian... how old is she?"

"A little over eight hundred, I think... Why?"

"I thought maybe I recognized her. Is she native to Cidarian?"

"Yeah... I'm not sure what part, though. Never asked."

Alec nodded and said nothing more. Cae furrowed his brow as he leaned back, Alahir settling down behind him. "Why does it matter wuh... where she's from, though?"

"It doesn't, I was just curious... she's quite powerful, I can feel the Light radiating off of her."

Cae nodded, tracing the scar on his cheek. "She's been there for me... I trust her with my life."

Alec nodded, then turned and gazed back into the forest. "We're not too far from Dane now. Maybe three days out, four, at the latest. Let me scout ahead, see if I can find the girls and send them back. Even with you in your current condition, we don't have time to stay here another night." He turned then to Leon, who had pulled out a pouch of herbs from his own magic bag. "Don't let him get up. Keep him warm, try to treat him, and wait here until I return."

Leon arched a brow, but he nodded. Alec turned and melted into a mist, and he whirled off into the woods.

* * *

"In the sight of Xanith, the great Mother of the Sky, let this child take wing!"

Siahra stood, shivering atop the highest tower of the Alabaster Palace, the icy wind threatening to blow her across the floor. Gathered around were Eldur and Burúm, along with all of Twipari's drakes. Siahra had been here before, had performed this ritual once already. A new Dragoon stood amidst a flight of drakes and form a bond with one of them. The drake would wreath the Dragoon in their flame, and from the flame would form the dragonspear.

Siahra remembered how awestruck she had been undergoing the ceremony the first time. To be named worthy of the magic bond between drake and rider was a powerful experience, one that opened her mind and helped her realize her worth both as warrior and queen.

But, when she stood in the midst of the drake flight this second time, the moment rang hollow. She wore the same ceremonial leather garb she had worn when she bonded with Kéldi, now charred and blackened form exposure to his flames, but with a word etched into the breast. *Maéste*. The word was Udán, meaning "lost."

Burúm bore three such markings on his armor. One marking for each drake he had previously flown with.

Siahra swept her eyes across the flight of creatures gathered around her. They watched curiously as she kept her arms tightly crossed and her head down. She was not quite bothered by the cold wind, the dragonfire inside of her saw to that. But she was not exactly comfortable. Standing there among those wise creatures, creatures who had known Kéldi long before she had... she couldn't help but wonder if they suspected her. She wondered if they blamed her for what happened to their friend... maybe because she still blamed herself. She wasn't sure.

One by one, each drake gathered met her eyes. One by one, each drake turned away. Part of Siahra was relieved. Part of her did not want another drake. To discard the bond she had made with Kéldi in such a way... part of her was pushing them away.

At the same time, though... would Kéldi want this? Would he want her to hide away when her people needed her the most? She thought not. Kéldi understood what Siahra was, what she had to be. The maotu people needed her. She hadn't realized it before but, perhaps, that was part of a drake's duty. To raise the Udári up and make them what they needed to be.

Maybe she was reading too much into it, but she couldn't deny that she had become better for meeting Kéldi. She had to stay that way. She had to be strong, for his sake as much as for Tamia's.

She turned and met the eyes of another drake. This one was female, having a broader wingspan than the males gathered there. She would be faster. Her scales were a light green that seemed to fade to red at their tips, and her eyes were sparkling ruby. The other drakes stepped back then, and this drake stepped forward.

"*Böth napen fe,*" said Siahra. She reached out with a hand wreathed in her blue dragonfire and placed it against the drake's cheek.

The drake eyed her for a moment, then nodded. "*Gershi.*"

Gershi stood tall then. The blue flames from Siahra's hand rested on her cheek. Her eyes flashed as she drew in a long breath. The other drakes leapt into the air and began circling overhead, and Gershi's flames bathed Siahra in emerald light.

The Diamond Queen squeezed her eyes shut, falling to her knees and clenching her fists. Gershi's fire was intense, just as hot as Kéldi's had been. This drake was strong, in her prime. She would serve well. The flames swirled all about Siahra, and with her hands the maotu began to form a shape in the flames. The fire coalesced in her hands, shrank down and concentrated there, solidifying into its new form.

Then all was quiet. Siahra opened her eyes to see the drakes all eyeing her grimly. Burúm and Eldur nodded, but she could see frowns beneath their mighty dragonhelms. She looked up at Gershi, whose eyes spoke understanding alongside sadness. She looked down at the weapon she had crafted...

A shortspear.

Siahra sighed. She should have known she wouldn't be able to make another full spear yet. Not so soon after losing her last drake. The shortspear would do its job, but she couldn't help feeling that pang of disappointment. The bond between Siahra and Gershi was incomplete. And she knew exactly why.

"*Zir-ik Kéldi, Udári,*" Gershi said, "*on Zin filg mefi.*"

Siahra bowed, tracing a line between the two of them with the new spear. The line burned with the Diamond Queen's blue flame, and Gershi scraped the line away with her wings, enveloping them both in flames of green.

"Let these two become one!" Burúm bellowed. "May their wings protect this land until the end of their days!"

Siahra looked out at the drakes circling overhead. Some of them peered down at the pair with grim eyes, but Siahra ignored them. This work needed to be done. The Oceanguard were preparing for their march on Creddon even now, a day before their departure. The Wild Rose would die. He had to die.

Siahra pressed her forehead to Gershi's. The drake wrapped her wings around the Queen. It was not just an embrace, Siahra realized, but a shield. She remembered then what Gershi meant in the Dragon-Tongue.

Mother.

* * *

"Guys, can we talk for a minute? We need to... I have something to say."

Alahir turned his head to Caeleen and nodded. Leon looked up from the tea he'd been preparing. Leon thought Cae might have a fever after looking over him, and so he'd decided on a tea with coriander and fairybloom to help fight the sickness and restore some of his energy.

"I just... people keep saying something to me that's been bugging me." The young knight leaned up against a tree and crossed his arms. "I... I haven't been checking in at home enough."

Alahir let out a sigh. This was true; Caeleen had hardly even visited his home village since he'd come home with Priestess Rumoré. "Yes...I meant to ask you about this when you came home two Frostpeaks ago."

"Your sister has been asking about you," Leon added. "Since you left for Tamia, she calls in every now and again to see if I've heard from you."

Cae frowned. "I just... things have been really weird for me lately, and I have a lot on my—"

"Caeleen."

Cae stopped and looked up at his eagle. He knew it was time to come clean. Cae could not lie to Alahir. He looked down at his feet, his fingers clutching the sleeves of his coat and his arms pulled in tighter to his body. "... When we got home, and we fixed what was wrong with Ma... I went to visit Pa while I was home. Had a heart-to-heart."

Leon turned away. He couldn't help but feel that this was a discussion the bird and rider needed to have to themselves. Caeleen rarely spoke to Leon about his father. He knew the man had been a great Ranger of the Dokk, and that he died killing a dragon, but other than that... it wasn't really his place.

Alahir's eyes softened. "What did you say?"

Cae paused for just a moment. He'd done his best to

bury the thought of it away in the back of his mind, but... "I told him I had to leave. I told him I couldn't stay home any longer." He reached out to the side then and wrapped his fingers around Sal'tera. "This sword... this sword revealed itself to me for a reason. I know it did."

Alahir looked down at the holy blade still resting in its sheath. The great bird had little understanding of the ways of magic weapons or destinies, but he could feel something there. Something was oddly alive about the blade his Whisper now wielded. "You believe the blade chose you, then?"

"No. Not...maybe. I dunno, it..." Cae pulled the sword into his lap, holding it in both hands. "I'm sure it could have been somebody else, anybody else, who could have taken it. But I was there, and I fit the part it needed. Sal'tera has... it's meant for something greater. But a sword needs a wielder."

Leon continued to stir the tea. "That's why you left the Dokk?"

Cae nodded. "I... I wanted to stay. There's nothing I..." He cut himself off. That would have been a lie. There was still one thing he wanted more. But... best to leave it be. "... I wanted to stay home so bad. Believe me, I did."

Alahir's eyes focused on the sword. "But you serve a higher purpose now. You serve the God of the Forest."

Cae stared at the jade-laden guard of the weapon. His fingers tightened around the leather sheath. "... I hate this sword."

Leon looked up then. "What?"

"Yes, I do." Cae felt a tear sting his eye. "I hate it. I

don't want to be some chosen warrior, or some folk hero like Mull made me out to be." His hands trembled, and he wiped his tears away with his sleeve. "I don't want to be the Boltwalker anymore... I want to go home."

A quiet fell over the camp then. Leon poured a mug of tea for Cae in silence, and the older Ranger drank slowly. The tea was warm and citrusy, but he could taste the bite of fairybloom underneath. Fairybloom tasted vile and bitter, but it did its job. It wasn't long afterward before Caeleen was back on his feet, tending to the holy blade. He couldn't help feeling a little awkward about it then. He'd never spoken aloud how he felt about Sal'tera, and yet it was so imperative that he take care of it.

What was left of him now without it? He still had Gem'shil, and it wasn't as if he could never go back to a steel blade. But the magic coursing through him, the magic now keeping him on his feet, came from the Bolt of Peace. He was of more use to everyone with Sal'tera.

And yet...and yet.

The others returned soon after. Isi and Iómi carried bundles of firewood in their arms, and Alec had scrawled out a map of the township ahead onto parchment. Alec had found no hindrances on their path to the town, but he was still troubled. Evidently, the letchya had made a few passes overhead and had its sights set on the town.

Cae grimaced at the thought. They couldn't let the town fall to the devil's magic. It didn't take much talk to prepare everyone to head that way.

Three or four days. They had to hurry.

12

"*Y*ou called for me, *fidas*?"

Siahra looked up from her desk to see Lady Suressa walk into her study. She smiled and gestured for her cousin to sit, which she did.

"Suressa... do you remember my mother?"

Suressa nodded. "I do. Not much, but I remember she was kind. Gentle, but... strong. Unyielding."

Siahra looked down at her desk. She put her quill and ink aside, and she ran a finger along the edge of the parchment upon which she'd been writing. "I remember yours."

"I'm afraid I don't," Suressa replied. "Everyone is always quick to tell me how kind she was, how she adored me..."

"She did," Siahra said, "but she was so vicious in some ways. I always admired her for it. She could have been the chief Mo-Lamai, were she not—"

"Not a siren?"

"Not a royal..." Siahra frowned. "But, yes, that, too."

Suressa looked down at her hands, her fingers running nervously along her fins. "Forgive me, fidas, I didn't mean to..."

"Don't apologize for the truth, Suressa." Siahra replied. "Never again."

Suressa tilted her head to one side. "Cousin, what is it you called me here for?"

Siahra gripped her hands tightly together on her desk. "I've been... ever since things started happening around here, I realized that I needed to prepare for the worst-case. I am my father's daughter as much as my mother's, and I am an Udári. I will not sit idly by as my knights and soldiers carry out my will throughout my kingdom. I will lead the Oceanguard to Creddon to destroy the Wild Rose."

Suressa frowned. "Your Grace, do you...I feel perhaps that... do you think, perhaps, this is too dangerous?"

"I do. I do not know if I will survive." Siahra slid the parchment across the desk to her cousin, who took the document and began to read over it. "If I do not return, I need someone I believe in on the throne."

Suressa's eyes widened. "Y...Your Grace, I don't know..."

"I do." Siahra stood. "You are more powerful than you give yourself credit for, Suressa. You are wise and kind, and you are strong. Stronger, perhaps, than me. You will make a fine Queen."

Suressa laid the parchment back on the desk and rose to her feet. "... I will sign this decree. But I pray to all the Gods that you survive. I do not know if I could lead these people."

"I was uncertain as well when I was crowned. Some days, most days even, I still am."

Suressa shook her head. "I... I do not want this."

"I know," Siahra replied, "and I hope you can forgive me for putting this on your shoulders. But that is why you will be a good Queen, should the need arise. The greatest rulers I've known have clung to their humility."

Siahra stood then, pulling her hair into a tail that she let run down her shoulder. Her eyes crackled with blue lightning for a moment, and from the corner she summoned Kéldi's spear to her. Suressa grimaced.

"This has to be done," the Queen said in response to one last unspoken protest.

Suressa sighed once more. "Just...just try not to die."

Siahra placed a hand on the siren's shoulder for just a moment before the two of them left the study.

In the armory, Siahra frowned as she looked at the resplendent, iridescent-white armor before her. The scales of Sturamtönn had never failed her yet. Every battle she wore them, her victory had been decisive. And it had seen many battles; her rule had kept her busy at far more than just rebuilding.

Her handmaidens were there then, and they helped her don her armor. Most days when they did this, they spoke with light hearts about the days to come, of festivals and gatherings, of their lessons and other duties throughout the capitol. But not today. Today the armory was quiet, save for the sound of scale clinking against scale, of belts tightening, of light mail rattling beneath and between the different pieces of the armor.

Siahra stepped forward once it was done, and she

fastened her long blue cape over her shoulders. It fluttered gently to the ground behind her and trailed along behind her as she walked. The armor was stiff at first, when she first began to wear it, but now she moved as effortlessly as if she were wearing a nightgown. She was an Udári, a mighty Dragoon, and she would do what needed to be done.

Gershi's shortspear hung from her hip. Over one shoulder she slung Kéldi's spear. One handmaiden carried her father's glaive, and another carried her trident.

Together, she walked with her girls through the halls of the Alabaster Palace and out to the gate where Gershi was waiting. They had armored the drake with the finest barding forged in the Makao-Toai, the plating a smooth silver-grey interspersed with swirls of white. She was laden down with her rider's arms, and Siahra climbed onto her back.

The Queen looked back at her faithful attendants, only for a moment. No words passed between them, but each beat of quiet hung heavy in the air. The Queen turned then, and drake and rider joined the other Udári in their procession through the streets of the capitol.

CAE RUBBED HIS HANDS TOGETHER AS HE WALKED, trying his best to get enough warmth in his fingers to restore their proper use. It was dreadful, and unusual, being so cold that he could barely use his hands and feet, and yet so dreadfully hot inside that he might drop at any moment. Leon had been right, he was definitely fighting a fever. He wished they had time for more of that coriander and fairybloom, but they had to move on.

Instead, he leaned into Isi's solid arm as he helped him fumble along through the snow. The powder itself was less of a problem now; it had occurred to Iómi to clear a bit of it away with her magic. Cae wanted to chew her out just a moment when she started, to ask her why she hadn't started doing that sooner. But, then, he hadn't thought of it either. Who was he to argue?

They were just hours outside of Dane now. On Alahir's back, Cae was certain he could be there before in mere moments. Unfortunately, the snow refused to let up, leaving the two of them utterly grounded. It was strange how sudden the storm had come in; it hadn't been that long ago that the air was clear, had it? Maybe...or maybe not. Cae wasn't so sure anymore.

The days were bleeding together. Everything was a bit of a haze with this fever, this ailment even Isi could not break. The worst part of it was that no one was certain what the affliction was. Isi had, at some point, wondered aloud if it was hand-rot from the mauling Cae had experienced at the river, but she was certain she burned the infection out of him already. After giving him another quick examination with her magic, Isi had concluded that the illness Cae was fighting was thoroughly unknown to her. She did comment on the fact that his chest was absolutely sweltering, hotter than even the poor Ranger's forehead, but Cae didn't notice. His body was cold and numb all over or, at least, it felt so to him.

"We should stop for a bit," he heard someone say. "Look at the Ranger, he's barely standing."

"We have to keep moving," Isi said, her voice muffled in Cae's ears. "Yes, he's sick, but Dane needs our help. Here, help me get him up onto the horse."

"They can wait another hour," the other voice said again. "One moment more won't kill them."

"It might."

"But it might not. But him? Look at him, he might be about to fall over dead right now."

Case felt jostled as Isi took him by the shoulders and stood him up straight. She held a hand to his forehead and grimaced. "... Fine. One hour."

Someone, Leon maybe, helped him down into a seated position against a tree. He reached for their hand, and held it for a moment, before it slipped away. He couldn't open his eyes any longer. He leaned his head against the tree and tried to sleep.

"...and scout ahead. The snow seems to be letting up."

"But what if he needs more medicine?"

"I'll watch him. It isn't that hard to make tea. Go on, be quick."

A sudden wind against his face. The sound of wings beating in the wintry air. Leon and Alahir were leaving. Who all was still here? Iómi and Isi were gone again, likely to gather wood for their fire again. Cae took labored breaths, his hands empty. He reached for Sal'tera and pulled the sword into his lap. Something about the blade's energy pushed a little more feeling back into his fingers.

"Wake up, Boltwalker. You need more tea."

Cae wasn't sure when he fell asleep, but he awoke to a warm cup of something being pushed into his hands. More tea. Fairybloom and coriander. His nose was weakened, but it still didn't lie. He sipped at the medicine, braced at the taste of fairybloom. His eyes crept open to find Alec kneeling in front of him.

"Hey..." he croaked. "How we doin'?"

"We'll be at Dane in the next few days," Alec said. "By then, we need you on your feet and ready to fight."

"I can be ready," Cae replied. "The sword..."

"I've heard about it, and I have to say... I don't like the sound of it." Alec gave a half-frown. "The sword draws on your strength to give you your powers. You have little strength left."

The viltar placed a hand over Cae's. Cae sucked in a sudden breath; Alec's hand was ice cold. Cae didn't think the weather was getting to him, but...

"You..." the Ranger struggled to form words. "You need t... tuhhh, tuh, t-to get warm."

"I'm fine," Alec replied. He threw his own cloak over the hunter.

"Oh." Cae fidgeted under the cloak.

"Hmm?" Alec tilted his head.

"N-uhh, nothing," Cae stammered. He took another sip of tea.

Alec offered a small smile. "That what you did at the river, the way you took command of the situation... It impressed me. I'd heard you were a skilled hunter, but you've a mind for tactics."

Cae shrugged. "Well...didn't help me much, did it?"

"Suppose that's why you have the sword."

"I didn't know it could do what it did."

"You didn't know you could move like that?"

"No."

Alec shook his head and laughed. "I take it back," he said. "You might be a bit foolish."

"Pshh... it's part of my charm," Cae replied, weakly.

They both laughed. Alec tossed his hair back with a hand, a flutter of vibrant red.

Cae blinked at the sudden smell of rain... Early morning rain that illuminates the earthy scent of the forest floor, and accents it, with the smell of clean water. All at once, just for a moment, it was like he was home, in the Dokk, skulking through the forest just before dawn, when the haze of night still obscured the world.

Then as the smell faded, he returned to the snow and the Ías, and the crippling fever.

Alec fell back and sat in the snow, brushing the flakes of white from his shoulders.

Cae crinkled his brow as he felt red blooming on his cheeks.

Alec looked up at him. "You alright?"

"Y-yeah," he said, sipping his tea. He pulled his hands out from under the cloak and lowered his eyes to his drink, still red-faced. His hands trembled with sick and cold, splashing a bit of tea onto Alec's cloak.

Alec frowned for a moment, leaning forward to press a hand to Cae's forehead once more. He sighed quietly, and his hand briefly slid down to Cae's cheek. The cheek was a bright red.

"We need to get you warm," Alec said. "Here." He

laid his hands on the cloak, and it grew warmer at his touch.

Cae pulled it closer around him, tucking his hands and his tea into his chest and burying himself beneath the black fabric.

Alec smiled. "Finish that tea, then try to get some rest. I'll be back soon, and we'll eat."

Cae nodded, and nestled into Alec's warm cloak. He sipped at his bitter tea a bit more, but soon drifted off.

* * *

THE GROUND SURROUNDING CREDDON WAS blanketed with a layer of fresh snow, now crunching under the feet of a force of almost a thousand Ocean-guard soldiers. A fraction of the whole Guard, naturally; they had other matters to attend to in the city, it would be foolish to pit the lot of their forces against one man.

But, even so, their number was enough to kill just the one... had it not been for his choice of location. Many of them shuffled uncomfortably in their boots, their merfolk skin dried out in the open air. The flakes pricked what few hairs they had on their aquatic bodies, but offered some reprieve to their discomfort when they melted into frigid droplets on their faces.

There were plenty of whispers, few of them very confi-dent, about their reasons for advancing on the abandoned settlement. It was common knowledge by now that the Wild Rose killer had been seen nearby, and Queen Siahra believed him to be hiding here in what remained of the old town. But for all the Gods' good graces, why did it have to be here? Why Creddon? So many stamping steps were sure to awaken the beast below if it still lived, which it very well might.

Siahra sat atop Gershi ahead of the legion, with Eldur and Burúm keeping watch overhead. Strapped to the barding of the beast she rode upon were her three favored arms: Kéldi's dragonspear, her old trident, and the Glaive of the Diamond Kings. Over her shoulder was strapped her new shortspear. She suspected she would need all four for this fight.

By her side walked Omani the Sea-Father, apparent to only her. She knew some of the Guard on the front could see her speaking. She was certain she knew what they would whisper behind her back. "Who in all the Hells is she talking to? Has she finally cracked? I bet it was all the pressure. First Kéldi, then the quarantine, then whatever happened to her new Knight, the woodsman."

Siahra felt Omani touch her mind ever so lightly with His own, easing her down from her rising panic. She had been dreading this day since Kéldi had died, but part of her knew since the moment they returned to the Palace that night that she would have to face the Rose again. Not just for Kéldi, but for everyone on her Shores and in her Seas.

She had wished Caeleen could be at her side for this, so he might find a bit of closure after the death of his horse. And because... well, it just would have been nice to have him here for this. But he had other duties to attend to. The Blade of the Covenant, it seemed, had a habit of foisting grand responsibilities onto poor Rakau's shoulders.

Omani and Kh'anora had been in communion earlier that day. The Forest Lord was keeping a careful eye on Caeleen and his Company, as they made their way north-ward. The other Ranger, Leon, had joined with them the previous night, and they seemed to be on the way to the Township of Dane, just at the edge of the Tamian border. Caeleen's own strength was waning, but Sal'tera would sustain him until he could rest.

Siahra hated the sound of that. He was just a boy and, for all she knew, he was at death's door at this very moment. Perhaps all that kept him from the dark now was that length of holy mithril that he so resented. He never said it, but she saw it in the way he carried the thing, like it weighed a thousand pounds. He wanted to be done with it, she knew, to put it away in some temple somewhere and move on.

He deserved a rest, she thought. He'd done enough for his people, and for hers. Any man or God worth their spit could see plain as day that the both of them had done enough to deserve some time for themselves. But Siahra held her tongue in the presence of the Ethereals. What right had she to question the machinations of the Gods? She was but a mortal girl. A Queen, yes, but still barely more than a child. If this was indeed the will of the Gods, then she could not refuse Them.

"It is not the way We would have these things happen either, little one," Omani said, responding to musings the Queen had not voiced. "To send children to fight on Our behalf... it disgusts Me. Truly."

Siahra turned then to the Sea Father. "... My lord, I do not question Your judgment. You know I would never."

He turned and looked at her, His eyes speaking His wisdom as clear as any words. "And, yet... you cannot help your doubts."

Siahra lowered her eyes, shaking her head in shame. "I just... He's even younger than me, and You and I both know how confused I am. I have no idea what I'm doing, how can we expect any more from him?" She bit her lip. Her wording was... it wasn't perfect.

"I take your meaning, young Queen," Omani assured her. "You're afraid for him, I know. So am I. So is My Brother. Know that, if any of this could be done differently, neither of you would have gotten involved."

Siahra nodded. "I am proud to carry out Your will, my Lord. Always."

"If there is aught We might do to ease your situations after this conflict ends, We will do it. But for now... for now, you are all We have."

Siahra peered into the bones of Creddon, fixing her eyes on the old tavern where she had found the Rose before. "And we will be enough." She did not need to look back to see that Omani was not beside her anymore. She instead stroked Gershi's neck softly and whispered a command into her ear as she drew her shortspear from her back. The green drake turned slowly around, and the two of them faced the legion of Oceanguard.

"Mo-lamai," she called out, "hear my voice! Hear now the words of your Queen!"

"We hear you, K'kanu!" the guard called in response.

Siahra took a deep breath. "You have all served this Kingdom faithfully for as long as I can remember. You fought for my father, and his mother, and her father before her. The Oceanguard has stood watch for all the Kings of the Old Tide, since the land first emerged from the seas."

Siahra could see a few of the Oceanguard shuffle in their boots. Perhaps some were too young to remember the Kings of old. Perhaps remembering brought back harsh memories.

"... But some of you didn't." Siahra looked down at Gershi. "Some of you did not wear the colors of an Oceanguard until the crown was already upon my brow." She looked up and met some of the Guards' eyes. "I'm sorry this is where your duty has led you so soon.

"I have no right to ask any of you to follow me this day. Where I go, death and ruin wait. If you follow me today, you may very well fall. If any of you wish to return now to your families, go now without consequence."

A moment of quiet passed over the field outside Creddon. Not one soldier moved from their position. Siahra allowed herself a small smile as she reached to her saddle and gripped her iridescent helm. "I believe in you, Mo-Lamai. I ask you now to believe in me!"

Gershi let out a roar, echoed soon by the drakes of Eldur and Burúm. The Oceanguard raised their voices and followed Siahra as she charged.

Gershi soared into the abandoned settlement, and the Diamond Queen locked eyes on the lonesome figure standing in the center of the road outside his tavern. He knew she was coming. How did he know she was coming?

Siahra didn't plan on giving it time to matter.

The Queen Dragoon leapt from her drake and swirled toward her mark, azure flames spiraling around her. Together, Siahra and Gershi bathed the Rose in their breath, a torrent of blue and green and white fire. Within the blinding flames, Siahra could make out a thick purple haze. Some sort of shield; the man was unharmed by the flames.

A fraction of a breath, and she had sped through the barrier with a dash. She thrust with her weapon, green spark of dragon-magic lighting up the air as she did so. The shortspear glanced off of the Rose's wicked axe. Quickly, *too* quickly, the axe's beard hooked onto the shaft of the spear, and with a sudden heave, the weapon tore out of Siahra's hand and spun aside. Siahra gritted her teeth and reached for the weapon, and it darted back toward her. Again, the man batted the spear aside.

Gershi came upon him, her wings beating furiously as she launched at the man. He weaved around the drake's jaws with an ease unnatural, almost appearing to meld into the air as he moved.

Siahra dove for her shortspear, launching it toward the man as his attention was on her mount. The spear passed straight through him, with only a puff of mist showing it had ever made contact. Siahra growled and made for her drake as the Oceanguard came flooding into the street, arms at the ready. She snatched her trident from the drake's armor and caught the Rose in the chest with its three prongs. Not a sound came from the man, but a spurt of red across Gershi's helmet showed his pain well enough.

"Wild Rose, you are a trespasser in my Kingdom, and a danger to my people." Siahra spat her words out quickly and angrily as she pressed her weapon further into the man's flesh. "By my right as Queen of the Diamond Shores, I sentence you to die."

Under his mask, the Rose peered up at the Queen curiously. She could not see his face, but she felt eyes on her. A chill ran up her spine then. She had him. It was done. It had been so easy. She had expected so much worse...

A wall of dust exploded into the air all round the settlement. The very ground they stood upon trembled. Siahra's eyes widened as she looked down. The Rose's hands were sparking with magic.

"Oh, Gods..."

All at once, the whole town began to rise. Scores of Oceanguard tumbled down into the cloud of dust and earth, their screams muffled by the sound of ground churning.

Siahra found herself pressed hard against the ground, her trident still gripped tightly in her hand, as she watched in awe and horror. Through the cloud of dust, an immense form rose out of the earth. The shape was unmistakable: a giant pincer. A low, thunderous clicking filled the air as the crustacean made itself known.

Creddon was alive. Or, at the very least, it was moving again.

Siahra gritted her teeth and heaved up into the Rose's wound, attempting to lift him up onto her trident.

The man simply stepped back, seeming to melt off of the weapon. How was he *doing* that? His axe whirled in his hand, and the sound of metal against metal rang amidst the chaos as the Rose launched his offensive.

Gershi lurched back into the fray, but was met with a fierce blow across her snout. The Rose pried the axe free with a foot, then brought it whirling into a parry against the incoming trident. Siahra cursed under her breath; he was just too fast. Quickly, she slid her hands into position on her trident, using it to halt blow after blow from that wicked axe. Each strike sent jolts up her arms, nerves lighting up like lightning.

He whirled around then and struck again at Gershi, his axe embedding itself deep into her brow. The drake jerked away ferociously, the axe coming free with a sickening sound, and blood seeped down into the creature's eye. The Rose thrust upward with the blunt of his axe, cracking it against Gershi's chest. The drake let out a weak puff of flame as the air fled her lungs, and she collapsed.

The axe came up over her head once more, but its beard caught on something. Siahra's trident. The maotu heaved on the weapon with her own, dragging it to the ground. The Rose tossed a wild fist into Siahra's face, and it stuck with such force as to crack the scales of mighty Sturamtönn. The Queen whirled on her weapon, bringing a flying knee into the killer's ribs. With the crack of bone, he fumbled to the side, his hands slipping off of the axe. The trident lifted into the air again, swirling over Siahra's head as she prepared to bring it down into the man. The Rose leapt aside in a sudden haze, and the axe leapt back to his hand. What foul blood-magic kept the man standing after all his injuries? Siahra wondered.

The Rose darted off down the abandoned street, his movements blurred by a strange mist bleeding from his form. Siahra tore after him with incredible speed, staying ever close on his tail as he zipped through the town. Another blow of her trident glanced off of his axe just as the two slipped into the long-abandoned temple to Omani. At once, the Rose swirled into mist as he slipped upward through the ceiling.

Siahra leapt after him, crashing through rotted wood into an empty old bell tower. Higher and higher she flew, chasing wildly after the fleeing haze. The Rose reformed for just a moment, long enough to cut a length of ancient rope. An enormous mass of copper dropped through the tower below, and he slid out of the tower once more. Siahra quickly bounded off the wall behind her, throwing all of her weight into the bell, crashing out of the tower behind it. It crashed to the dirt street below, mere feet from the Rose. Siahra tore down after it, a vicious kick batted aside by the mad figure she chased.

The crab let out another rumble of clicks as it began to walk, sending the poor souls atop it tumbling and fumbling across the empty streets. The Oceanguard still on the ground scattered, many vanishing under the clouds of earth at the creature's tread. Javelins and arrows flew, bouncing off the ancient chitin. Spells screamed though the air, fire and frost crashing against the mighty shell. The creature slowly rose one monstrous, rotting claw into the air, and brought it to the ground, onto the swarming maotu, with such force as to dislodge the ancient dirt from its form.

Siahra did her best to put the screams out of her mind, to focus on her own fight, but the voices of her dying people shook the young mermaid.

"You will answer for each of their deaths!" Siahra screamed as she thrust madly at the Rose. Her trident clanged against his axe again and again, darting past his form again and again.

The few Oceanguard who had not fallen off of Creddon as it jostled about made their way stumbling toward their Queen.

The Rose put his weight into a shove with his shoulder, sending Siahra tumbling to the side as he raised a hand toward the Guard. At once, a column of swirling flame descended from the clouds. It crashed into the town, destroying several abandoned shops, and scattering the ashes of countless Guard to the wind. Another swipe of his hands, and a bolt of grey lightning crashed through the old temple, blasting the building to splinters and scattered even more of Fartide's forces. A stamp of his feet, and the very ground atop the crab gaped open, swallowing up most of the remnants before closing. As the earth sealed up, a muffled scream just barely rode the air before it died off.

Siahra got to a knee as she watched the Rose's magic in horror. Such destruction wrought by one man, to say nothing of the deaths caused by this incessant crab on its march to... where? As the Queen wobbled to her feet, she questioned just what the crab was doing. Naturally, it was there to sunder her Oceanguard, but clearly the Rose didn't need much help with that. No, Creddon was moving for something. Moving toward something, even.

For just a moment, the Queen's eyes darted out in the direction they were headed, just long enough for her face to drain of color. Creddon was headed for Twipari.

They intended to bring her city down.

"Absolutely *not*."

Siahra darted past the mad killer, and took her father's glaive from Gershi, wielding trident and glaive together furiously. She was unwieldy with a polearm in each hand, but her dragon-magic made her strong. Two mighty weapons whirled wildly in her hands as she pressed onto the Rose, leaving marks on his ragged clothes as he fumbled backward. Another swipe, and the axe flew from his hand. Siahra leapt up with a twirl, cracked her shin across the man's mask. Blackish-red sputtered out as she landed.

The Rose stumbled, and Siahra thrust her glaive into the snow-covered ground. With both hands, she drove her trident into the man's belly, and screamed as she heaved him up over her head.

"Udári! Give me your fire!"

Eldur and Burúm descended on their drakes. Though Gershi could not aid them, they would be enough. Together, two drakes and three Dragoons unleashed their breath, bathing the unholy man in searing dragonfire. The Rose writhed atop the trident, letting out some kind of screech as he twisted in agony. His rags smoldered on his flesh.

All at once, something broke in the air. The great crab trembled beneath the town, then fell. The remains of a long-dead crustacean crumbled to dust, leaving all the maotu to fall into a roiling cloud of rotten debris and swirling earth.

Siahra clung viciously to her trident as she fell, and she allowed herself just a moment of relief as she felt her drake swoop up underneath her. She joined her teachers in the sky overhead, watching the cloud of destruction settle onto the ground below. Far behind now, they could barely make out a few groups of Oceanguard from the ground. There was no way of knowing how many Guards had fallen. It would take weeks to sift through the wreckage to find all the survivors... or, more likely, to find all the bodies. Weeks of uncertainty for their families, not knowing whether their brave loved ones were still holding on, or if it was too late. For most, Siahra knew with a grim certainty, it would be too late.

There was one more great burst in the cloud, like the air had exploded. A charred form lay in the center of the clearing, his ragged clothes smoldering and smoking. Siahra's hands trembled as she stared down at the unholy thing before her. The man, if such a force could be called a man, had utterly rent the Diamond Ocean's greatest defenders.

She had hoped that they hadn't killed him yet. She wanted his death to be an example, a public display to dissuade any further evils on her kingdom. He had much to answer for.

Siahra turned to her fellow Udári. Eldur and Burúm had their spears in hand. Her own hand reached for Kéldi's spear, sliding the trident back into its place on Gershi's barding. Together, the three Dragoons leapt from their mounts, their drakes trailing after them. Six swirling comets of bright dragonfire screaming down the sky, claws and spears rocketing toward their foe.

The Rose did not move to defend himself, but he sat up slowly as the Udári surrounded him. He did not even lift his head when the tip of the Queen's spear just barely pressed against his chest. Siahra gritted her teeth and stilled the trembling in her hands before she spoke.

"Wild Rose," she recited again, "you are a trespasser in my Kingdom, and a danger to my people. By my right as Queen of the Diamond Shores, I sentence you to die."

The Rose lifted his head. Then, beneath the tattered hood, Siahra could see a single eye, tired and black.

"The fight is over," she continued. "My best hands are here now, and you will not defeat all of us."

At this, the two other Udári raised their spears. The Wild Rose looked to each of them, then returned his sight to the Queen. In a gravelly voice like fire and ash, he spoke.

"Not all of them."

Not all of them? Please. The Dragoons were the most capable warriors in all of Cidarian, and these two stood more powerful than any in all of Tamia's forces. Who had a better hand than—

Siahra's eyes widened. *Caeleen.*

The Rose smiled under his mask.

"I have to go, now." Siahra turned and leapt onto Gershi. "You two, bind him and prepare him for execution."

Eldur and Burúm nodded, closing in on the madman with their spears.

Siahra gripped tightly at Gershi's reins and shouted "North! To the Ías! Go!"

Gershi leapt into the air, and her wings carried them rocketing toward the mountains in the distance.

* * *

THE TOWNSHIP OF DANE WAS QUIET AS THE company shuffled through the street. Larger than Even-wood, yet still smaller than Brookridge, the little cottages of Dane held no light in them at the fall of the day, when the world all around took on a sort of bluish tint. Not a soul came out to meet the travelers. Leon crinkled his brow, worried that something had already happened to them. He turned to ask his old teacher, but stopped as he saw the Ranger half-awake, hobbling along as he leaned heavily on Alec's shoulder.

The viltar shook the hunter gently. "Caeleen," he whispered. "We've reached Dane."

Caeleen lifted his head slowly. His fever was waning, thankfully, but he was still weak. "W... what?"

"We're here, Cae," Isi said as she helped him stand on his own feet. "We've made it to the town."

"That doesn't, th... no," Cae stammered. "We... there should... shouldn't someone be..."

Alahir ruffled his feathers as he cast his wizened eyes all round. "There should," he growled. "Something is amiss." The bird looked skyward, to Frostpeak. They were at its very foot now, and the eagle had been keeping watch on the mountain for a while now. Every now and again, he could see the silhouette of the letchya and the other creature circling above but, now... nothing. Even their quarry had vanished.

Cae shook his head, still dazed but now able to stand on his feet. "Where are all the Danesmen?"

Iómi shook her head, standing in Alahir's shadow alongside her wraith. "I... I can feel something. There was a lot of death here, and it was recent."

"Were we too late?" Leon asked.

"Maybe..." said Iómi. "If anyone is still alive, they'd probably be in the big house."

Cae nodded. "Then, let's take a look." Pulling his wolfbear cloak tighter around him and drawing his hood, the Ranger started toward the mansion. Alec fell in line behind him, and the rest followed.

The gate to the manor was not locked, but it was heavy enough to require both Isi and Alec to push it open. After a brief saunter up to the entryway, Caeleen gave a quick three bangs against the door.

No response came.

He tried once more.

Still nothing.

"I don't like this," Leon said, aloud.

"Me neither..." said Cae. "Come on, let's have a look up high."

Together, the two Rangers made their way to the old stone wall, just off to the side with their boots crunching in the powder. Leon produced two pairs of long spikes, and soon the two of them made their way slowly up the old wall.

Alec started after them, but Isi held out a hand.

"They'll move faster on their own. Trust me, I've seen them work."

"Let me pass," Alec whispered. "He isn't well."

"And Leon can tend to him," Isi insisted. "We need you down here."

Alec paused for a moment and looked at the Priestess. Just barely, ever so faintly, his brow furrowed.

As Cae and Leon climbed higher, Leon couldn't help but notice Cae's hands. Despite how difficult it had been to get him here, despite how weak and ill he'd been since before Leon had even arrived... Leon was struggling now to keep up with the older Ranger.

Cae made his way up to a darkened window and wiped away a layer of frost to peer inside, his breath just a bit heavy. "Leon, come help me out... Y'see anything in there, maybe you have a lantern on you or something?"

Leon heaved himself up onto the ledge. "No, sorry. Didn't think of it," he replied. He looked his partner up and down for a moment. "Good to see you're feeling better."

Cae opened his mouth to reply, then closed it. His brow furrowed. "I...huh." He placed a hand to his own forehead. Leon was right. He felt fine. Great, even. A little winded, and his chest was still oddly warm, but...

He reached into his coat, but jerked his hand away when something burned his fingers. He looked down, and his eyes widened.

His feather pendant was searing hot.

"What is it?" Leon asked.

"I... I don't know," said Cae. "I guess we're here..."

He looked up to see a maw of gaping teeth.

Cae leapt from the wall and drew Sal'tera. "*Kän!*"

The window exploded as white lightning streaked down from the sky and struck the Ranger, darting from him to the beast. Leon and Cae crashed hard on their backs into the snow. The letchya spiraled for a moment, landing hard, but on its feet.

Cae spun onto his feet, sparks crackling from his body and his weapon. He gritted his teeth and gripped his sword tight, his veins glowing with white lightning. Leon slowly heaved himself up, not fortunate enough to have such magic. The former brandished the holy longsword viciously, lightning crackling high above them.

It was then that Leon noticed, as he drew Seeker from his back, that the snow had stopped falling.

"And, thus, does the blade come to me once more," the letchya hissed. The creature was missing several teeth, and it bore scars from each strike the company had landed before.

"And me with it, to carve those wings clean off you," Cae hissed, full of vigor. "I'm betting devil leather makes a fine cloak."

Seeker spun in Leon's hands as the younger Ranger stepped forward. "So is it you, then? Did you do all this?"

"I am but a servant of my Emperor," the moon devil answered. "All these things which unfold now do so in accordance with his will."

"I don't buy it," Cae replied. "Cestus might be a dirt-bag, but he wouldn't ally with devils."

"Your Cestus is but a pretender," the letchya barked, each word dripping with venom. "The true master of these realms will drink his soul like wine, and all shall bear witness."

Cae frowned. "Well, I guess that answers that question..."

A spark, just behind Caeleen's ear. His movement was lightning as he brought the holy weapon back to parry a long, thin blade. A rapier.

Cae stood firm as he stared into the viltar's cold black eyes.

"Alec?" Leon's voice was shaky, uncertain.

Alec responded with a crack of his whip, catching hold of the magic axe in the boy's hands. With a slight tug of the viltar's hand, Leon fell forward into the snow.

The viltar whirled his whip to strike once more, but Cae spun in a flash, and his blade cleaved the weapon before it could come down. Another thrust from the rapier, the tip piercing naught but the edge of a cloak as the Ranger wheeled back through the air. He had drawn his dagger before he ever landed, and he fell quietly into stance as soon as he hit the ground.

The boy scrambled back to his feet, and his face flushed as he saw them all around. The Danesmen, all of them, shambling out of the dark. Men, women, children, elders. They'd probably been dead for months. They were eerily well-preserved, likely kept from rot by the cold. His eyes jumped back to the manor, back to his allies.

Isi was on the ground, uninjured, but unmoving. Iómi crouched over her. Whiskey and Alahir stood on either side with their wings outstretched, as scores of corpses shuffled slowly toward them.

As he brushed the snow off Seeker, Leon blinked for a moment. A flurry of snow whirled to life on the far side of Caeleen. The young Ranger blinked once more, and it was no flurry. Just coming into visibility now was the form of a young man in white furs. A bow across his back, a short sword in each hand. His eyes were a cold silver-grey, but his pupils glowed an empty white.

Alec turned his rapier slowly in the air, taking a stance of his own as his eyes bored into Caeleen's. "I see you've made a full recovery."

"Yeah, magic lightning'll do that to ya," Cae replied, his voice harsh.

Alec inclined his head, and the faintest hint of a smile played at the corner of his lips. "Oh, I know. I've studied swords like yours extensively in my career."

"Your career doing what, exactly?" Cae asked. "Maybe you really are a viltar, but somehow I doubt very much that you're just a common sellsword."

"Quite right, I'm afraid." Alec tilted his head just a bit, his crimson hair spilling over his shoulder as he did. "I'm no sellsword. Sure, I lend my blade out every now and again, but the more accurate title would be 'harbinger.'"

"Harbinger of what?" Cae snipped. "Cut the crap, pretty boy. Who's doing all this? Is it the Eighth Ethereal?"

"Eighth Ethereal?" Leon piped as he leapt to Cae's side, Seeker now gripped tight in his hands as he placed himself between Cae and the ghostly warrior. "What are you on about, Cae?"

Alec rolled his eyes. "Look, I really can't deal with you at the moment. If you'll just wait your turn—"

"You don't speak to him like that." Cae's words were harsh, laced through with menace. "Have some respect."

Alec sighed. "Longwatch. Look around you."

He did. Cae let his eyes glide around, taking in everything about him. The bodies. The letchya. The ghost. His friends. How much of this had been by design? How long had this man been watching him? Cae knew he'd seen him at Silvishi, but had he...

He had.

The bet at Silvishi. The guard who fought the dracowight. The Claw who greeted him during the Trials.

Alec nodded. "I've been there. Every step."

"How long have you been following me, Alec?" he asked, his voice just barely quivering. "Who are you?"

Alec's smile faded as he stepped slowly in a circle around the Ranger. "... my name is Denin. And you are right about one thing, Sir Longwatch: the Eighth Ethereal King has had a hand in my work since the very beginning." Again, the viltar let out a tired sigh. "But that is the way they are, is it not? They encourage your freedom, certainly, but... well, all mothers like to imagine plans for their babes. Before they ever even take their first steps."

Cae's blood ran cold. "N...no. Don't, don't toy with me."

"I'm not toying," Denin said. "Would you like to know Her name?"

"I'll kill you."

"Oh, lovely, you're going to strike down a demigod.

Wonderful plan, that. And then what? Will they give you another title?" The man not called Alec gestured boisterously toward Cae. "Raise your ciders to Caeleen, Boltwalker, Bowmaster, and Godslayer!"

"You'll stop mocking me. I'll make you stop."

"Do it, then," Alec, or Denin, said, his voice sad but firm. "Come on. Show me what your Godsblade is worth."

Caeleen trembled. His knees quaked, but he roared with a lion's might. *"Tuu'lákra!"* He tore through the air, a crack of thunder exploding behind him, and he attacked. Stroke after stroke, he flung madly at the viltar, and stroke after stroke Alec-or-Denin slipped past.

As Caeleen blasted off, the ghost came in from behind. Its two swords were met by the shaft of an axe. Leon stood firm, holding the phantom figure at bay. The axe spun, knocking the swords from the ghost's hands and twisting him off-balance. Leon cracked the blunt of the axe against the ghost's head with terrific force... or, at least, he meant to, but the weapon passed right through and flew from Leon's hands.

Seeker spun in the air as Leon leapt back out of range of a deathly swipe from the figure. Its swords leapt back to it, and it gave chase as Leon flipped and whirled back from its swings. Leon swore under his breath, wishing he'd asked for silvered weapons before he'd set out from the Alabaster Palace. The young Ranger instinctively threw a fist at the ghost. This time, his whole body lurched through. He cried out as he felt two sudden ice-cold strikes on his back. He twisted his body and kicked the blades aside again, and he took off running. He just barely heard the bowstring behind him, and he twirled through the air as arrows, or perhaps they were shards of ice streaking past him, deathly close to piercing the boy.

Seeker came whirling back to him then, and he shattered one more such shard with a quick swing before darting up the street. The icy arrows continued to rain down after him, and the ghost continued his pursuit.

A forceful thrust from Sal'tera sent a thunderbolt hurtling into the corpses in the distance as Denin batted the blade aside with his rapier. With the distance closed, Cae twirled and dug in with his dagger. The blade cut through the fine coat worn by the viltar, and a thin red line appeared on the shoulder underneath. Denin grunted, throwing an elbow into Caeleen's nose. The Ranger stumbled back, and Denin leapt back, following with a thrust. Sal'tera clashed against the rapier, and white sparks showered the snow, again and again.

The letchya lunged toward the manor doorway, a sound somewhere between a screech and a retch crackling out from its throat. Iómi drew her blade, and Whiskey flared up behind her. The devil leapt high over Iómi's head, coming swirling down into the wraith's form, scattering it in a cloud of black smoke. Iómi swiped with her blade of green fire, leaving a blackened cut across one wing, but the letchya responded with a strike of its own, knocking the Wizard to the ground with the swipe of one cold claw.

Iómi scrambled away from the creature as Whiskey reformed between them, assuming the form of a black lion. Inky jaws and claws flew at the moon devil, but the letchya met each blow with a strike of its own. Countless teeth dug into the lion's body and tore strips of darkness away. Each time the wraith reformed immediately but, each time, the healing came just a bit slower. The devil unleashed a great buffet with its wings then, and Whiskey tumbled aside.

Iómi charged, poised to skewer the beast, but a great beam of cold white light burst forth from its terrible mouth. The Wizard skidded across the snow, her robes tattered and frozen, and Graadrog tumbled out of her hands.

Cae fell back several steps before throwing a shin into the side of Denin's head. As he fumbled to the ground, Denin melted into mist, reforming just behind Caeleen as the Ranger planted his foot after his kick. Caeleen turned and was greeted by the rake of claws across his face. Hot sparking red spurted from his face as he lashed out madly with his dagger. His cheek stung with its fresh wound, but he would live.

Denin tore away in a cloud of mist, and Cae gave chase, white sparks arcing out of his body as he leapt and darted after his foe's formless mass. Past the line of shambling corpses, and up into the trees they flew, an occasional flash of sparks erupting as their blades continued to clash. Denin tore through the air then from the top of a great pine onto the roof of the manor.

Cae followed close behind, and their swords continued to clash with vicious force. Tearing on their feet across the snow-covered rooftop, Cae left a smattering of cuts across the viltar's chest and shoulders, and sustained a few wounds from the end of Denin's rapier in return. Both of them bled, but Cae bled faster. He pushed forward for another strike but, with a quick turn from the black-cloaked stranger, he tumbled over the edge of the roof.

A quick whisper of *uro,* and a small burst of thunder, and Cae tumbled, harmlessly, on impact with the ground. Denin came down harder, his landing scattering snow and shaking the ground. A flash of violent amethyst light erupted high above, a screech shattered the air, and something came crashing down yards away. The stranger let out a rough shout, and he leapt back upon the Ranger in white.

The corpses piled over one another as they clambered toward Isi. The Cleric was still dazed from... whatever Alec had done to her, but she shook it off as best she could, throwing up a solid barrier of golden light around herself to hold back the wall of bodies descending upon her. A strike with her morningstar sent bodies flying, and smoldering, creating an opening large enough for her to dart through.

Isi roared as she barreled through, her armor flashing into existence around her. The corpses gathered again, closing in a circle around the priestess as rising high above her head. She would bash at them with her magic, and her weapon, and still they wailed upon her shield. Her barrier had faded as she fought, her concentration fallen.

Soon, the dead piled into a mountain too high for her to fend off. Isi held up her shield and braced for their fall... but found herself hurled though the air, instead, crashing against the manor. Her eyes opened to horror as she watched the corpses descend with rending hands and tearing jaws over Alahir's singed and ragged form.

The great eagle let out one more loud screech as he disappeared beneath the bodies. Isi leapt onto the pile of rotted flesh and tore at the bodies desperately, but she could not find the bird beneath them.

Again, the thrusts came from the rapier but, this time, Cae was ready. With longsword and dagger holding the thin blade at bay, not one thrust found its mark and, this time, it was Denin who lost ground. Cae pressed into an offensive, his two blades coming in hotter and faster than Denin's. As Cae closed the distance, he cracked his head against Denin's nose with vicious force, and buried his dagger up to its hilt in the viltar's belly. Cae screamed as he pressed the dagger into the stranger as hard as he could.

Denin groaned, and his mouth became a straight line. Not an expression of pain, but of irritation. He grabbed Cae's off-hand and pulled the dagger out of him. Taking the small weapon by the blade, he grunted for just a moment as mithril shattered and crumbled in his fist.

The hilt fell to the snow as Cae stepped back for a moment, and Denin cracked the pommel of his rapier against the Ranger's nose. Cae felt bone and cartilage break under the force of the strike, and he cried out for just a moment before drawing a broad stroke across Denin's chest with Sal'tera. He stumbled for just a moment, now gripping the holy weapon in both hands.

Denin leapt back as he reached over his shoulder.

Cae aimed with Sal'tera just as Denin's hand came

back down, with something gripped tightly in front of him.

"Uro!!"

The word came, tearing out of both their throats.

A flash of white crashing against red. The air erupted with sparks.

Caeleen crashed against the stone wall of a barracks, his head throbbing where it bounced against their building. Both his hands still gripped the Bolt of Peace, but his feet gave way. He fell to his knees, his whole body aching. He struggled back to his feet.

Denin streaked through the electric air and struck, and not with a rapier.

Cae threw Sal'tera up just fast enough to clash against a longsword of spectacular make. The blade was a cold black, like Graadrog, but with no platinum lining. This weapon was forged of pure vothril. It sparked with red lightning the way Sal'tera sparked with white.

"I told you," Denin growled, "I know your weapon."

"W... what...?"

"Come on. Did you think it was the only Godsblade in the world?" Denin grabbed Caeleen by his hair and hurled him across the ground. "There are eight Ethereal Kings, why would they *not* have their own blades?"

Cae wobbled to his feet and looked around once more. His heart sank; Leon could not defeat this phantom warrior. Whiskey and Iómi could not hold off the letchya. Isi could not destroy the horde, nor could she reach Alahir, now buried under waves of ripping and tearing dead.

"A... Alahir..." Cae stumbled toward the mound

underneath which he could see the wings of his brother, but he knew. He knew it was too late.

Alahir was dead. First Tüli, now Alahir. Two companions, two partners. Two brothers. And he could do nothing for them.

"Gods above... look at you. Again, and again, everyone holds you up like some sort of chosen one, some kind of holy warrior." Denin drove his heel into Caeleen's back, shoving him into the snow. "But, no...no, you're just a boy. You're just..." He paused. "...You're just a boy."

Caeleen groaned as he tried desperately to push himself back to his feet. Elbows dug deeper into the snow, now stained red with hot, sparking blood. "Let them... let them go."

"I can't," Denin replied. "Believe me, I wish I could. But we're not quite ready to show our hand just yet. And your friends, the girls... they each have something I need."

Caeleen was back on his feet now, just barely. "No. No..." he turned, and he stared with weary, broken green eyes at the viltar. "I won't let you hurt them."

"Hush now," Denin replied, frowning. "It's over."

Cae knew his lightning had faded. He wouldn't have the strength to summon it again. As he stumbled forward, he barely found enough strength to raise Sal'tera up over his head for one last strike.

That strike never came. Cae froze there in the street as Denin drove his vothril blade through his belly and out his back.

Sal'tera fell from his hand, and he went limp, falling into Denin's arms. Slowly, gently, the stranger lowered him to the cold ground.

"I'm so sorry," Alec, or Denin, said. "None of this was fair to you. None of it was fair to them, either. It just... this is how it is."

Caeleen meant to raise a hand to strike Denin once more, but he couldn't find the strength. He lay, powerless, his life seeping out into the powder beneath him.

Denin scooped up Sal'tera. He looked down at it for a moment, then tucked it away, the blade vanishing underneath his cloak.

Far overhead, something else passed through clouds enshrouded in night. Denin looked up to see the bird erupt in violet flame before vanishing back into the darkness. It had found its own prey, but it had delivered its message.

You have them for a reason.

The viltar winced, then looked down at the Ranger with sad eyes. "... I don't want to do this." The viltar's hair fell down over their faces, and again the smell of morning rain flooded Caeleen's senses. He calmed for just a moment. Then, his eyes widened as he noticed a strange glint in the stranger's mouth.

"I hope you can forgive me someday," Denin whispered. He lowered himself to Caeleen's neck, and his lips brushed against Cae's throat.

Cae lay, frozen and helpless, as two fangs broke the skin of his neck. All at once, every vein in Caeleen's body, every last drop of blood still inside him, lit up with searing pain. The chill of encroaching death inside him turned at once to fire and agony.

With the last of his strength, Caeleen screamed.